Light Sister, Dark Sister

Light Sister, Dark Sister

Lee Walmsley

Random House
New York

Library of Congress Cataloging-in-Publication Data
Walmsley, Lee.
    Light sister, dark sister / Lee Walmsley.—1st ed.
      p. cm.
    ISBN 0-679-41455-X
1. Fathers and daughters—United States—Fiction. 2. Sisters—
United States—Fiction. I. Title.
PS3573.A445L54 1994
813'.54—dc20   93-10403

Book design by Tanya M. Pérez

Manufactured in the United States of America
24689753
First Edition

To John

All of us collect fortunes when we are children—a fortune of colors, of lights and darkness, of movements, of tensions. Some of us have the fantastic chance to go back to his fortune when grown up.

—Ingmar Bergman

Thanks to Kate Medina, for everything

Part 1

one

obbie runs through dark, decided, green, November trees. She has between her hands my new blue Mylar kite, a fragment of the sky. She starts to run, and when she gets going fast enough, she lets go.

The kite rises, pulling against the wind like an unhappy child. Bobbie yanks back at the kite and runs, spinning out down the darkened pavement with the kite spiraling after her, dangerously low and close to the bare trees. Soon all I can see is Bobbie's back, a swirl of leaves, the kite, and Bobbie running.

Now, trouble. The kite darts nervously up and down in the sky, fighting Bobbie to let out more line. She gives easily at first, then wildly. The kite bounds up, almost out of sight; suddenly it swoops upside down and crashes into the branches of a tree.

I run to catch up and by the time I arrive Bobbie already has her mittens off and is working to untangle the kite string. Her hands move with fine, almost surgical acuity. My own hands are clumsy, as if they were formed for some purpose I haven't yet realized.

"Now look what we've done," I say, as usual afraid, as usual careful never to accuse Bobbie without also accusing myself. She knows this and narrows her eyes at me. They are a rare color, *ultramarine*, a word that is brighter than it should be, like Bobbie's teachers say she is.

"You didn't do it," Bobbie says, "I did." She works the line loose and starts to free the kite from the empty witchy branches. She seems to know just how much play to give the line, when to rein in, when to risk. "Don't blame yourself for things you haven't done," she says in an even tone, free of reproach. "You only muddy the waters. Besides, you might actually *do* something someday, instead of just sitting there stupidly while I do everything."

She turns the kite over to me, and I catch the look in her eyes: pure devilment. Any minute she might become an angel, but with Bobbie there's no telling. "Your turn," she says lightly.

I reach out to take the line from her; the wind's come up and plays crazily back and forth with the kite, but Bobbie hangs on tight. Then, the moment I touch the kite string, I see her face is no longer light, as faces are in dreams, but deliberate, desperate, cruel. I want to yell *No!* but already I feel the kite slipping away from me. I can't keep it from happening; I can't get a tighter grasp because of the mittens.

And the kite's rising high over the red-tiled roofs; the New Orleans air looks black and sooty, Londony somehow, with the kite disappearing over the chimneys. It strikes me at once: Bobbie let my kite go on purpose. She knew I hadn't really taken hold of it, wasn't ready to be responsible. I go to say something to her, just to let her know she hasn't fooled me, but Bobbie's face is turned up to the sky, to the rooftops of all the houses on Harmony Street, one of which is our house, which the street lights have begun to silver. I know better than to interrupt Bobbie when she gets her faraway look.

• • •

I sit in the kitchen, crying. I can't get the tears to stop; they seem to come from some rich, secret source.

"Gray," Hannah says, "you know Bobbie got the devil in her. Always has. Why can't you learn?" She turns the broad slab of her back to me while she fries the chops. I think about the devil in Bobbie, how it is the color and consistency of a red-ant pile. I think of all her secretive, numerous ways. Then I think about our mother, Mudie, and how one time when Bobbie and I were in the backyard playing I looked up and saw her watching us from her third-floor window. The way the afternoon light shone, her face seemed overlaid with leaves, all colors but somehow sad. Maybe that is why Mudie sometimes doesn't leave the house much: She would have to carry this sadness with her.

Mudie is an artist, and our father, Max, calls her "my ruined beauty," which makes her laugh in a way Bobbie and I never can. Sometimes when I close my eyes I see Mudie, not laughing, but looking serious, as if she thought the world was too much for her.

"I told you and told you," Hannah says, "stay out of Bobbie's way."

"But she's my sister. How can I?" My question rides the air unanswered. Down the hall in the library I can hear Bobbie reading her Greek lesson to Max, a spill of nervous twittery bones.

Hannah says, "Gray, there will come a time when I am dead and buried and where will you be then if you don't learn to look after yourself?" When Bobbie and I were little and Bobbie hit me, Hannah would pin Bobbie down and command me to hit her back. "You call that a hit?" she'd say in disgust. "That ain't nothing but a little love tap."

Hannah recites from the Bible. When Isaac was dying he went to bless his elder son, Esau; by mistake, he blessed the younger one, Jacob. Hannah says there's meaning in that story for me.

"You mean because Max loves Bobbie more?"

It's true, he does.

"What's the Bible say?" Hannah asks in reply. "It ain't saying he loved the younger, it says he *blessed* the younger. Don't they teach you how to read in that fancy school?"

"I think I'd rather not be blessed, if this is what blessing is," I mumble so Hannah can only half hear.

"Don't say that," Hannah replies. "You not old enough to know what you got inside you yet. You little green pear."

"What happened to the younger son anyway?" I ask as an after-thought.

"Search me," Hannah says.

It is June twenty-first, the longest day of the year. At night the locusts seem to go on singing forever. Outside the screen, the sun going down casts shadows that move whenever the wind blows. It might be going to rain later on, it might not. The breeze comes in gusts through the screen and the evening light is pale, the color of mud.

Bobbie comes to the doorway. "Want to ride down to Audubon Park and see the sea lions?"

"The park's closed. You know that."

"Nothing's closed if you want it open."

I turn over on my side. "No thanks."

"Jesus." Bobbie puts two fingers in her mouth and gives a loud whistle, waking the neighborhood dogs. "You're worse than a corpse."

"I am a corpse."

"Funny, you don't stink," Bobbie says.

"Are you trying to cheer me up? Because you can't, you know. I just have to feel horrible until it goes away."

"How long's that going to be, Gray?"

"I don't know. Two, three weeks. Maybe a month."

"Like when I get my wild streaks."

"I guess so. Only you seem to distinguish yourself. You write good school papers, say funny things. I only wander around in this fog."

Later, when Max and Mudie are asleep Bobbie comes to the door again. I haven't exactly been sleeping, only turning back and forth in the bed fitfully. "Moonflowers are out," she says.

"So what."

"Come on, Gray. Unless you're actually dead."

We go out the back door into the yard. In my nightgown and bare feet I can feel the tropical heat rise through my body, making me feel more vegetable than human. "Look." Bobbie points. There, on the back wall surrounding the yard, a hundred moist, white, heavy flowers have opened in the moonlight.

Bobbie goes to the wall and pulls a few flowers for herself; she is drenched in light, in dew. In her white nightgown in the moonlight she looks delicate and ethereal, as if at any moment she might dissolve into something else, some other. I'm standing in the shadow of the house, the house on Harmony Street that Max dreamed about and began to plan when we were babies still in our cribs. It is the middle of the night, and I am unaccountably sad. I can't even cry because this is not that kind of sadness, it is dark, heavy, immaterial. The two of us are just standing there: light sister, dark sister. I have an eerie feeling that we are connected beyond just being sisters, our identities somehow fused into one. Of course I don't tell Bobbie any of this, because she might only laugh at me.

The library door is open a crack, enough to see the spines of all the books, and Max's shoes impatiently pacing. Max has blue eyes and a mustache and he's pale like Bobbie, but sometimes he gets patches of color on his cheeks. He wears starchy shirts and bow ties with what look like tadpoles on them that Mudie calls Liberty of London, a name I like because it has flags waving and a river in it. When Max sneezes he leaves behind a smell in the room of tobacco and leather and bay rum. I swear I could go in a room an hour later and tell Max had been there and sneezed.

"Report cards came today," Mudie says.

"How did Bobbie do?" Max asks.

"They think she could do better. She's *brilliant*, they say."

For a moment I hold Bobbie's radiance inside me, like a candle protected from the wind, and then Max says, "And Gray? The usual? She's the most desultory child I've ever seen."

"Gray's a late bloomer," Mudie says.

"Bobbie ought to go East to school," Max says. "She's not being challenged enough here. What sort of school is that? Run by a bunch of defrocked Jesuits. Half stuck in some Louisiana swamp . . . It's a wonder the girls don't both get yellow fever."

"I like St. Rita's," Mudie says, "it's low-key."

"Fine for Gray," Max says, "but Bobbie needs more. Bobbie needs a real education."

Mudie starts to protest but gives up; her voice becomes a sigh. I imagine her looking out of the tall French windows and yawning, sunk once again in a world of her own. She knows better than to argue with Max about two things, and Bobbie is one of them. The other is where he goes when he says he's going someplace else.

I ride the streetcar to Hannah's house. Along the way the words "late bloomer" hang in the air like the actual smell of gardenias. I hate thinking of myself as any kind of bloom; if anyone in our family blooms, it's Mudie, a wild, orphaned rose. I know Mudie only says things like this about me to Max to tease him about his way of thinking. It's not to protect me or champion me to make Max love me more. Even if she could. No, long ago Max made up his mind about Bobbie, and even I know he favors her because she is like him, the way the sun is like other stars. If you ask me, Bobbie needs protecting from Max and the weight of his dreams.

Hannah's house, at 934 North Johnson Street, is attached to the ones next to it, which gives them all a cozy related look, even if they aren't large or in good repair. Her front yard is full of flowers. Hannah is amazed that I got here without getting lost, on the streetcar and two buses, past the cemetery where four generations of my family are buried and where I will probably be buried too, someday. Hannah doesn't ask questions; she gives me lemonade, and James plays a game of checkers with me. James is Hannah's common-law husband and he cheats at checkers, but I let him get away with it. I like Hannah's family. She has a son named Brother, who is fat and the color of peanut butter. Her two sisters are named Sea and Sister. Sister is narrow and disapproving, like a skinny yellow candle in a church, and Sea is—Sea is large and sloppy and full of foam and surprises, like the sea.

At Hannah's house there is no talk of brilliance and how Bobbie is going to go to Harvard and do great things someday. At Hannah's house we have coffee as black as the street and talk about actual things. The weather. How the New Orleans summer is worse than usual, hotter than anybody can remember. How the electricity went off at Charity Hospital and they had to pack the bodies in the morgue in ice, to keep them for the funerals. In the cases where there weren't to be any funerals, they kept them cold anyway, out of respect.

Hannah says, "I know how come the weather's so bad. It's on account of the governor. Governor Eisenheimer and that atom bum. *That's* who done changed you-all's weather."

At Hannah's house words have a different look, a glow, like when my teacher writes in colored chalk on a wet blackboard. Nine thirty-four North Johnson Street: I wish I lived there and not at 2211 Harmony Street, in the house that Max built. In my father's house I am only Bobbie's sister, a desultory child.

At Hannah's house the talk goes on late in the evening until finally it is ten o'clock, and Hannah gives me a nod and rises out of her chair to call Mudie and tell her where I am and that I'm safe. There is no need to, really; nobody has called the police, and anyway, Mudie always knows where I am.

two

s a baby I had vivid pictures. Max walking home from work in a suit the color of rice paper and a lavender bow tie, the same color as the walls of my room. He and Mudie would dance around the living room to a scratchy mournful calypso record, and later on we would all sit down to a dinner of fried potatoes and fish. I thought then the fish were looking up at me with pleading eyes.

In the morning Mudie used to have Hannah come clean house. Except Saturdays when she and Max sat in marmalade sunshine drinking coffee and reading the morning paper. "Oh," Mudie said once, "I'm so tired of trying to be happy. Can't we think of something else to try for?"

"Like what?" Max said.

"I don't know, there must be something easier, something concrete."

"There is," Max said. "Try hitting the daily double two days running."

"I thought you were an architect, not a gambler," Mudie said. The ends of her black eyebrows ran together; her skin was pearly, the inside of an oyster shell.

"I am," Max said, "an architect and a gambler."

In those days Max tried to make money reading the *Racing Form*. He went to the track on Saturdays, taking me with him. Bobbie went to horse-riding class. Mudie stayed home and worked; she had a tiny studio on the back porch of the apartment. There was a rickety table and a galvanized can full of cold squishy clay and a beat-up Kelvinator full of beer and Max's smelly cheese. Max and I spent the afternoon at the fairgrounds, squinting through binoculars. We ate hot dogs and drank Barq's root beer, and Max let me keep his winnings in the pocket of my jacket.

There was real happiness. Then later when the money came the happiness left, not the money's fault. Happiness drifted through the open windows of the apartment like the irresponsible sunshine. Max stopped going to the track, became serious about his architectural career. He started going to work on Saturdays. We bought a house, the first in a series of long skinny houses that you could stand in the front door of and see all the way to the back. Like looking the past straight in the face. Max started spending Sundays at the big dining-room table drawing plans for a new house. His dream house, Mudie called it, but I didn't like the way that sounded; it sounded as if the house were made of something like spun sugar, too sweet, insubstantial, not real.

Max at the piano, drunk. The youngest man at his firm to make full partner, he has gone out and bought a car. The car, a '47 Buick with a convertible top, is named Bertha. Max bought Bertha for forty dollars. Something is wrong with the wiring; when Max drives any distance in Bertha, the floorboards get hot.

Mudie can't drive Bertha at all; the big hulking car pulls and bucks as if it knows how afraid she is. The car bullies her, and Mudie frequently breaks into tears. When this happens Bobbie scoots over and takes the wheel and Mudie just sits there and lets her drive home.

Bobbie never has any trouble with Bertha. Neither does Max; Bertha is his ally. He spends Wednesday nights after dinner working on the wiring; Fridays he waxes and polishes. Mudie hates the car, pleads with Max to get rid of it. Possibly Bertha is the first thing to come between Max and Mudie in their marriage. They snap at each other; I can smell electricity in the air, the odor of burning rubber. I don't tell anybody who might think I'm peculiar, only Bobbie, who listens to everything I say with a secretive smile on her face, as if she already knew everything I had to tell her, and more.

Pass Christian, the summer house Max rented. After swimming, Bobbie, Hannah, and I walk to the old cemetery, half buried in sand near the seawall where the tall grasses grow. We study the graves and discuss the lives of the people buried there and what they must have been like. We talk seriously, because Hannah doesn't like us to make jokes about the dead.

One day we come upon a grave that is newly dug but empty. It is small, a child's grave. Bobbie and I are standing on the edge of the sandy hole when all of a sudden Bobbie jumps into the open grave and lies down with her eyes closed and her hands folded. It takes me a moment to register what she's just done; somewhere in the little town are a mother and father waiting to bury the child in her stiff white dress, her high-top baby shoes, and here's Bobbie, clowning around. I have never seen anybody with less propriety than Bobbie.

"Bobbie," Hannah says, "God will punish you for that."

"He already has. He made me who I am today."

"I have a good mind to bury you myself," Hannah says.

"Be my guest."

Back at the house Max and Mudie sit on the porch, tired and sunburnt. Max is barefoot, wears white trousers; Mudie scrabbles in a pail of conchs collected that morning at the beach. After supper the sun drops. We eat tuna-fish salad and drink lemonade and feel the sandy floorboards with our feet. By the time we go to bed it is dark; the moon hangs like a new silver fishhook in the Gulf sky. We sleep back to back in the weathered old bed, Bobbie and I, each in our separate dreams. Mine are of castles and wise old men, hers of admiring crowds. In the middle of the night—no, later than that, judging by the light—I hear a scream. Down the hall, Mudie's room. We jump up and run to where Mudie is standing, bone-white.

"What's the matter?"

She points. "In there. Creatures on the wall."

By the dim predawn light I make them out, the small army of conchs with their spidery bodies advancing up the wall of Mudie's room. For a moment I see what she saw. Bobbie shrugs.

"I see things like that all the time."

Even so, Bobbie helps Mudie back to bed and takes the pail and picks the conchs off the wall. The two of us take the bucket of conchs back outside and let them go; we watch them scrabble in the sand. "Poor Mudie," Bobbie says, "she can't handle *anything.*"

Pass Christian again, the summer house. I am four. After swimming I have been sent upstairs to take a nap. I lie down under the still sheets. There is a window above me, and a pair of long, gauzy curtains blows in the wind, touching my face. I am almost asleep. Then somehow Max is there, offering me a sip of beer. One sip, more, I feel like I am drowning in the golden foam. "Take it easy," Max laughs, but he gives me all the beer I want. Most of all he and Mudie want me to be no trouble. Bobbie is all the trouble they can stand. "Poor Gray," he says, giving me an affectionate pat. He stands up and drains the beer mug. I am the girl he sees in the bottom of the glass, small and distorted. An afterthought.

On the fifth day I run out into the Gulf and have to be rescued. I am disappointed that I didn't die, that I am still here, a child of four on a summer vacation. They pull me out of the drowning water and Hannah towels me off with swift, harsh caresses. Afterward I am confused about Max. Should I love him anymore? Does he realize trying to drown myself in the brackish water comes from having so little value in his eyes? I vow never to speak to him again, never to love him.

My resolve weakens when he shows up with a doll I have been longing for. Poor Pitiful Pearl, she is called. I have to love him, he is my father, I have no choice. Anyway, he buys me dolls. I vow instead not to remember anything bad about him.

I am seven, Bobbie is nine. Max and Mudie are at one of their many parties. Mudie doesn't like to go out much: She claims she hates crowds. Max forces her to go to parties with him because he wants people to see how beautiful Mudie is. But Hannah and I, and Bobbie, know the truth. So, probably, does Max, if he thinks about it. These days, though, his mind is on other things.

This evening Bobbie is antsy. She sits in Max's armchair so heavy with boredom she might as well be swimming in it.

"I've got an idea," I say, "let's dress up."

Bobbie rolls her eyes.

"Not the way we used to. For real," I say.

"What do you mean, for real?"

"Come and see."

In Mudie's bathroom Bobbie takes Max's razor and shaves off the blond hair on my legs and arms. It doesn't hurt but I make a face like it does. Then I find some underwear of Mudie's, a lacy-looking thing called a teddy that Max gave her that she never wears. Bobbie makes me put it on. We fill the top with toilet paper. Bobbie makes me put on Mudie's torn black stockings. She takes scissors and cuts gashes in the underwear thing and rubs deep blue makeup on my eyes like bruises. I'm starting to tire of the game, of Bobbie's zeal for it. "Keep still," she keeps telling me. Then, finally, I am done, and both of us look in the mirror. We can't believe how I look. Like I've had to grow up fast. "But you're beautiful," Bobbie says. I scowl. I keep looking and looking because it's the first time I've ever seen it: I am beautiful and sad and wise in a way Bobbie will never be.

I like to remember when Max first bought the land for our house on Harmony Street. I was with him when he saw the lot and the old house being torn down, layers of walls the color of tea cakes crumbling, the ornamental plaster icing smashed. The next day we drove by, there it was. A corner lot full of rubble, poison ivy, banana trees. Too large, Max said. Irregularly shaped. His eyes shone with love. He bought the land at an auction, simply came home with the deed. The house itself he'd been planning for years, all during our poor days.

Max tinkered with the plans and pestered the contractors. On Saturdays Bobbie and I went with him to watch the building. He argued with the mason over the delivery of bricks, engineered the accidental collapse of a hod of mortar on my foot. Max was in love with the chaos of building, with its near disasters and serendipities, its unexpected gifts. It was the only time he preferred what is natural to what is planned; he said this was what made architecture come alive.

Rich days, those. Fall afternoons the color of cider, we watched the walls rise. Windows and skylights were hoisted in place; the copper roof reflected the October sun, and in the atrium downstairs, a cylinder of glass connected with the sky. A modern house, we said, looking down the block at the Greek revival and Victorians. What will people think?

"They'll think we're fools," Max said with obvious delight. "They'll think we're crazy."

He explained to us what the house meant, how even though it was modern, it paid homage to the history of houses going back to the ancient Romans, how there were architectural clues embedded in the design. We didn't have to understand it to love it, he said. Love it now, understand later.

When the house was finally finished, we drove over with a case of champagne. Max was wearing a white linen suit, the one he wore to get married in, and a poppy in his lapel. Their friends came streaming in, I remember light and laughter blending, and the house became ours. In the middle of the party, I went upstairs to Mudie's studio on the third floor. Max had designed the room especially for her, with long, large windows overlooking the yard. Mudie was standing at one of the windows with her arms crossed, looking out. She turned and gave me a mysterious half-smile that made me realize for the first time that there were whole shimmering areas of her I knew nothing about.

"Is anything the matter?" I asked.

Mudie turned, her black eyes full of tears, of a reluctant love. "Natural light," she said. "It's what I've always wanted."

Max, Mudie, and Mudie's best friend, Kendra, in the front seat of Bertha, Bobbie and me in the back. The three grown-ups are laughing, their hair rumpled by the wind. Max drives the wrong way down a one-way street, trying to go after the Roman candy man. The Roman candy man's cart and mule are stopped at the corner; Max and Kendra pile out, return to the car with fistfuls of long sweet taffy wrapped in wax paper. Bobbie chooses a vanilla stick, I choose chocolate. We eat our Roman candy in silence, chewing carefully so as not to miss the grown-ups' conversation. Kendra tosses us a look in the back seat. "Childhood is charming," she says. "Why can't adulthood be charming?"

"Most people get over that," Mudie says petulantly.

Kendra, defiant, says, "Well, I haven't."

Max drums his fingers on the steering wheel of the car. The wheel is grooved, and Max explores the grooves nervously. "I'm going to miss this car," he says. "You should always have reminders from your poor days."

"We have plenty," Mudie says. Her voice is sweet and sour, like lemon drops. Max drives home. The air is thin, bitter, citrusy. Kendra takes a cab back to wherever she is staying; I have the feeling adult days are often like this.

three

"There's a powerful odor of mendacity in this house," Bobbie says. She drags a long white rag across the row of shutters a recent hurricane has blown off. The windows to the breakfast room shine like newly polished teeth. Bobbie sprays, I wipe.

"A powerful odor," Bobbie says.

In the last year she has gotten thin; parts of her keep disappearing. Sometimes she seems to be all arms and legs, other times all eyes. My own eyes are gray. I like to think I was named Gray after the color of my eyes, but of course Mudie couldn't have known when I was born what color they were going to be.

"What do you mean?"

Bobbie squints. "Max and Mudie took me to a shrink. Some British guy on Prytania Street named Dr. Cavendish. An *adolescent* psychiatrist." She says the word *adolescent* with disdain. "Of course Max is pretending it's just for some tests so they can send me to that hotshot school in Virginia."

"How do you know it's not?"

"Because of the powerful odor." Bobbie tweaks my nose. "Mendacity. You can smell it a mile away."

I know what Bobbie means: the smell of lies. Something is going on between Max and Mudie, something having to do with Mudie's best friend, Kendra. The odd, bashed look that crosses Max's face when Kendra's name is mentioned. Also, something inside Bobbie is increasing these days, some force that makes her do wild and reckless things that she makes me promise not to tell Max about. Shoplifting, smoking cigarettes, having more than our usual one glass of wine at dinner. Telling lies; stealing things from Max and Mudie's drawers. One day she brought home a black goat for a pet. Hannah made her take it back. Max, preoccupied with order and beauty, acts oblivious. But not Mudie. These days Mudie hardly leaves the house; that has to tell us something.

The windows, finished, reflect a fall sky streaked with clouds. Bobbie puts her arm around my neck, pulls me to her, mugs in the newly polished glass. There are perhaps twelve of us, thirteen. "So," Bobbie says, "what do you really think of me?"

"Nothing."

"Come on."

"What do you want from me?"

"The truth. What you think."

"About what?"

"Am I ethereal, or what?"

"Sure, you're ethereal."

Bobbie is playing now, stepping on my feet and trying to dance on them, but I'm not in a playful mood. "You think I ought to see that guy," she says, "that something *is* the matter with me. That I'm crazy."

"I don't know what you mean."

Bobbie breaks away from me, twelve Bobbies in the blue window-panes. "Well, I *feel* crazy," she says.

I look around, and for a second there are only reflections of Bobbie, none of me. "Don't say that, Bobbie" I say.

"But you know it's true."

"No."

"Liar." Bobbie turns away from me and faces all twelve of her reflections in the breakfast-room windows. She makes a fist and whirls around and, pop, breaks the windows, pop, pop, just like that, every one of them. When she's done, she's hardly even bleeding.

A week later two policemen stand in our driveway looking crest-fallen. Mudie invites them in with a nervous smile. One of the men found Bobbie's purse under a bar stool in the Napoleon House downtown on Chartres Street. The purse is stuffed with Max's aunt's jewelry. "Your daughter tried to hock the pieces at Adler's," the policeman explains. "Fortunately they recognized the stuff and called us in. Some of it's mighty valuable, ma'am."

"Officers," Mudie says, "I think this is a family matter—"

"Sure thing." The officer winks and hands Mudie over the bag, obviously relieved. "Take care now."

"We will," Mudie says. "You too."

From the second-floor hallway I wait for the policemen to leave, then go to Mudie in the library. She is standing by Max's desk, holding out Bobbie's purse full of jewelry. "Gray," she asks me, "what do you make of this? Was Bobbie in some difficulty that she needed to sell Aunt Elise's jewelry?"

"What's in there?"

"Two quite valuable necklaces that your uncle Stanton gave to Aunt Elise. They went to Max when she died, since Uncle Stanton raised Max, after all. But why should Bobbie take them?"

"I don't know. She does weird things sometimes."

Mudie looks at me, and a current passes between us, a dangerous current that neither of us touches. She sighs, blows a strand of hair from her forehead, and puts the jewelry back in Max's drawer. Later, over coffee, I hear them discussing it.

"But why should Bobbie want to sell the jewelry, Max?" Mudie is saying. "It seems, well, peculiar."

"Don't ask me. You're her mother. If you didn't spend so much time up in your studio you'd probably know. Maybe Bobbie was going to give the money to charity. Plato says we pursue the good and beautiful. Why do you assume otherwise?"

"I don't assume anything," Mudie says, "certainly not where Bobbie is concerned. I try to be her mother, but she manages in most instances to . . . to prevail. I never have had much influence over her, you know that. This jewelry thing is a mystery to me."

"Not at all." Max waves her away. "Bobbie's just bored, that's all. She'll be fine once she goes away to school. You'll see."

In the kitchen Hannah declares, "I don't care *what* Plato say. Your daddy is so crazy about that child, she could steal the sun out of the sky before he'd notice. Or else he'd say, 'Don't worry, we can just wear sweaters, we didn't need that old sun nohow.' "

Bobbie says, "I hate psychiatrists. You can hear their thoughts rattling around in their heads but they don't ever solve anything. All Dr. Cavendish does is listen and nod, and every once in a while he says, 'And what do you think?' "

"Otherwise, what's he like?"

Bobbie narrows her eyes, concentrating. "He's British. About as old as Max but more ruined-looking. Smokes a lot. Wears turtleneck sweaters. Buys a lot of antiques he can't pay for. I overheard some guy calling him on the phone, dunning him for money. Makes him seem more vulnerable, don't you think?"

"What do you talk to him about?"

Bobbie shrugs. "Max and Mudie and all their friends. Businessmenartistes, I call them. So much flair, so much style. Of course, we talk about sex, too."

"Sex?"

"Don't look so concerned. I'm a virgin as far as I can remember but I told Cavendish a lot of sexual experiences that he wrote down on his legal pad. God, sometimes I'm in awe of my own lies. They stream out behind me like a phosphorescent wake in a calm ocean. I lie, therefore I am. Our family motto."

"What does Cavendish say about you?"

"He thinks I'm a genius. He says all my problems come from Max and Mudie."

"How?"

"Because they're thwarted. Bottled up. Prevented from being their true selves. They *use* us, Gray."

"Everybody's thwarted," I say.

"Not like they are." Bobbie says. "Look at Max. Obsessed with order and beauty. Everything has to *look* perfect. And Mudie. Ever wonder why Mudie sometimes can't leave the house?"

I think a minute; Mudie is at home a lot, but I don't think of her as avoiding the outside, only as filling the house on Harmony Street with her wraithlike spirit.

"It's called agoraphobia," Bobbie says, "fear of the marketplace. Of open spaces. An open life."

"Mudie goes out sometimes."

"Not regularly, like other people. Some days she's hot and shoots up like mercury. Other times, she sinks." Bobbie smiles craftily, the way she does when she is deliberately twisting a story. She does it to Max and Mudie all the time; sometimes I barely know what's true, what isn't. It's typical of Bobbie to come home from seeing a psychiatrist and say things are wrong with the rest of us. It's just like her.

I know where to go to find out everything Bobbie thinks. Bobbie keeps a journal. She doesn't hide it; she leaves her black book lying right out on the pine desk Max gave her for her eighth birthday. Sometimes I feel guilty reading her thoughts—it feels like stealing—

but then with Bobbie I figure I need everything I can find to go on. Besides, there's something about the way she leaves her black book lying around that makes me think she *wants* me to find it. I think she wants me to talk to her about her life because she's so busy living it she doesn't have much time to interpret what happens to her.

There's a page in Bobbie's journal I keep turning to, with sexual things about Max and Mudie. The first time I read it I didn't believe it. Bobbie came home one of those days when Mudie was out and saw Max through the keyhole in bed with Kendra Hamilton. Watched the whole thing through the keyhole because of course Max was stupid and classical enough to install hardware with big, elegant keyholes on all the doors. Afterward Kendra straightened the sheets and Max picked blond hairs from the down pillows. Would Bobbie tell lies in her journal? Why would she bother? Why would Max be stupid enough to go to bed with Kendra in our own house? I don't know. Since we were small Bobbie has had the kind of mind that likes to make things up, but Bobbie's not small anymore, and neither am I. This time I wonder if she's telling the truth.

I decide to confront Max and Mudie. It's Sunday morning; the newspaper is spread open on the glass table in the breakfast room. Mudie is wearing a frayed silk nightgown and ballet slippers; Max wears a white robe cinched tight at the waist.

I hang around the doorway. Sunlight pours in the windows, blinding me.

"What is it, Gray?" Mudie asks. "Is there something on your mind?"

Still blinded, uncomfortable, I blurt out the words. "I want to know if Max is having an affair with Kendra."

"My Kendra?" Mudie asks. "Kendra? Where did you get that idea?"

"From Bobbie's journal. She leaves it around so everyone can read it."

Mudie starts to laugh, spitting hot coffee over the comics. In a minute she controls herself and turns serious. "You know very well

Max isn't capable of that kind of deception. And Kendra is my closest friend. You have to stop believing everything Bobbie says, Gray."

I look at Max. His Adam's apple bobs up when he swallows. He's got that same odd look I've seen before, but it's obvious to me he's trying to control himself. "Gray," he finally says, "you shouldn't put stock in everything Bobbie says or, God knows, writes in that journal of hers. She's trying to get attention, pulling your leg. How many times do we have to warn you, Bobbie has a very vivid imagination."

"I know. She's brilliant." I say the words with sarcasm that comes from not being heard, or taken seriously.

"Very brilliant. Listen, I think all she was doing was playing an elaborate game with you, inventing stories to get your goat. Having fun, really," Max says.

"Fun."

"Do me a favor. Always take what Bobbie says with a grain of salt. She's so bright that ordinary life just bores her sometimes."

He's off, Max is, talking about how smart Bobbie is. You'd think he'd created her out of the dust in his own backyard instead of just happening to be her father. I let him talk; Max likes to hear the sound of his own voice, deep, gentle, reassuring. A voice I can almost believe in. Almost, but not quite.

"I love you, Graycat," Bobbie says, "I don't mean to be bad. To wreck things. It just happens."

"I know."

"I keep trying to be what Max wants, God knows it would be easier on all of us, but I just can't. His picture of me and my picture of me are different.

"You're my sweet sister Gray," she adds. "You've always under-stood."

"Bobbie, you do the things I sometimes feel like doing but don't dare. Everything you do stands out, people notice. Me, they hardly see. But it doesn't mean I don't have some of the same feelings."

We're sitting at the soda fountain at Smith's Drugstore on St. Charles Avenue, next to the Pontchartrain Hotel. The drugstore is patronized mostly by guests from the hotel; Bobbie and I look out of place. We're here because Bobbie wanted to buy me all the ice cream I could eat.

"Another chocolate shake, please."

"Make it two," Bobbie says.

"Are you sure you want to do this?"

"Positive," Bobbie says. "Don't worry about the money."

After the ice cream we go next door and buy records. When it comes to music, Bobbie is insatiable, and today she's in one of her buying moods. She buys the new Stones album and some old jazz. "Anything you want," she tells me. She flips through the classical for about twenty minutes, comes up with Mahler and Sibelius. She only knows about this music from Max; Max loves music. When she's done selecting ten or twelve records, Bobbie takes out a big roll of bills.

"Anything you want," she repeats, flashing the money.

I look around. I don't want anything.

"Gray," Max says, "is this your handwriting?" He holds out a yellow bank check. It's made out for five hundred dollars and signed "Henry Maxwell Maubry." An obvious forgery.

"No."

"Are you sure?"

Bobbie gives me a nudge. We're standing side by side on the library carpet, close but not touching.

"Dishonesty after the fact is worse than the original deed," Max says.

Bobbie sighs.

"Neither one of you is leaving this room until I get the complete story of this check. In the first place, forging my signature was unnecessary. You girls have everything you want."

"Not Stones albums," I say, "not Sibelius."

Bobbie kicks me. She wants to take the blame for this one, doesn't even want me to act rebellious.

"Bobbie," Max says, "why did you write my name on this check?"

"I don't know, Max."

He looks at both of us. It might be my imagination, but when he looks at me, his eyes turn weary. "You know," he says, "when I was at Yale there was this extremely gifted student who kept robbing stores. When he finally got caught, it came out that he was bored with his studies. He needed more stimulation."

"Max," Mudie intervenes, "what's your point?"

"I think the analogy is obvious."

Mudie rolls her eyes. "You would think that at a time like this in our family, you would stick to facts."

"I'd like to know the real truth," Max says, "that's all."

Bobbie, Mudie, and I look at one another. It's plain Max has the idea lodged in his head that Bobbie's intellectual superiority excuses all kinds of behavior. This reasoning allows him to be proud when he should be wary. What does it mean that Bobbie hocks necklaces and forges checks? And why now, just before she is going away to school? I look at Mudie for help, but she looks away. When I look at Bobbie she gives me a pleading glance, like that of an animal caught in a trap.

four

obbie is going away tomorrow, to St. Anselm's School in the Blue Ridge Mountains. I don't want her to go but I pretend enthusiasm so nobody can say I'm jealous of Bobbie. I'm jealous but it's more than that: I'm afraid to cut the cord that has existed between us since babyhood. What will my days be like now, what will my world be like now, without Bobbie?

Somewhere in my picture of where Bobbie will be is a choir singing: impossible sweet voices. Bobbie is going to St. Anselm's because Max thinks she will have more opportunities there to develop her potential. This is just like Max—no place is good enough unless it has a reputation. Bobbie wants to become an actress, and they have a drama department at St. Anselm's; they don't just put on a play once a year the way they do at our old school.

I hate St. Anselm's and I've never even been there. Bobbie went with Max for an interview. She came home describing the brick chapel with a white spire rising in the Virginia air and stained-glass windows in the cafeteria. The school smells like cut grass and lemon polish, not dusty old chalkboards and rotting cypress and rain, like our old school.

Mudie helps Bobbie get ready to go. She orders Bobbie's school uniform out of a catalogue, and a week later a heavy package arrives on our doorstep, like a bomb. Bobbie puts the uniform on to show us her new self: pleated plaid skirt, brown brogans, a white oxford blouse with a button-down collar, navy blazer with the school insignia on the pocket. "So," Bobbie asks us—Mudie and I are the ones watching—"what do you think?"

Mudie hesitates. She has that quality of a shy child trying to say the right thing, but then her natural wildness bubbles up. "Bobbie," she says, "you don't have to go to St. Anselm's just because your father wants you to. You can still change your mind."

Bobbie glares. "What do you mean, change my mind? I've wanted to go to St. Anselm's for years. It's the best acting school in the country."

"There are other places," Mudie says.

"I don't want to go to other places. I want to do this." Bobbie frowns, appraising herself in the mirror. I have the feeling that if the moment had taken any longer to pass, she would have broken.

"Well, all right." Mudie lets go, her mind already wandering off on to other things, places of her own she goes to when she can't be here. I want to shake her and say, *"Stay here,"* but Mudie is gone. She hates conflict.

Bobbie turns to me. "What do you think, Gray?"

"I like our old uniform better. Wrinkled brown khakis."

"You're just jealous," Bobbie says.

Later that night I go downstairs for a root beer and overhear Max and Mudie in the kitchen.

"I just don't know, Max," Mudie says, "you might think it's crazy of me, but I have a bad feeling about Bobbie going away."

"Mudie, we can't decide important issues on the basis of bad feelings. We have to do what we think is best for Bobbie."

"I know, but . . ."

"Cavendish approves, doesn't he? It was practically his idea in the first place. He thinks it would be good for Bobbie to be challenged more. To be where there's some real competition for the spotlight. Maybe it would help straighten out some of her recent strange behavior."

"I don't know."

"Don't project your own neurotic fears onto Bobbie," Max says.

"Max, that's not fair."

"Isn't it?"

I'm not even in the room but I can feel Mudie recoil like a sea creature and go back into her shell. Max hears me creaking on the staircase and calls, "Gray, go back to bed." I do, but I don't fall asleep. There is such a nervous feeling in the house.

As the time gets closer for Bobbie to leave, everything becomes like an old movie played too fast. It is as if we are afraid time won't pass if we don't hurry it along. Max speeds off to his office in the mornings, gleaming with new purpose. Mudie bangs away furiously in her studio. Hannah packs Bobbie's clothes, whistling or singing to herself. She doesn't say much, and when Hannah won't talk I know she disapproves.

Bobbie visits all of her friends and buys them lavish going-away presents with money I saw her snitch from Max's top drawer. Max has this beautiful mahogany dresser with shiny brass pulls on it, so much brass that he and Mudie call it the General. Do other people give names to their furniture, their cars?

I am the only one going slow.

Tonight, on Bobbie's last night, Hannah serves Bobbie's favorite dinner of Creole mirlitons stuffed with shrimp. We have lemon doberge cake from Gambino's Bakery for dessert. Max uncorks a bottle of wine, a Sauternes, that tastes sweet and oily and makes me feel sick. I go upstairs to the bathroom. Bobbie follows me and knocks on the door.

"Go away."

"I have something to show you, Gray. If you promise not to tell."

As usual, the invitation is irresistible. I unlock the door and walk down the hall to Bobbie's room. Downstairs, Max is playing Vivaldi.

Bobbie is standing near the window, where the greeny elm-tree light is cool, like a pocket of forest in the room. "Over here," Bobbie says.

She has a double-edged razor blade wrapped in a square of glassine: one of Max's razor blades we aren't supposed to touch. "What are you doing?" I ask.

"You'll see."

Bobbie unwraps the razor blade and holds it between her thumb and forefinger, like a surgeon. The glassine blows away. There is a look of destructiveness in Bobbie's eyes I recognize from somewhere in our history: the black blowy day she lost my kite.

"Careful, that thing is sharp."

Bobbie smiles a beatific smile. She lifts her skirt and turns toward the light and draws the razor blade straight across the side of her thigh. Nothing happens, but then there's a sudden blooming of the blood.

"Lovely," Bobbie says.

"Doesn't it hurt?"

"No. If you do it fast enough, it doesn't."

Bobbie draws the blade across again, and this time I hold my breath until I see the blood bleed; it's like magic or some miracle or some terrible disease we share. The third time she does it, I say, "Stop."

Bobbie draws up, as if I've shaken her out of something, some trance or distant place. She turns to me fiercely. "Swear you won't tell Max and Mudie."

"I swear." Easy, because I cannot imagine ever telling our mother and father a thing like this. And what would I say anyway? I sit numb, wordless, while Bobbie puts the razor blade away and washes her cuts. They look deeper than washing will fix, and even with gauze on them, they still bleed. We go back downstairs and sit in the library while Max and Mudie have coffee and listen to Vivaldi. Neither one of them sees the blood running down Bobbie's leg.

Right then I begin to see something I have always known about Bobbie: Something is wrong with her, with the way she thinks and feels and is. Something inside her has been cracked, like the crystal glass Mudie dropped once that didn't shatter, only remained cracked inside. Sometimes Max holds this glass up to the light marveling at its survival, but even he can never get the cracked part out nor can he accept it as part of the pattern.

October, and Bobbie's first grades from St. Anselm's arrive: all A's. She gets the lead in the school's winter production of *Antigone*. Already I feel like she is light-years ahead of me.

To bridge the distance I go to the library on St. Charles Avenue, the enormous brick house under the soft old oaks, the library that was Bobbie's and my childhood refuge. I check out Sophocles' *Antigone* and that night, instead of doing arithmetic, I read the play through. Antigone and Ismene, two sisters like Bobbie and me. Antigone, the daring one, tries to induce Ismene to commit the crime, but Ismene refuses. Later, when Antigone is about to be killed, Ismene begs to share the blame with her, but Antigone refuses. The story reminds me of the times Bobbie and I both did something wrong and Bobbie would take all the blame herself. "There has to be a bad sister and a good sister," she told me once when we were still children, "so that way Max and Mudie can go on thinking we're an ordinary family."

At the time I thought the remark was cryptic, typical of Bobbie. Now, thinking of Antigone locked up in her stone room while Ismene goes unpunished, I start to cry. More than anything I miss my sister, my other half. It feels strange to go about my daily life without her, getting dressed in the morning, daydreaming through school, keeping Hannah company in the kitchen.

"Child," Hannah tells me, "you got moon eyes."

"I miss Bobbie. I'm bored."

"Bobbie's kind of excitement we don't need. You know, most of the time she was a torment."

Bobbie writes me once or twice and then the letters stop. There's an occasional weekend phone call, but since I have to share it with Max and Mudie, it doesn't feel like mine. A lot of the time I hole up with botany textbooks and draw leaves; I start a leaf collection, each specimen dried and affixed to a separate card, labeled in Latin. The beauty and precision of my own work astonishes me. It's the first thing I've ever done that I've admired.

At night when Max and Mudie go up to bed I begin going to Max's library to read. Biology books, Darwin, *Gray's Anatomy* are my favorites. With the rest of the family dominating the arts I feel more comfortable with science. I keep my own journal now, filled mostly with sketches of plants and birds.

One of my school friends, Tessa, has a house on Bayou Liberty, in St. Tammany Parish. I go there on weekends and we take a canoe out on the bayou, paddling the dark green water. I love bayou country more than any other place; it makes me feel part of earth's beauty. When we get tired of canoeing, we flop down on the deep grassy hill that rises to Tessa's family's house and look up at the sky through amazing gnarled oaks. Cypress knees press into our backs. When I'm in bayou country I don't feel as tense and bottled up as I do on Harmony Street.

At first Max read my withdrawal into my own pursuits as jealousy of Bobbie. He even teased me about it. "Max," Mudie said, "that's enough. You know how touchy adolescents are."

"I'm not touchy," I said. "I'm not an adolescent. I'm old, way older than either of you."

I retreat to my room, which has begun to be transformed with plant and animal life. I have several aquariums, and a terrarium, and my favorite illustrations of leaves are mounted on the walls. I got Mudie to let me tear down my flowered wallpaper and paint the walls a color called celadon, a mossy gray-green.

"You could have consulted me," Max says when he sees the results. "After all, I designed the house."

"Bobbie gets to have her room however she likes."

I can almost hear Max say, "That's Bobbie," but he doesn't, he closes his mouth on the words. "You're growing up," he says instead, almost with a sigh. "Sometimes I think of you as still a child."

What we don't talk about is my restlessness, my anxiety. These days I mistrust my surroundings, and myself. I keep thinking something is going to happen that will throw me back into my former life, the childhood I shared with Bobbie. How I loved Max then, how we both did.

I remember liking to play with the gold chain he wore on his vest that had a small gold ivy leaf and a mythical creature called a wyvern dangling on it. Max belongs to a club called the Wyvern Club that meets once a month upstairs at Antoine's. The members take turns reading papers on arcane subjects—the history of beekeeping, legal conundrums, the real identity of Shakespeare—and all the club's correspondence is written in Latin. I used to think that Max was charmed, and that his life was perfect. Now I know, but don't yet understand, that the life Max and Mudie live isn't ordinary. I keep expecting a loud crash, the dropped crystal glass, or an ugly incident over Kendra. I build my life around this certainty, certain it will come.

A drama critic attends the opening-night performance of *Antigone* at St. Anselm's and writes, "Bobbie Maubry is incandescent. She has a quality, call it the pure acetylene of Antigone, that makes her burn and shine above the rest."

I keep the clipping in my wallet next to my library card, another talisman of Bobbie. The last few times I've spoken to her on the phone she has sounded so elated, so false, that I didn't know what to say to her. She's become very popular as a result of her dramatic success, and while I'm happy for her, something about the way she talks makes me agitated. There's a high, out-of-control pitch to her conversation. Even her words spill out too fast.

It's only been a few months since Bobbie went away, but in my mind ten or twenty years have passed. Yet, I think, not for Bobbie— Bobbie will come home young as the wind while Max and Mudie and I will be old, changed. Deprived of Bobbie we flounder, mistrustful of our own selves. She gave us a focus, a center, someone to worry about, admire, and endlessly discuss.

Now we pick at our dinners, listen halfheartedly to Max reciting items from *The New York Times*. Our own paper, the *Picayune*, isn't sophisticated enough for him. One night, suddenly bored and ready to explode at this routine, I get up from the table in the middle of dinner and leave. It's never occurred to me to do this before: I never realized before that I don't have to be hostage to Max's need to control us all. How many times has he made me hysterical with boredom? Meanwhile, true to Mudie's prediction I am beginning to bloom—one large, late flower. Or am I simply ready to self-destruct?

Nathan Kentor, a friend since nursery school, becomes my best friend. His father, Darwin Kentor, has been a friend of Max's for years and is a fellow member of the Wyvern Club. Darwin became an inventor when he had a nervous breakdown after twenty years of practicing law. Nathan looks exactly like his father: brown hair, tortoiseshell glasses, and an expression of mild curiosity on his face. In all the time Nathan and I have known each other, it's only lately he's started to take any real interest in me.

Nathan sits on the hood of Max's car. He does this to irritate Max, but Max is too polite to say anything. Also, Max sees Nathan as a potential suitor for me. He doesn't want to drive Nathan off.

Nathan shreds a cigarette butt. Nathan has a habit of shredding things: cigarettes, matches, newspapers, anything he can find. His fingernails are bitten to the quick of his gentle, tapered fingers.

"My father's invented a smoking machine," he tells me. "To demonstrate how bad it is to smoke. The machine has this little pair of lungs that get clogged up instantly with tar. It has a pair of chrome lips. You insert a cigarette between the lips and the machine smokes for you. Wave of the future, my father claims."

"What's the point?"

"To keep people from smoking. Me, actually. My father is totally opposed to smoking. This artist friend of his painted a picture for our downstairs hall, a pair of blackened lungs. Acrylic on canvas, signed, everything. Turns out my father *commissioned* the painting. Can you believe it? He's so afraid I'm going to get lung cancer or something. Keeping me from smoking has become my father's purpose in life."

"Does the machine kiss?"

Nathan laughs. "Probably not. My father's not a romantic man. He doesn't approve of kissing. I suppose if you had two of the smoking machines you could put them together and they could blow smoke rings at each other."

Nathan flicks his cigarette away, looks at me with an expression of gentle mockery. He has a way of making me happy in small, idle ways. Sitting on the hood of Max's Mercedes, smoking in the afternoon sunlight, talking, trying things out.

We ride our bikes to Audubon Park. Under a canopy of trees near the lagoon Nathan abruptly hops off and flops down on his back.

"What are you doing?"

"Gray," he says, "I've decided to make you my project. My father thinks I should never be without a project."

"Is your father really an inventor?"

Nathan shakes his head. "Patent attorney. He only became an inventor when his law firm fired him. He had a manic episode. Started calling the firm's clients in the middle of the night and inviting them to go out in his plane. He has his pilot's license, but flying with him isn't too safe."

"Why not?"

"He's manic-depressive," Nathan says. "When he gets on a high, he'll do anything."

"Max says he's brilliant."

"He's okay. Quirky. It was his idea that I should have a project, but choosing you was my idea. Just in case you come to think the whole thing is gratuitous."

"I've never been anyone's project before," I say.

We lie on our backs awhile, looking at the clouds in the sky. Nathan points out shapes: an eggbeater, a broken nose, crows' feet. Then Nathan begins kissing me. After a few minutes he breaks off.

"Do I have your permission, then?"

"For what?"

"Making you my project."

"Yes."

At home I look up gratuitous in the dictionary. "Given or done without good reason," it says. That's it. That's what I want. I want nothing between Nathan and me to be given or done without good reason.

Nathan and I meet on the sward of grass in Rosa Park near my house. We lie on the grass and smoke; in only two weeks I've gone from having coughing fits to being addicted. When we're not smoking we make out.

In a quasi-scientific way I find endearing, Nathan has made a study of me. "You don't eat regular meals," he reads from his chart, "and your sleeping hours are erratic. At school, the only class you show interest in is science. You're antisocial, although you claim to like other people. Your hair always needs brushing and you wear the same thing three days in a row, suggesting indifference. Plus, you're morose. My conclusion: You're depressed."

"I could have told you that."

"My project, as I see it, is to cheer you up."

Mostly so far we've done a lot of talking and kissing and smoking; sometimes we go to movies and make out under an old Indian blanket. Another element Nathan believes in is risk. He thinks I need to take more risks.

"Like what?"

"See? The fact that you can't think of anything risky is proof that your wilder side needs developing."

"*Nathan.*"

"All right. Let's say, for example, you managed to sneak me up to your bedroom at four in the morning, without your parents knowing. That would qualify as taking a risk."

"How do we do that?"

"Think, Gray."

"Okay, but I don't see the point."

"The point is to change your outlook. Most people, including you, see the world through the wrong end of a telescope. A dark and diminished place. No wonder you're depressed. I want to turn the telescope around, or better, throw it away entirely. I want more for you, Gray. I want everything for you."

That night I go to sleep with my window open. Tied to my big toe I have a piece of kite string, which runs out of the window down to the ground below. At two in the morning, Nathan starts tugging on the string. I untie the end that is around my toe and go down to the back door and let him in. He insists on coming into my bedroom with me; that way we risk Max catching us. I can't help thinking this whole thing is a comic variation of a wedding night, except Nathan doesn't touch me. We smoke a few cigarettes and talk. Then Nathan kisses me good-bye and climbs out of the window and down the elm tree. I hear him drop softly onto the gravel driveway; he waves good-bye without turning around.

The phone rings just as I am falling back asleep. It's three in the morning.

"The Reverend Mr. Hadley calling from St. Anselm's School. This is terribly unfortunate news about your daughter Bobbie. We've taken her to Mercy Hospital in Charlottesville. About an hour ago she tried to kill herself. Razor blades, I think. She's listed in critical condition. I feel it my duty to inform you that St. Anselm's assumes no further responsibility for your daughter's welfare. You must pick her up within twenty-four hours. I'm sorry, but you understand our position, Mrs. Maubry?"

"I'm not Mrs. Maubry," I say. "I'm Bobbie's sister, Gray."

"Well then, put your mother on."

I put the phone down and walk to the other side of the house, where Max and Mudie are asleep. It kills me to deliver this news, I don't even have the right words in my head, but before I can finally knock I realize Max is on the line, cursing the Reverend Mr. Hadley.

They appear in the door of their bedroom, pale and grieved. Max was once a man; now he is a shirt and tie and shoes; the rest of him is fear. Mudie's face is clenched tight.

Max starts to rant. "The lousy fucking tight-assed Episcopalian bastard. 'Assumes no further responsibility,' does he? The lizard. They ought to cut his collar off and hang him by it. I'm going to get Bobbie myself. My child, Bobbie. Take care of your mother," he tells me.

Max goes to the airport to catch a plane to Virginia, Mudie and I go to the Allgood Restaurant on Prytania Street, open all night for the doctors and nurses at Touro Infirmary going off duty. Once inside, I know why we have chosen the place: for its soft old linoleum, mirrored walls, aroma of coffee and waffles, the feel of sanctuary against the night world. Bobbie was born across the street, at Touro. So was I.

We order, and Mudie starts talking. She talks mostly about herself. How she grew up in an old tumbledown house on Esplanade Avenue, back of the Quarter, and how as a young woman she went north to Bennington, Vermont, to study pottery. In New York she met Max.

"He was so charming, and so charmed, he was like a line drawing by Cocteau—witty and elegant yet fresh, new—I fell in love."

Bobbie was born. At two she had a prodigious vocabulary and spoke in complete, grammatical sentences.

"You know, Gray," Mudie says, looking around the mirrored walls at the tired doctors, the nurses slumped in chairs reading the paper, "the first time I realized something was radically different about Bobbie was the time she painted brown bears on the walls of the nursery using caca from her pants. I was desperately afraid Max would find out, do something silly. I called up Hannah on her day off and made her come over, and then I lugged paint in from the shed and repainted the entire room. When Max got home for dinner, the walls were still wet. He looked at me strangely, but he didn't say anything."

"Why didn't you tell him? Why did you go through all that rigmarole?"

"I was afraid. I didn't want Max to think Bobbie might be imperfect in any way. Disturbed. Sometimes when a child plays with feces, it's an early warning sign of a mental disorder. And you know Max— he's only happy with perfection. I wanted our life to keep being happy. I believed I could make it so. There wasn't any room for Bobbie's behavior."

"A lot of babies smear poop," I say.

"Yes, but not like *this*. There they were, all lined up on Bobbie's walls: big, smelly, malicious brown bears. Not cute baby bears."

We go on to other things—her parents' romantic marriage; her older brother, damaged by the war. When the waitress comes, she brings waffles, and the lightness, the impossible lightness and butteriness of those waffles, seems a revelation. We eat without talking. When we are done, we take the St. Charles Avenue streetcar home and I lie awake until daylight, listening to the distant snarling of the lions at the zoo, carried upriver by the wind.

five

I n the morning there are no sounds of Mudie.
Usually she is up early, pacing the floor of her
studio. Then the phone rings and I hear her voice muffled behind the
bedroom door. I'm afraid for her, afraid because she is so easily
disturbed by small events. What will a big event like Bobbie's suicide
attempt do to her?

I knock, get no answer, go in. The bedroom is barely disturbed; for
a second I almost don't see Mudie lying coiled in the middle of the
bed. The phone is off the hook. "Max called," she says. "Bobbie's
going to live. She lost a lot of blood and they gave her several
transfusions. The doctors want her to stay in the hospital a few days
longer. She's on a psychiatric ward." Mudie pulls the covers up
around her and closes her eyes. "When I talked to Max, his biggest
concern was that she was on a psychiatric ward. He thinks it's a
disgrace."

"Aren't you getting up?" I ask.

"Why?" Mudie opens her eyes again and stares at the ceiling. "What is there to do? Where is there to go?"

"You might feel better if you acted normal."

"I doubt it," Mudie says. Her eyes are the deep green-black of the bayous, filled with tears. She smiles uncertainly at me. "Tell me it wasn't my fault."

"What?"

"Tell me Bobbie's suicide attempt wasn't my fault."

"It wasn't your fault, Mudie."

"We won't ever be the same, Gray."

"I know."

I feel so sad, and disoriented. It's obvious I'm not going to get any comfort from Mudie, she's so submerged in her own feelings. I wish she'd open her eyes and tell me it's going to be all right, but Mudie can't bring herself to do that. Either she's too sophisticated or she's too childish, that's how Mudie is. She's too sophisticated because she knows that Bobbie's suicide attempt is a clear message of something very wrong; she's childish, wanting me to comfort her. I'm only thirteen. I'm her daughter too.

If Max were here he'd make her get up, shower, have breakfast. Max insists it's good to keep routine even in the face of hardship. Maybe he's right.

"Mudie," I say, "I want you to get up. I'm going to run a hot bath for you and make us a delicious breakfast."

"We'll never be the same again," Mudie says. "Bobbie didn't kill herself, but she killed us. I already ate breakfast at the Allgood."

"That was hours ago," I tell her. I go in the bathroom and run a bath in the tub and then I go downstairs. I ask Hannah to make some scrambled eggs and toast. And coffee. Lots of hot coffee. Made properly the old New Orleans way, spoonful by spoonful of hot water dripped in the white enamel pot.

In the bedroom Mudie is still in bed. The sight of her angers me; I try to haul her up out of bed, but she collapses in tears. "Go away," she keeps crying. For a minute I'm afraid she's going to bite me. I lean next to her ear and sing one of the songs she used to sing when Bobbie and I were little, the Creole song "Fais Do Do." Mudie listens and grows quiet. Then she gets up and takes her clothes off and slides into the bathtub.

While she bathes I lay out some fresh clothes for her. A white shirt and slender black pants. At forty, Mudie is a beautiful woman. I don't have any adolescent hatred of her yet, only wistfulness and a longing that she would stand up for herself more.

On her bureau is a photograph, a black-and-white photograph of Max and Mudie taken the day they met. He was studying architecture then, and she was on her way to sell her father's old Royal typewriter so she could afford to buy a winter coat. The picture shows Max and Mudie, their arms linked, standing on a windy corner. They have an unguarded look on their faces, like people who are not afraid to have experiences. Max has on a three-piece suit and bow tie; Mudie is wearing one of those funny half-hats with a veil, and open-toed shoes. They are looking not at each other, but ahead, into the future. It is winter in New York, you can tell because you can see their white breaths in the photograph. Their whole lives lie so clearly in front of them you can almost see those lives; they are so young, so trusting, so full of promise.

Everybody on the bus turns to stare at me.

"It's true, isn't it," Boy Legendre says. "Bobbie Maubry tried to kill herself. She swallowed a bunch of pills or something. My mother heard about it at Piggly Wiggly."

"Don't answer them," Nathan says. He is sitting on the back seat of the bus next to me, working a mathematics problem.

"I have to, Nathan. They're going to know anyway."

"They're animals," Nathan says. He rubs out an answer with the eraser on his pencil and fills in another.

"I have to go to school here," I say. "I can't act afraid of them."

"You're right." Nathan looks up. "I hadn't thought of it that way."

"Come on, Gray, tell us," Boy is saying. "Did she swallow a bunch of Seconal or what?"

"Go ahead," Nathan says, "tell them."

"My sister slashed her wrists. She had ninety-six stitches in all."

"Jesus," somebody says.

The bus is quiet. Everybody is embarrassed except Nathan and me. "The press conference is over," Nathan finally announces in his mild, clear voice. "Is everybody satisfied?" He slumps back in the seat next to me, resumes writing the proof of a theorem. "I don't think anybody will bother you again," he says. "If they do, let me know."

"Thanks, Nathan."

After a moment of scribbling Nathan says, "You aren't as afraid of things as you think, Gray."

That night Max calls. Bobbie is coming home tomorrow. He had a consultation with the staff psychiatrist at the hospital, and they think she can live at home "while she's being evaluated."

Mudie comes into my room at bedtime.

"So," she says, "tomorrow Bobbie comes home."

"Right."

"How was school?"

I switch off the light. "Fine."

"You know, Gray, some of the students are going to be curious. They might ask a lot of questions, say things about Bobbie that are going to hurt or even embarrass you. I just thought I'd warn you, so if the subject comes up, you'll be prepared. People can be cruel sometimes."

I flop on my side, hitch up the covers. "Don't worry, Mudie," I say. "Nobody's like that. They're not a bunch of animals." My lie is a gift to Mudie, a small sentence of comfort she can take to bed with her. Why should she have to worry about both Bobbie and me? I can worry about myself.

• • •

I wake up early the day Bobbie is to come home. The house is quiet, as if it is fragile, afraid. Then I hear the distant tinkering of Mudie upstairs in her studio. I can almost hear her thoughts gathering, the house is so considerate. I try to think for myself what all this means, but Mudie's thoughts fly up to me suddenly like birds disturbed from a tree. I have no thoughts of my own. And anyway, I know she will do whatever Max says should be done, her own thoughts gone like birds.

I drip coffee in the familiar enamel pot that is so much a part of Mudie it is almost alive, hesitant and fragile as she is. Mudie smiles when I bring up two cups in black mugs from Bennington Potters. They are almost Greek, these cups; they speak to me of fate and liveliness. I have a sense today that whatever has been set in motion by Bobbie's suicide attempt will unravel us. Mudie's eyes quaver with light and uncertainty. She has green eyes today; tomorrow they may darken with sadness.

"I was really just puttering around in here," she admits. "I was trying not to think. Sometimes thinking is the worst thing you can do."

"Max always tells me to think first, but I can't seem to."

"You're too like me," Mudie says, "gifted in feeling."

It's the first time she's given a name to how I am, how she is. I imagine Max would only sneer and say, "Where does feeling get you?" But then Max is one of those people who think of the world as a series of destinations, not a series of places.

"Oh," Mudie says, looking out of the window, "here they are."

We watch as Max's old cream-colored Mercedes pulls up in the circular gravel driveway. His headlights throw two beams of light against the fog off the Mississippi. Mudie clutches at me but I push her away. I want to scream, "You're supposed to be the mother, I'm the child!" Mudie stares hard out the window at Max and Bobbie getting out of the car, but in fact the scene looks pretty natural. Max goes around to the passenger side and opens the door, as if we weren't all passengers but some of us actually drivers, in control.

Bobbie glances up at our window. She knows we're there watching. The sunlight must be blocking her vision of us because it feels like she is waving blindly.

"Poor thing," Mudie says. "How should we act?"

"Just be yourself."

"I wish I knew what that was."

"You're her mother, remember?"

Mudie cries harder. "I guess you're right," she says.

"Come on, Mudie. Go down there."

I stay upstairs, partly because I don't want to be in the way when Mudie goes to hug Bobbie, partly because I don't know what to say. I go to my own room, arrange myself on the bed, compose a face for the occasion, but by the time Bobbie knocks on my door, I've let my expression lapse. A glimpse in the mirror tells me I look rumpled and sad while Bobbie looks neat, pale, efficient.

"So," she says, "want to see my stitches?"

"No."

Bobbie closes the door and takes a cigarette out of her pocket. I see that in her absence we have both taken up smoking, which Bobbie does with a nervous, quirky grace. She is wearing a long-sleeved oxford-cloth shirt and baggy gray flannel pants, not that preppy school uniform. "I really did it this time, didn't I, Gray?" she says.

"I guess so."

"Cigarette?"

"Thanks."

"You can't fool me"—Bobbie grins—"I bet smoking isn't the only thing you've picked up since I left. How about sex?"

I blush, think of Nathan. Bobbie flips open a box of cigarettes and lights one for me with a gold cigarette lighter I haven't seen before. "Dunhill," she says, "a present from Ted White. My drama coach."

"It's beautiful," I say.

"He was the one who found me, the night I did it. He found me on the floor of the girls' room. The *little girls'* room, as Mudie used to call it." Bobbie exhales and looks around my room as if it's a place she doesn't quite recognize. "Well, well," she says, "I guess we're not little girls anymore, are we?"

"I guess not."

"Good-bye, Graycat," she says suddenly.

"Why are you saying good-bye? You just got home."

"I'm telling you good-bye because you and I both know it's never going to be the same. I've crossed the line. Neither of us can ever go back."

"Bobbie, don't." My eyes well with tears; I don't want to hear Bobbie telling me this. I want to hear her say that things will be mended and we can go back to being sisters together on Harmony Street. Except that deep down I know Bobbie's right. I can feel how far we've drifted away already.

I don't usually have much interest in the mail but when it comes today I notice a funny letter on flyaway blue paper. It's addressed to Bobbie, and when I hold the blue envelope up to the light, I think I can see the name *Ted* through the thin paper.

In the library, a fire is burning although nobody is in the room. Max and Mudie come in and find me holding the letter. "What's that?" Max asks, lifting the twin arches of his eyebrows as he looks at me.

"It's a letter."

"For whom?" Mudie says.

"For Bobbie. It's from St. Anselm's."

"Where is Bobbie?" Max asks.

"Gone for a walk."

It might be my imagination, but Max's hair looks grayer than it did when he left to bring Bobbie home, and his skin seems looser on his body. He watches without comment when I hold the blue edge of the letter out for the fire; it nips the edge, then eagerly consumes the rest. The letter burns rapidly, all but the last pale letters of the word *Yours*, which turn purplish, then ashen. Max gives me a cool look of new regard. There's no need for either of us to say anything.

Mudie looks alarmed. Is it because she senses that something in me has changed?

"I didn't think you'd want Bobbie to read any letters from that school," I say with quiet authority. The truth is, I don't want Bobbie to have anything to do with those people, especially not Ted White. Still, I'm not going to say anything to Max and Mudie about him; my loyalty to Bobbie goes at least that far.

"I hate theater people," I say, more vehemently than I feel. "They're all phonies. Giving each other presents, sending flowers. They'd probably applaud if Bobbie had killed herself right on stage, *Bravo!* I can just imagine the reviews."

Max says, "Since Bobbie's not going back to St. Anselm's, I see no purpose in encouraging any friendship that flourished there. We'll find another school for Bobbie. Maybe a place in New England."

Mudie gives Max a queer look, as if she can't be sure she heard him right. "Max," she says hesitantly. She is on sacred ground now, and she knows it. "The school term is half over anyway. I think we should wait until Bobbie is feeling better to decide on a new school."

"Nonsense," Max says, but without much heart. "I always thought that place was flaky. Too full of high-strung, inbred Southerners. They're enough to make anybody loony."

Mudie says, "So what you would choose for her instead is a lot of intense, bitter, inbred New Englanders. That would be so much better for Bobbie, wouldn't it?"

Max looks like somebody hit him on the head. He is so unused to sarcasm or any argument at all from Mudie that it's as if she had spoken in tongues. "I really think you should put your own needs second and Bobbie's first," Mudie says, quietly. Her quiet fills the room, seems to fill the whole house.

Max stares at her; his quiet matches hers. "I thought I *was* doing that," he says. He is in unexplored territory now, this foreign land of Mudie's challenge. Now he looks small and lost.

Hannah comes in and draws the library curtains while the three of us just stand there. The sun has gone down without anybody noticing.

Bobbie comes down to dinner. Her hair is neatly combed; her face looks as pale and composed as a child's. She says grace, to please Max. I had forgotten how pure her voice is, how resonant its tones can be. Nobody says anything that might upset anybody else, yet even so we are all upset. We try to be normal, we *are* normal, or at least what passes for normal in most places, but none of us *feels* normal. Max keeps pulling on his mustache; Mudie looks out of the window. Hannah serves carefully, holding out the dishes tenderly to each of us. Especially to Bobbie, tender offerings.

The food looks beautiful: filet mignon with mushrooms, rice pilaf, fresh string beans, but everything tastes like sawdust to me. Mudie's china and crystal look unnatural, too fragile on this dark November night. Bobbie pushes her food around on her plate and gives me a smile, faintly mocking. I find myself grinning at Max: Save us, Daddy, save us. He dominates the conversation as usual, and as usual he steers us clear of any subject that might remind us of our emotional pain.

I am thinking, What are we going to do about this, about Bobbie? We are too small, too ordinary, for something like this to happen. I always thought that as families go, we were more than ordinary, we were somehow larger, more heroic than other families; but now I see that we are small and ordinary and afraid.

Max carefully pours each of us a glass of red wine. Careful, we are all so careful. If we are careful enough, maybe nothing more will happen to Bobbie. It will be like one or two careless drops of red wine on Mudie's good tablecloth, no more. Somehow, I don't have much faith in this; and, what is worse, I know that no matter how hard we try to undo what Bobbie has done, we will never be restored. When Max first built this house and the roof leaked, nothing could keep the rain from pouring in, nothing. It was worse than a leak in the roof; "It's fate," Max had said, and we laughed at him. But we don't laugh anymore, not tonight. Bobbie laughs, but then she has to. She needs to try to make us all feel all right. Normal, ordinary, unafraid.

The next day Hannah comes in the morning to unpack Bobbie's trunk. Bobbie and I are in the kitchen when Hannah opens it and takes out Bobbie's Antigone costume, a white toga stained with blood. This was what she wore the night she tried to kill herself; the dramatic touch is somehow embarrassing in our humdrum New Orleans kitchen. Hannah, who always has claimed to have seen everything, merely runs water into the basin, adds Clorox and baking soda, then soaks the toga. The next day I see it hanging on the line.

"So all the multitudinous seas incarnadine *can* be washed clean," Bobbie says, watching the toga flap on the line.

"What's that?" Hannah says.

"Shakespeare. He wrote plays."

Hannah shrugs. "Good for him."

A lot of meetings among Max, Mudie, and psychiatrists. Bobbie stays home while her fate is being decided. She has her stitches out but goes around wearing long-sleeved shirts. She closets herself in her room a lot and reads, and sometimes I hear her banging away at her typewriter, a portable Olivetti Max bought her to take to school. She smokes cigarettes, lighting them with her beautiful gold Dunhill lighter.

Sometimes we take the streetcar to visit our great-grandmother on Coliseum Street, in her lost old house surrounded by a neglected rose garden. Aunt Byrd, as we call her, is ninety-six. Bobbie and I sit in her bedroom and eat peanut brittle while Aunt Byrd tells family stories, which are mostly about how the Maubry family was once great but now has run to seed. "I hate to have to tell you girls this,"

Aunt Byrd says, "but we're a vast ruinous empire of idiots and savants, mostly idiots."

"Not Max. Not Uncle Stanton," Bobbie says.

"Heavens no. I had thirteen children, and how I managed to produce such a diverse range of offspring baffles me. From the no-good Charles to brilliant Stanton. God, he was something. Head of surgery at Tulane when he was twenty-six years old. But he was always surrounded by controversy. People thought it was sacrilegious that he continued an operation after the patient had died just to demonstrate to his students the proper procedure. Nothing wrong with that to me. Stanton always did as he liked. And it was characteristic of him to take in little Max. But one thing your father hasn't told you: Be careful when you pick husbands. Mental illness runs in the family. Pick from good, non-eccentric stock."

At dinner that night Bobbie asks Max, "Is it true that mental illness runs in the Maubry family?"

Mudie chokes on a fishbone; Max turns white. "I'd prefer it if you didn't spend so much time with Aunt Byrd," he tells Bobbie. "She's got a screw or two loose."

"I think she's hilarious," Bobbie says.

"Byrd always makes perfect sense to me," Mudie says.

"Nevertheless," Max continues, looking at Bobbie and me, "as long as you are under my roof, you'll listen to me."

Bobbie pokes me under the table, then says, "Yes, Max," which is her way of letting me know that she has no intention of obeying him. That night I lie awake wondering whether what Aunt Byrd said is true. A vast ruinous empire of idiots and savants. Why is it only the truth that Max forbids us to hear?

I go to Nathan's house after school. He lives four blocks away, and his house is the exact opposite of the one Max built: Nothing is planned. The Kentors have crumbly plaster and an assortment of furniture that reminds me of the mismatched people left at the end of a party. Nathan says his parents have been through so many reverses of fortune they've stopped trying to live in the material world. Max claims they have more money than we do; Mudie says, Who cares?

Nathan's mother, Alice, is a psychologist. She's the most absent-minded person I know. She spends her days wandering in a fog, looking for things she's lost. She speaks in a drawling, gravelly voice. "Has anybody seen my checkbook?" she'll say, and when nobody has: "Oh, then it must be *really* lost. I haven't seen it in about a year."

Nathan claims his mother once lost a pair of diamond earrings. His father filed an insurance claim, and two years later Alice found the earrings stuffed in the bottom of a shopping bag in her closet. Nathan says there's no telling how much money she's thrown away thinking it was junk mail.

I go to Nathan's to avoid going home. I hate the way our house feels these days. Too guarded. I can't get comfortable anywhere, even in my own room. I keep waiting to find out what's going to happen to Bobbie, but no one will tell me anything.

Nathan distracts me. We take the streetcar places, or we ride bikes, or else we sit on the Kentors' sun porch on a faded old chintz sofa and do our homework. Sometimes we make out. Nathan chain-smokes cigarettes and then shreds the filters into ashtrays all over the house. He criticizes my English themes, gives me books to read. I have the feeling that someday I am going to marry Nathan Kentor, but I have no idea what shape my life will take until then.

For Nathan things are more settled. He will go to Harvard, the fifth generation of his family to go there, and then to graduate school. He already has the money saved in a special fund in case his father suffers another disastrous reverse, and this knowledge adds to Nathan's aura of calm. He doesn't seem to mind the predictability of his future; anyway, he says, "it's the small surprises make us who we are."

Nathan likes to spend time in Audubon Park, under the lush overgrown oaks. One afternoon after school we're sitting by the lagoon when I see Bobbie walking with a man I don't recognize.

"That's Chester de la Cruz," Nathan says. Nathan knows who everybody is and what they have a reputation for. "He's a director. He owns a small experimental theater on Magazine Street. He's known for liaisons with young, impressionable women."

"Bobbie's not supposed to get involved with anything having to do with the theater. Max thinks she's too emotionally unstable—vulnerable, you might say. He made her promise to agree the theater would be off-limits."

I start waving to Bobbie. She finishes her conversation with Chester and comes over to me. "Graycat," she says, "my sweet sister Gray." She's wearing dark glasses, and her skin looks white; her hand shakes as she lights a cigarette. Nathan gives me a wondering glance; he thinks Bobbie is taking drugs.

"Bobbie," I say, "Let's go home."

"That was Chester de la Cruz," Bobbie says, "he's a director. He's going to audition me for *Viet Rock*."

"Bobbie, Max will have a fit."

"Let him," Bobbie says. "Just unloosen his tie and stick a spoon under his tongue. A silver spoon." She offers Nathan and me a cigarette.

We sit down and Bobbie resumes talking. Her voice is fast and light, punctuated with laughter that strikes me as coming at the wrong places. She just talks. Tells us all about St. Anselm's School and how after she tried to kill herself the rest of the students were prohibited from writing to her or calling to see how she was. "They managed to make me a leper and then they made me disappear," she says, "so in a way, they succeeded in killing me. They shouldn't have tried to save me in the first place. They should have just let me go. I don't belong here, on this earth. Especially if I can't be in the theater." When she finishes talking, Nathan and I don't know what to say.

• • •

Somehow I'm at Hannah's on a Sunday morning. Max and Bobbie are in Boston staying at the Ritz, which is supposed to make Bobbie feel better while she goes for psychiatric tests, but which really only makes Max feel better. The quietness, the opulence of the hotel calm him, he says. Bobbie doesn't care: anything to keep Max happy until she's done with the tests.

I remember we stayed at the Ritz once when Bobbie and I were children. To us the best part of the whole trip was the sign above the revolving door that said THIS IS NOT AN ACCREDITED EGRESS DOOR. We laughed and laughed at that sign.

Now I'm standing in Hannah's front yard up to my knees in cats. They belong to her next-door neighbors; Hannah hates cats. She says they make her nervous. I put my face up to the screen door and though it's dark in Hannah's house I can see all the way through to the backyard, big red poppies flopping in the sun. They make me want to lie down in them and go to sleep.

Hannah's at church. When she comes home she sees me sitting on her front porch. Sea and Sister skitter into the dark corners as Hannah draws the rocker up next to me and sits.

"To what do I owe the honor?" she says. What she means is, What am I doing at her house in a poor colored neighborhood on a Sunday morning when I could be in Audubon Park, feeding the ducks?

"I'm worried about Bobbie," I say. "What's going to happen to her."

"You always been worried about Bobbie. Has she ever been worried about you?"

"I'm okay. I'm safe. I don't have Bobbie's energy or intelligence. Do you think she's really crazy or is she just trying to tell us something? That's how Bobbie is—she talks in actions."

Hannah looks at me so hard and for so long that I feel worn away. The blanket of cats undulating in the backyard shifts in the sunlight. Eventually Hannah says,

"Let me tell you about madness. One time Sea read the Bible

straight through three times and when she was done, she turned crazy."

"What'd you do?"

"I took her Bible from her and sealed it up with wax and wrote 'Sea' on it and made her promise never to open it again. I put her name on it so God would know about it and come help her."

"And did he?"

"She ain't crazy now," Hannah says.

I'm thinking about Hannah's story and how it could possibly apply to Bobbie, but I can't see a way. For one thing, Bobbie's a completely different person than Sea, more complicated probably, which would mean she would need a more complicated remedy. I'm shocked to even be thinking along these lines, to even consider that Bobbie might be crazy, but then people don't usually slash their wrists after performances of *Antigone.*

"I just want to know, will she get better?"

"Gray, you asking me things you ought to ask the Lord."

I cast my eyes down, and Hannah does too, but hers are cast down in prayer while mine are just restless, looking for answers. Everything I know about God I learned from Hannah; Mudie was always too busy or too general about God and Max thinks all you have to do is study medieval churches. Maybe so, but you have to study a long time to get stone arches and crypts to say what God is. Bobbie and I used to lie awake summer nights under the drone of the ceiling fan and talk about God and tell each other stories and dreams and little ends and bits of conversations and things that happened to us, hoping if we talked long enough, we'd understand.

six

obbie comes home from Boston, and two weeks later her psychiatric evaluation arrives. When everyone's asleep I sneak down to Max's desk and rummage around until I find the information I'm looking for, Bobbie's diagnosis: *schizophrenia, undifferentiated type.* I can't believe this, it seems so final, so removed from the changeable Bobbie I know.

At breakfast the next morning Bobbie says, "Well, isn't anyone going to *talk* about it? Come on, we're all grown-ups here."

Max looks up from his paper. "Talk about *what?*"

"The big S," Bobbie says. She bites into her toast. "Schiz-o-phrenia."

"Exquisite timing," Max says.

"Gray already knows everything," Bobbie says. "She read the report."

Max flushes. "My desk and its contents are my private domain. I thought you girls understood that."

"Max." Mudie's voice is quiet. "Your desk is beside the point. Bobbie and Gray are right; we can't go on blithely ignoring the truth."

"No one's blithe," Max says.

Bobbie looks at me, gives a low whistle. She finishes her toast, licks the marmalade off her fingers, swoops her coffee cup off the table, and says,

"If you two devour one another, you won't have any room left in your stomachs to eat me. Morsel by succulent morsel."

Then she's gone, up to her room to lie on her daybed and listen endlessly to Mozart. Mudie leaves the dishes in the sink and goes up to her studio but I don't hear her start banging in there. Max leaves for work.

That night Max comes home laden with books from the Tulane medical-school library. As Stanton Maubry's nephew he has been granted special library privileges, and he has decided to learn more about schizophrenia before making a decision about Bobbie.

"Fantastic," Bobbie says, "a reprieve." Mudie gives me a long sideways look. I can tell she thinks Max is absurd but has decided to humor him for now. I'm kind of angry that Max is making a hobby out of Bobbie's illness, if it is an illness. To me it feels like he's avoiding the pain of the real situation. Make Bobbie's schizophrenia the focus and his and Mudie's shortcomings fall away. Only Bobbie is lacking, only Bobbie is the problem.

I tell all this to Nathan. "Bobbie's not crazy," he says, "she's being the perfect daughter."

"How?"

"Look at her behavior. So outrageous. Anything your mother and father do pales by comparison. She's letting them off the hook."

"Maybe."

"Count on it," Nathan says. "You grew up with Bobbie. You know her better than anyone on earth. Is she crazy?"

"No."

"Well, then."

Max goes off in the mornings to survey the progress on his new building. He says good-bye, ruffles Mudie's hair, tosses Bobbie a tidbit of praise and me some worthy advice, then he's gone. He acts as if he has everything under control. The three of us—Mudie, Bobbie, and I—look at one another in astonishment; then Mudie shakes her head, her eyes dark with worry. Bobbie smokes another cigarette. Eventually we get up and find our ways into the day.

Some mornings Bobbie comes with me to school; the headmaster at St. Rita's, Mr. Root, told Bobbie to come whenever she wants, to take art or listen in on an English class, no restrictions. The arrangement is temporary, of course, and sometimes I see Bobbie skulking around the art room or sneaking a cigarette behind the bookstore.

Friday after school, I stay to play on the soccer team. I am dribbling the ball downfield when I see Bobbie standing on the sidelines, watching me. She's wearing sunglasses and an olive-green raincoat that comes down to her ankles. Seeing her there makes me mad all of a sudden. I stop, let the ball be stolen from me and carried off. The other team scores.

"Smart move," Bobbie says. "Why did you do that?"

I shrug. "Felt like it."

"You could have scored."

"I want to talk to you," I say.

"Now?"

"I want to see them. The scars."

Bobbie comes with me into the locker room, where we are alone. She takes off her raincoat and hangs it up, then unbuttons both her sleeves and rolls up the cuffs. She turns her hands over, and on the inside of each wrist, running horizontally, are fourteen scars, so new they are still violet, so deep they cut forever into my image of Bobbie. When we were children we made cuts that deep in blocks of wood and inked the designs which we carried home to Mudie in the rain, Bobbie's an old woman, mine a shoe, the new ink running. But with Bobbie's scars I look and look, I can't stop, and each look is like a fresh cut. Then Bobbie rolls her sleeves back down and buttons the cuffs and takes her raincoat off the hook and puts it on. She buttons the buttons and ties the belt. "Don't say I didn't warn you," she says.

After that it gets easier to talk. A week or two later I ask her, "What was it like?" and even though we are in the kitchen peeling figs Bobbie knows exactly what I mean. The night she cut her wrists, what did she think about, what did she feel? Bobbie stops peeling to wipe her upper lip with the back of her hand; a fig explodes into the bowl. "Too soft," Bobbie says. "California figs." She's wearing a thick fisherman's sweater with the sleeves rolled up and big silver bracelets to hide the scars.

"I don't remember," she says eventually. We look into the bowl of peeled figs, sweet and pink and vulnerable as babies. "That's the funny part. You'd think if you were going to do something as dramatic as kill yourself, you'd at least remember it."

"Not if you thought you were going to die."

"Maybe *that's* why I didn't bother remembering," Bobbie says, laughing. I laugh too.

"How about from now on *you* being my memory for me," Bobbie says. "I'll do things and you remember them. You can even write them down if you want—only I wouldn't because as soon as you try to write the way something was, you change it. Have you ever noticed that? No, for memory to be real, it has to be entirely mental. Something infinitely fragile and changing, like frost on a window."

I think about having to remember her whole life for her, and how I once thought Bobbie's life was going to stand out and eclipse mine, no matter what I did. Now that I'm beginning to have a life of my own I'm not so sure I still believe this. I hate to admit it, but when I heard what Bobbie had done to herself, there was a small part of me that was happy I was going to get some kind of chance. I'd never tell this to anyone but Nathan because he's about the only one who would understand, who wouldn't consider me immoral.

When Bobbie and I are old maybe she'll say to me, "Gray, remember the time I slashed my wrists?" and maybe I won't remember it so vividly after all. My own life will rise up and take precedence. Oh, I'll have some dim recollection, but the events of my own life will be more vivid. Bobbie's life will be like scrim on a theater set, a backdrop against which my own life will shine stronger. People always say it's impossible to remember all the details I do, but they're wrong. Details are what you remember the big things by, details like the chipped bowl and Bobbie's violet scars, since you don't always know at the time which are which, details or big things.

Dr. Cavendish doesn't believe Bobbie is schizophrenic. Max says he wants more time to think about her treatment. Mudie withdraws as usual, spending long days in her studio. Meanwhile, the fake feeling of winter in New Orleans sets in. I can feel the chill from the river in my bones even on warm darkly flowing days.

My mind is on Bobbie, on what will become of her, of us, of me. Max says about Bobbie that the next step is not to be taken lightly, whatever it will be. Mudie says in her breezy airy way, Oh well, it will be Christmas soon. She fills the house with constant hammering. I know she doesn't care about Christmas at all, it's just an excuse to put things off.

Bobbie rides to school with me on the bus; her being here at all feels uncertain and slight, as if a child were tugging my sleeve. I try to ignore the whispers and gossip behind us, around us; Bobbie looks like danger to the other kids. At the same time, she's a kind of hero, someone who crosses into forbidden territory, someone who suffers and acts, which is how our literature teacher defines what a hero is. Still, I don't like it. I'd rather be inconspicuous and gray, a moth on a wall.

At school Bobbie's appearance seems flamboyant. She's dyed her hair platinum blond and she wears bizarre clothing from Salvation Army stores which she embellishes with rhinestones and paint. I know she smokes a lot of grass; her breath smells both acrid and sweet. She makes a lot of crazy-person jokes. "I wish you'd cut it out," I say after the fourth or fifth one, "you aren't helping yourself any."

"What's the matter with you," Bobbie says, "don't you even have a sense of humor anymore?"

"Not about some things," I say.

"Those are the things you have to laugh at," Bobbie argues.

We part ways; I go to algebra and Bobbie to the art room, where she spends entire days smoking and throwing pots. She makes a series of Greek urns, and the days of December turn black like the clay on Bobbie's fingers. Between classes, I find myself standing next to my locker. Our lockers are old and made of cypress; I can smell the ancient sunken bayou smell, feel the wood worn smooth by children's hands. In a classroom nearby someone recites, "Thou still unravished bride of quietness, / Thou foster-child of silence and slow time . . ." I rest my head against my wooden locker, close my eyes. A teacher brushes past, wondering probably but not daring to ask why I am not in class with the others. Forty years pass. In the classroom the unseen voice has gotten as far as, "Thou, silent form, dost tease us out of thought / As doth eternity: Cold Pastoral!" and without being ashamed I start to cry.

Bobbie comes up behind me, touches my shoulder. In the whole labyrinth of the school she has found me. "Come on," she says, "let's go home."

"Won't we get in trouble?"

Bobbie shakes her head. "No, they'll figure we've already got enough trouble of our own."

• • •

Bobbie says, "Max has a double life."

"A what?"

"A double life. Another life besides this one. He's got an apartment in the French Quarter, on St. Peter Street."

"Kendra Hamilton."

Bobbie nods.

"But she's Mudie's best friend. How can she do this?"

"How can Max do it?"

"His own apartment! How did you find out?"

"Max showed me himself. He couldn't resist showing me how cleverly he'd orchestrated everything. He took me down there one Sunday and made me a Ramos gin fizz and showed me his new stereo and his dishes. They're black, in case you're interested."

"I'm not," I say.

"After two or three drinks he took me aside and made me promise not to tell anybody. Said I was sophisticated enough to know how the world works but would I please not tell Mudie. 'These things only upset her,' he said. Upset her? What about me?"

"And me?"

"Sleeping with Kendra is one thing. But a double life? He must be really unhappy with this life to go to so much trouble," Bobbie says.

For the first time in my life I think of my father as a man with his own sorrows and uncertainties, a man eating his way through daily disappointments like a worm though roses. I wish I could have a double life, a life away from Harmony Street and all our problems. Maybe that's what Nathan is trying to offer me. Though I can't leave my family physically I can still leave them mentally. Nathan's constant attention and gentle pushes, all of these are designed in a subtle way so that I can have a double life too.

The day before Christmas Max goes to his club for lunch, then shops for our Christmas presents at Godchaux Department Store. It is his

yearly ritual, and this year is no exception. He seems bent on showing us that nothing has to change, that we can still be the people we
were before Bobbie tried to kill herself.

Max's presents always have a bought-at-the-last-minute feeling
about them that make them seem extravagant, luxurious even. One
year he bought me a knitted scarf that was twelve feet long, with
intricate woven colors, green and blue and mauve and soft grays; for
Bobbie that year it was a complete set of Shakespeare's plays, a
separate blue cloth volume for each play, and one for the sonnets.

Mudie's just the opposite. She usually pretends she doesn't care
about Christmas at all, but at the last minute she produces these gifts
balled up in tissue paper, things she ordered months earlier from
catalogues: pottery from Bennington; or necklaces and earrings from
little shops in Italy; or, for Max, rare art books from Rizzoli in New
York.

Mudie calls me into her studio. Hannah's in the kitchen making
oyster stew for Christmas Eve supper; Bobbie is out rehearsing for
Viet Rock. When she got the part she made me swear not to tell Max,
but she really didn't have to worry. I won't tell. I know that being
in the theater is Bobbie's way of having a double life, of being
someone other than a failed suicide.

Upstairs in Mudie's studio the winter light reminds me of an Emily
Dickinson poem, the one that goes, "There's a certain Slant of light /
Winter Afternoons— . . ."

It strikes me, thinking about the poem, that Mudie reminds me a
little of Emily Dickinson, hiding up in her studio. I picture Mudie's
mind as a series of even polished steps, old wooden steps like the
ones Emily Dickinson climbed to her writing desk. "I bought something special I wanted you to see," Mudie says. She rummages in old
paper sacks until she comes up with a red shopping bag stuffed with
tissue paper. "I thought this was fun," she says, and holds out an
oversized canvas schoolbag, chocolate brown with brass zippers and
flaps and different compartments, a bag to keep secrets and surprises
in. "It's a Danish schoolboy's bag," Mudie says. "Do you like it?"

"I love it," I say, thinking she bought the bag for me. A moment of happiness floods the dull afternoon.

"I thought it was perfect for Bobbie," Mudie says, and my happiness drains like color from the afternoon sky. "You know how much Bobbie likes to carry pens and pencils and notebooks and books and postcards around," she goes on, oblivious to my sadness. I watch her wrap Bobbie's present back up in tissue paper, and with it go all the days of carrying that schoolbag on my shoulder, the spring mornings of walking down the street with that bag on my shoulder, the fall evenings of coming home again, tired and replete, the brown bag thumping softly on my shoulder. I am surprised at how deeply I feel the disappointment, but Mudie goes on to other things, and the afternoon progresses, while I stand there, wanting.

Bobbie comes home in time for supper. She talks fast and her eyes look glittery. Probably from drugs. After rehearsal Bobbie goes to a friend's apartment and gets high; once she invited me, but I said no. I'm trying to separate from her, to unravel the tangled thread between us, but it's not easy. I have to keep reminding myself of the project, have to remember that Bobbie only wants me there as some kind of witness.

She doesn't see any of our old school friends anymore. Bobbie calls them "narrow and parochial," which is just fine with me; it means they're comfortable and funny, but Bobbie doesn't want that in people. She likes novelty. In my opinion the people she sees are novelties, and not friends.

She doesn't dress like the old Bobbie, either. In addition to the Salvation Army clothes, she wears cast-off sweaters of Max's that make her look thin and leggy. Too much mascara. Her favorite perfume is one that makes me gag, called Tea Rose. Her clothes are often torn. The rips aren't careless, like the ones in Mudie's clothes; they look deliberate.

When she sits down to dinner she pushes the food around on her plate and gazes out the window. Usually talkative, she's silent now. Max tries not to look, or not to interpret what he sees, and Mudie says, Oh well, and has a glass of wine. After all, it's Christmas. Max does most of the talking.

After dinner, champagne and presents. I feel very sorry when Bobbie opens hers, except my own sorrow lessens when Bobbie's whole face lights up when she opens the Danish schoolbag. Bobbie loads it up immediately with things from her desk, and into it go my mornings, my afternoons, the days of writing I was looking forward to. I hate myself and feel ashamed. I must try not to want anything from Max and Mudie, must try to be my own person.

I excuse myself and go into the bathroom. On the wall there's a small oil painting on display, just three slashes of color, painted by an artist friend of Mudie's. I sit there looking at the painting; Bobbie and I have this private joke about how Mudie's friend probably got a lot of bills in the mail that day and thought to himself, Now, what can I do to pay these bills, quick, and so started painting these little canvases of three colors, slash, slash, slash, just to get the bills paid.

I start to laugh and soon I can't stop. Mudie knocks on the door. "Gray, are you all right in there?"

"Of course she is," Max says. "We won't let her have champagne if that's how she acts."

"I thought that was the whole *point* of champagne," Bobbie says.

"Moderation is best in all things," Max replies. "Theognis."

"There is moderation even in excess," Bobbie says. "Disraeli."

They go on like this until it's hopeless, I'm crumpled up and laughing on the bathroom floor and it's Christmas and I can't remember when I've laughed so hard or felt so sad.

seven

n February, a change. Green leaves still on the trees make the cold seem unnatural, a trance. On Bobbie's opening night Nathan picks me up and we ride the streetcar downtown together. Max and Mudie still don't know anything about the play. I don't like having to be so secretive, so devious, but Max's rigidity forces me into it.

I can't believe how good Bobbie is. I had a feeling she would be a good actress but I didn't think I could watch her perform and not keep thinking, That's Bobbie, that's Bobbie.

Bobbie invites us to the cast party. We walk through the Quarter past Max's apartment to a rundown house in the Fauberg-Marigny District, where Mudie grew up. The houses are all pretty dilapidated now.

The apartment is lit with candles. It's dark, with these huge, wavering shadows everywhere, and laughter. Somebody offers me a

---

joint, and while I've refused them before when Bobbie offered, I accept it. Nathan comes back from the kitchen with two Dixie beers and sees me smoking.

"I thought you'd decided not to," he says.

"Well I changed my mind. Part of the project."

"Part of the project," he repeats. He takes the joint from me and tries it himself.

I start to think about Bobbie's performance, how she seemed to fit so perfectly into her role that the outer Bobbie disappeared. In contrast, I feel like I'm stumbling around in the dark, feeling for the light switch. I have no idea where I really fit. There are things I like doing, and people I like, but nothing in my experience corresponds to the way Bobbie looks, standing under the lights.

Max is furious. He holds out a clipping from the paper with a picture of Bobbie in *Viet Rock*.

"You knew about this?" Max asks.

"Yes."

Mudie stands in the doorway, behind me. "Max, don't you think Gray feels bad enough?"

"Does she? How bad is 'bad enough'?"

"Bobbie's not Gray's responsibility. She's ours. Yours and mine."

"Oh sure," Max says.

I go up to Bobbie's room. She's sitting on the bed cross-legged, smoking hash in a small enamel pipe. "Bobbie unrepentant," she says, starting to laugh. "How badly did Max work you over?"

"Cuts and lacerations," I say, "no internal damage."

"Jesus," Bobbie says, "I had no idea Max would read the theater section of the paper.

"Is he going to let you continue?"

"I don't know. I'm sorry he yelled at you. I didn't mean to get you in trouble."

"Don't you see, I *am* in trouble. I mean, if I go along with everything Max wants me to do. He wants me to be some kind of guardian to you."

"Your sister's keeper."

"Yes. He doesn't think I have any ability of my own. I may not have a talent that stands out now, but I'm only thirteen."

The next day Bobbie knocks on my door. I'm drawing a colossal fern, with spores on the back that wait hundreds of years to revive.

"Max saw the matinee of *Viet Rock*," Bobbie says. "He said I was excellent."

"Is he going to let you finish the run?"

"No. When I explained that I didn't want to let everybody in the play down, he said I'd let *him* down."

"I'm sorry, Bobbie."

"It's okay. I'm sorry I dragged you into it and made you lie."

It doesn't feel like a lie so much as a new way of seeing. Whatever I know about Bobbie and myself is such a small portion of what there is to know, I wonder if I'll ever reach a point high enough to make sense of it all. When Bobbie and I were younger Max took us to Brittany, where we climbed the stone steps of a lighthouse. The stairs kept getting higher and more dark, the top more unreachable, undesirable even; I almost lost faith it would ever come. Then finally, I pushed open a little door and there was an old crone in the stone doorway, and a sudden flood of light, and a wedge of slate-gray sea.

I'm lying on my bed listening to a Beatles album when Bobbie comes to the door and says, "Guess what? They're putting me into St. Vincent's Hospital."

"I thought St. Vincent's was—"

"—for crazy people. It is."

"But when? Why?"

"Tomorrow morning."

"Oh, Bobbie," I say, "I'm sorry."

"Don't be." Bobbie sits down on the edge of my bed; her head in her hands. When she finally looks at me, I'm the one who's crying. "Don't cry, Graycat," she says. "I *want* to go there."

"Why?"

"They expect too much of me here. Max does. And Mudie won't interfere with him although she doesn't agree, not really. Max wants me to be special, and when I am special, he says I can't be in the theater. He doesn't understand, being in the theater fits me. Oh fuck it, I'd rather be in a psych hospital than here, continually in the wrong."

All I can think of is St. Vincent's Hospital and my beautiful sister inside. The whole thing is so twisted, so awful, so fundamentally wrong that I am stunned that Max and Mudie could let this happen.

Bobbie starts packing while I'm still taking in the news. I'm crying, without sound, without words, because it seems to me that having Bobbie sent to St. Vincent's Hospital represents a different kind of loss than when she went to St. Anselm's. At least when she went away to school I could pretend it was going to be better for her, but how could this be better?

"Don't cry, Graycat," Bobbie says, "try to enjoy your life."

"What life?" I say.

"Look around you. Look inside of yourself. You have no idea how good you are."

Bobbie stops packing and holds me to her. I can't do anything but cry; I can't even hold her. "I want you to promise me that you'll never make yourself smaller than you are. Not for me, not for Max, not for anybody. I want you to be as big as you are."

"I don't feel big."

"*Promise,*" Bobbie says. She lets me go and whips a blue denim shirt off the hanger, folds it, and puts it in her suitcase.

"That's my shirt," I say.

Bobbie smiles. "You're going to get my life. Is it okay if I take this shirt?"

"But I don't want your life."

"Sure you do. You want a chance to grab people's attention. To shine."

I look away, ashamed for all the envy I ever felt, the meanness, the contriving to make Max love me more. The sons of Jacob: Bless me; love me first. And now that Bobbie is going to St. Vincent's, her place seems suddenly unfillable, unique as her shadow, her footprint at birth, her grave. She stubs out her cigarette in an ashtray, shaped like an open hand. I made it for Mudie when I was five. The two of us stand at the window a moment, looking out.

"I didn't hear you say it," Bobbie says finally.

"Say what?"

"I'll never make myself smaller than I am."

"I'll never make myself smaller than I am."

"Good," Bobbie says, "because the world out there is going to try to cut you down. Don't let them. And don't lie about me, either. If somebody at school asks what ever happened to Bobbie Maubry, tell them. Tell them I'm in St. Vincent's Hospital. Don't be ashamed."

"But Bobbie—"

"Just do it," Bobbie says, "don't worry about me."

Part 2

one

D r. Cavendish's office. I am here because he wants to talk to me about myself, so Mudie says. I agreed to come, but I'm skeptical. Since Bobbie left for St. Vincent's, I feel the need to lay out my life like a suit of clothes and see how it looks from someone else's vantage point. I want to know what's happening, what accounts for the strange mixture of feelings I've been having. One minute I'm happy, the next I'm unaccountably sad.

When Bobbie left for St. Vincent's, I expected to feel bereft, and I do, but there's something more. Parts of me that were in hiding are beginning to show. Parts I don't even know if I like. I'm starting to want things for myself, not just to win Max's love. I'm starting to feel angry at all the attention Bobbie gets, to want some attention myself. These are new feelings and I am ashamed of them.

"A family is like a tree," Dr. Cavendish explains. "When one branch is diseased, all the other branches gnarl and warp in its direction to compensate for the lost limb."

"So," I say, "my whole life I've been growing gnarled around Bobbie."

"Not just Bobbie. Your mother and father, too."

"I know I can't really please them so I try not to displease them."

"That doesn't sound very conducive to the growth of your character."

"It's strange, but sometimes I have the feeling I was given the things Bobbie wasn't. Character-wise. Or else we developed in two entirely different directions so that together we'd make up one person."

"That's a dangerous idea Gray. It leads to the creation of a false self. Your genuine self lies buried."

"I don't care. I love Bobbie. I can't grow apart from her."

"You can't tailor-make your personality to compensate for Bobbie."

"Yes I can."

"Only at great peril to your own self."

"I don't care about that," I say.

"You will." Dr. Cavendish offers a sad smile. "You already do. How old are you?"

"Thirteen."

I tell him all this and more, how with Bobbie gone I am finding it harder to maintain my old image of myself. Gray, the undistinguished one, the sister on the sidelines, lacking in brilliance, an observer, prone to deep, private depressions. Yet, at the core I am strangely growing, new buds out of blasted wood. I tell Dr. Cavendish what I understand about Bobbie. She has intelligence, wit, and the ability to amuse herself and everyone around her. She has no continuity. Bobbie is brilliant, like light; she illuminates whatever is close by. Dr. Cavendish swivels back in his chair, hands folded behind his head, eyes closed.

"I want you to stop trying to be the opposite of Bobbie. You can't anyway, it's humanly impossible. Bobbie is Bobbie and you are you. I want you to take the opportunity of her absence to be yourself. I know it isn't easy. Do you have friends? A boyfriend?"

"I have Nathan."

"Spend time with him. Try as much as possible to challenge old ideas you harbor about yourself."

In the evenings I lie in the beds Bobbie and I slept in as children and think about our lives. Sometimes I read through some of the books we loved then and wonder whether all that time Bobbie and I were reading different stories. There's one book in particular I think about that Bobbie gave me one summer when we both had mumps— Bobbie first, then me. Our favorite book that year was *Pudd'nhead Wilson* by Mark Twain. We used to lie in the semidarkness and feel the hot breath of the ceiling fan trying to cool the room down, and read aloud to each other. When Bobbie recovered first, she gave me the book so I wouldn't be lonely. She even inscribed the flyleaf:

> *To Gray Maubry, when she had mumps*
> *From Bobbie when she didn't (anymore)*
> *August, 1959*

We laughed so hard over the inscription my jaws ached. Are all things like that, I wonder, things that seemed funny once, or sad once, do they always lose their power after a while?

"Gray, we're going to Gentilly," Nathan says when I get in the car.

"What's in Gentilly?"

"Nothing. That's why we're going there. It's easy to have a good time in places designed for good times. It's having a good time in ordinary places that's a challenge." He gives me a wry look and passes me a fat rumpled joint.

"Nathan, I thought we'd agreed only to smoke on special occasions."

"Granted," Nathan says. "But I found this at school on Friday, on the floor of the science lab. I think we have a moral obligation to smoke it. Looks like a miniature Claes Oldenburg, don't you think?"

"Nathan."

He hands me a pack of matches. "You're always saying how tired you are of being the dutiful daughter."

"I am. I'm just not sure that becoming a drug addict is the way to change that."

I light one of the twisted ends. A cold, delicious feeling of happiness sneaks over me. I feel like I've just slipped out of my skin and into someone else's, someone lighter, more carefree.

"Here," I hand the cigarette to Nathan. He holds it in one hand and drives with the other.

Nathan draws in some smoke, starts coughing, nearly wrecks the car. When he gains control he says, "I don't feel anything yet. I thought narcotics were supposed to make you feel good."

"It probably takes time."

We pass it back and forth. Nathan drives. Now that he has his learner's permit we don't have to take the bus anymore. From the passenger's window, the city looks charmed. I don't know whether the marijuana is affecting me or if it's just the feeling of doing something out of character, but I feel happy. The rest of my life, the life outside of Nathan's car and the city streets going by in the dusk, seems oddly formal and far away.

We go to a movie theater, the Gentilly Orleans, which is a spiffed-up old fifties cinderblock building next to a hamburger restaurant. The theater has an arrangement with the restaurant; they let you buy beer in the restaurant and carry it in paper cups into the theater. Nathan goes and gets the beers and settles next to me in the dark theater. The movie starts. It's about this man who grows tired of his life, and one day arranges to have an accident in his car that makes it look like he's dead. He moves to another city, makes up a different name, starts a new life. Then he finds out, after a few years, that he's just as bored with his new life.

"Poignant," Nathan says when the movie's over.

I smile. I'm standing on the street corner with Nathan, and the wind is blowing just a little. Nathan's wearing this brown leather jacket, not a bicycle jacket but a leather blazer. His parents gave it to him for his birthday. I'm standing there with Nathan, under a flat New Orleans sky, thinking about the movie.

I don't know whether it's possible to change your life; maybe like the man in the movie you can go to all kinds of extremes, but your life still catches up to you, like your shadow or a dog you decide you don't want anymore that you keep trying to lose, and it keeps finding you.

two

I wait in Mr. Root's office. He's the school principal, an ex-Jesuit from West Feliciana Parish, balding, well fed. The students call him Root of All Evil, a joke because the man is mild and ineffectual, not given to punishment or strong decisions.

"Glorious day," he says when he comes in, although the day looks ordinary. "Please sit down. I haven't often had the opportunity to talk to you, Gray. Of course, I know Bobbie."

"Of course."

"But this isn't about Bobbie. It's about you. How are you doing these days?"

"Fine."

"Good. Happy at St. Rita's?"

"Pretty much."

"Good. You see there's something that's been on my mind for a while, a rumor probably, you know how teachers gossip."

"What rumor?"

Root settles back; he's into his talk now, swims in his element as easily as a fish. "There's talk about you and Nathan Kentor. Nathan's an unusual boy, the brightest in your class, as you probably know. Lately he's gotten kind of restless here. Acts up. I don't think this is a diverse enough environment for him so he does things to liven it up. You know what I mean."

"Not exactly."

"Look." Mr. Root takes off his glasses, as if this is going to make me see more clearly. He looks at me hard. "Nathan can afford a little trouble in his life. He's highly motivated, despite his rather eccentric appearance. A gifted young man. He'll go on to Harvard, as I believe he wants to do. But you—"

"What about me?"

"You have to be careful, Gray. This is a difficult time for your family."

Is he telling me I'm not as smart as Nathan? That I have to be good because of the things Bobbie's done? I look away out of the double French windows, at the class playing soccer on the football field.

"I don't mean to pry, but I just wanted to tell you to be careful," Mr. Root says. "For your own sake. Don't assume you can do the things Nathan does and survive."

"Thank you, Mr. Root."

"A family has to pull together," he says. "When one member is sick, the others have to rally." We are standing up now; he has a hand on my shoulder, although he knows I am lost to him, lost to this place. I choke out another thanks and go out to the parking lot to wait for school to be over and Nathan to come.

• • •

Nathan takes me on the bus to City Park. There, back of the art museum, the grounds are full of ponderous old oaks, some of them with branches so long and meandering they wind down to the ground. Nathan shimmies up first. He's got a jug of cheap wine in a paper bag.

"What did Root want?" he asks when we are settled on a branch.

"To warn me about you."

Nathan unscrews the cap, swigs from the jug, and passes it to me.

"He says you can afford to do wild things but I can't. I guess what he meant was you're special and I'm not."

"*Radix malorum est stupiditas,*" Nathan says.

"Still, what if he's right?"

Nathan grunts; he doesn't want to dignify this theory with a response. We sit in the tree for a while and drink the wine. The landscape begins to soften.

"Maybe he's right," I say, "maybe my whole life I will spend trying to make up for Bobbie. Like Dr. Cavendish says, I'll get as gnarled and funny-looking as the branches of this tree."

"That's why I'm here," Nathan says, "to prevent that."

"Maybe you can't. Maybe no one can. Maybe my whole life I'm going to be crouched in the shadow of Bobbie."

"You're wrong," Nathan says.

"You don't understand. Bobbie is everyplace. She has everything I don't have."

"Like what?"

"Everything that counts. All she needs is something to help her hold it together."

"Like you?" Nathan says.

We drink some more of the wine and then climb down out of the tree and lie on the ground beneath it, looking up. We lie like that for a long time, looking at the sky through the amazing pattern of the old, black branches. I think about me and Bobbie, and how in the country you see a dwarf apple growing in the shade of a big live oak like this one and the apple is stunted, doesn't have much chance of growing by itself. Then one day, driving past, you see the ground is blasted, the big oak split by lightning, dead, and only then does the apple tree bear fruit.

My birthday today; I am fourteen. All Saints' Day in New Orleans feels sacred to me, the ground austere and warm, the trees barely blown, the cemeteries decorated with white chrysanthemums. I was actually born at midnight on Halloween. In ancient times a girl born on Halloween was taken off and drowned. I find myself on every birthday thinking of the accident of history that spared me.

I have a photography assignment for school but I'm having trouble talking Nathan into coming to the cemetery with me. "I don't like dead people," he says, "they're poor conversationalists."

"Come on, Nathan, part of the project."

"It's your character we're working on, not mine. Besides, I hate New Orleans cemeteries. What a misnomer. The whole place is a cemetery, more tomb than city."

"Never mind. I forgot you were superstitious."

"Oh, all right."

"You have nothing to worry about. I'll just wear one of those huge strands of garlic you see at the French Market."

Nathan picks me up. We drive together through the Garden District, past the pre–Civil War house on Second Street that once belonged to the Maubry family. Both Nathan's family and mine are very old, very settled. It's something we understand about each other, and something that gives rise to our ambivalence about living in New Orleans. To have so many, and such close, ties can make a person feel suffocated as well as needed.

At the entrance to the walled cemetery Nathan takes out a little package. "Happy birthday, Gray," he says.

I open my present. It's a small, lovely prewar Leica in a soft old leather case. Nathan and I go in the cemetery and start photographing tombstones. I'm using black-and-white film, which does a better job of capturing light and shadow than color film does. Nathan sits and smokes and watches me. I'm climbing in and out of the tombs, snapping the shutter. The old Leica works so smoothly I almost feel it is part of my hand.

In back of the tombs are the graves for poor people. In this cemetery the poor are buried in a single wall, each grave a single cell, sealed with an iron plate. Now the wall is falling down, the iron plates missing. Nathan reaches in one of the grave cells and holds up what looks like a small pelvic bone. Snap, snap, I don't stop taking pictures to think about what he's doing. Snap, snap, we wander back between the graves, decorated with white chrysanthemums. Nathan kisses my neck, snap, I take his picture. He has a loony grin on his face. Then he takes the camera and snaps me, not once, but three times.

When I develop the film in photography class, the pictures have areas of dramatic contrast: light and darkness. There's Nathan smoking, and the ruined graves, and Nathan mugging for the camera. There's me smiling, and me looking sad, and me looking like a girl I hardly recognize. This girl is neither happy nor sad; she's not ruled by her moods. She is strong, purposeful, she can do anything she sets her mind to do.

At night I pore over the pictures. How can I become the girl in the photographs, my rightful self? Is it something that happens naturally, or are there specific things I must do? How can I find out? Can Dr. Cavendish tell me? Nathan? I look at the pictures over and over. I'm mystified. It seems like there's this narrow band of what—personality?—that belongs to me. Only I don't know how to make it mine.

three

On Christmas we are going to be allowed to see Bobbie. Dr. Fergus, who oversees Bobbie's treatment at St. Vincent's, warns us to be careful; Christmas is an emotionally charged time, he says, we must keep the mood tranquil.

Max, Mudie, and I are nervous about the visit. What to bring, what to expect, what to say to Bobbie when we finally see her; this seclusion is like a river of dark water, dividing us. Max refuses to acknowledge it; he treats Bobbie's hospitalization as just another phase; he busies himself with plans. Mudie frowns and chews on her pencil, looking down at the yard from her attic windows. Frost barely touches the ground; the leaves on the trees are coppery and firm, like the enameled leaves Mudie puts on the copper fresco she is making for Bobbie.

I spend an afternoon shopping for things to bring Bobbie; I

consider fancy chocolates, perfume, a Toulouse-Lautrec poster. Everything seems insubstantial; I am afraid of going to the hospital, my insides lurch wildly like the bus I am riding. The other passengers seem warm, content, oblivious. Finally I settle on three gifts for Bobbie: a red sweater, a box of pastels, a giant drawing pad.

Christmas Eve the house is preoccupied, drawn into itself with thought. There is a feeling of readiness: What will come will come. We feel ridiculous for being so self-conscious, Max and Mudie and I. We drink hot tea by the fire and watch the live logs split and hiss. Into the flames we throw bills, old photographs, wrapping paper. It is as if we are preparing for a journey we will never return from.

Before she leaves for her own house and her holiday, Hannah motions me into the kitchen. A heavy, fragrant box, wrapped in tinfoil, sits on the counter. "Take this and give it to Bobbie," Hannah says. She looks embarrassed, as she always is when caught in acts of kindness.

"What's inside?"

"Pecan divinity."

An old custom, going back to the years when Bobbie and I were small; Hannah used to make us boxes of the sweet white fudge, and we'd exchange them for things we'd made in art class—misshapen ashtrays, pot holders with holes, a paperweight shaped like a hippopotamus.

"Merry Christmas, Hannah. Bobbie will love it."

"Hmm," Hannah says in her gruff voice, "put some meat on her sassy bones."

She walks toward the avenue in the early dusk, her own packages under her arm, her head lowered. My love for Hannah, and for the past of which she is inextricably a part, wells up; I put my nose to the window and watch her disappear. I think of all the times Hannah tried to protect me from Bobbie and her wiles, and how I never learned, being willing, out of desire for Bobbie's time, Bobbie's attention, to be duped again and again like a puppy. Now Bobbie is in St. Vincent's, and I am here. It doesn't make sense. We have the same parents but such different lives. I wonder what Max and Mudie think about it; Max probably just thinks Bobbie's got a flaky artistic temperament and Mudie thinks Bobbie inherited the Maubry family's flawed genes.

Christmas morning is crisp. Mudie makes breakfast; Max brews coffee and whistles bits from a Brandenburg Concerto. His eyes are pale, concentrated. Mudie is so distracted she burns the first batch of scrambled eggs. We eat the second batch along with the flaky pastry that Bobbie and I used to call Prussians, from the Four Seasons Bakery in the Quarter.

Then Max drives us to the hospital. He has both feet on the pedals. The streets are full of children on new roller skates, their movements gawky, touching, exuberant. I can tell how nervous Max is by his feigned nonchalance; he acts as if visiting Bobbie in St. Vincent's is an everyday occurrence. Beneath his collar his neck looks dark, flushed. His white shirt gleams, immaculate.

Two nuns are tending a small garden near the front entrance. They are wearing winter habits; their black garments fan out on the stone steps as they move. They are pruning the red-pepper bushes; hot red peppers the size of the cardinal's little finger glisten on the vine. One nun carries a small basket, clips expertly, careful not to nick the peppers.

"Good morning, Sisters." Max stops to speak to the nuns. He expresses interest in the red peppers, says he hasn't tasted peppers like them in years. Oh, but you must have some, the sisters say. They pinch peppers from the vine with their white soft hands. Max wraps them in a handkerchief; for the moment he has forgotten why we are here, he is in the kitchen preparing shrimp with peas and these red peppers. We are pilgrims, anxious only to survive.

Bobbie's ward, Seton, is named for the first American saint, Elizabeth Ann Seton. All the wards have saints' names except for the violent ward which is called Rosary. Bobbie is lucky to be in Seton; it is where they keep the patients who have some hope of recovery. Still the ward is disappointing when we get there.

All these months I have been imagining a classic scene: crazier-looking people, distorted laughter, orderlies wrestling with ghostly, straitjacketed figures, forced injections. If any of this goes on here, we can't see it. Max, Mudie, and I walk through the dayroom on our way to Bobbie's room, and I am struck by the ordinariness of the place: the hum of the television, the worn stacks of magazines, the blue haze of cigarette smoke, the casual chatter. The patients on Seton look like people told to expect an indeterminate wait in an airport; some look hopeful of reprieve, others indifferent.

Bobbie seems glad to see us. She hugs and kisses us warmly, with nothing held back, the way children do. She is thin, her fair complexion a shade fairer, her blue eyes clear—remarkable blue eyes, their irises outlined in a darker blue. She shows us her room with its scrubbed cypress dresser, four-poster bed, mahogany armoire, and says it reminds her of a convent room in the Louisiana countryside she saw once on a tour, it's not like a hospital room at all.

"I'm so glad it looks like this," Mudie says, patting the white coverlet. What she means is the room doesn't look clinical.

"So how've you all been?" Bobbie asks.

"We've been fine," Max says.

"We miss you," Mudie says.

"Gray's doing well in school," Max says, "for a change." He tweaks my nose. "All A's, wasn't it, Gray?"

"Stop it, Max," I say.

Bobbie doesn't miss the exchange; her smile fades at its brightest and the room suddenly feels cold. I make Bobbie unwrap the package and put on her new red sweater; she's gotten so thin it hangs on her, she looks like an orphan. Oh, Bobbie, I think, how come this happened to you and not to me?

Bobbie opens her other presents, Mudie's first. It is a fresco of heaven, enamel on copper, with a host of angels flying in a navy sky, the stars in their constellations. "Mudie, it's beautiful," Bobbie says, her voice hoarse with tears. "I can lie in my bed and see angels every night before I fall asleep."

"It's my wish for you," Mudie says.

In the dayroom we sit with the other patients and families and try to look natural. Poor Max, give him a hundred years of practice, he will never manage to look natural in the visitors' lounge of a mental hospital. His face looks queerly pulled; his hands in the pockets of his tweed jacket seem like puppet hands, muffled, inarticulate. Mudie does better; she is not as afraid of the experience as Max. She asks Bobbie about the other patients, who her friends are. Bobbie has one friend she introduces to us, a small redheaded girl named Robin whose father is a prominent judge. Robin steals things, Bobbie explains later. She steals things and takes her mother's credit cards and runs up enormous balances. There's a whole room in Robin's house full of the things she's stolen and bought. St. Vincent's is her third hospital. "She keeps getting kicked out and told nothing is wrong with her but her parents keep on having her committed," Bobbie says.

"That boy's in love with me." Bobbie points. "His name is Billy Fitzsimmons. He looks like the young Truman Capote, you know that photograph by Cartier-Bresson of Capote in a T-shirt, hostile and lovelorn like a child. He's a pianist," she explains, "he plays jazz. He kept asking me to go out with him and when I wouldn't, he set his hair on fire. It's growing back now."

Max looks as if he would like to fall through a hole in the floor. I can tell what he is feeling: sorrow that Bobbie should have as her friends these people, pyromaniacs and thieves, the forlorn and lost. It doesn't fit in with his picture of Bobbie, with his dreams. He is like a wounded animal, nursing himself. Bobbie senses this and says, "Not exactly Harvard material around here."

Mudie is more wounded for Bobbie than for herself. She's the kind of person who feels her way through new situations instead of making her mind up beforehand that something is intolerable. She's nowhere near as uncomfortable as Max, having more of a tendency to accept what is real than to cling to what might have been.

The punch and hors d'oeuvres are served; patients and parents stand around awkwardly nibbling at shrimp toast on paper plates, commenting on things like how good the pineapple punch is. Soon we will go back to our house on Harmony Street and let the patients have their Christmas meal in peace, without the strain of having to appear normal for their families. "I don't see why you-all can't eat with us," Bobbie complains. "What are they afraid of, that somebody might sabotage the turkey?"

"Oh well," Mudie says, "there'll be other times."

"And other Christmases," Max says, "won't there be, Graycat?"

"Of course. I'll bet your turkey is moister than ours is. You know Mudie."

"Still," Bobbie says, her voice tentative.

"Merry Christmas," Max says. For the first time there are tears in his blue eyes, making his eyes seem bluer. I know what he is thinking: He is asserting that there will come a time when this will all be over, when Bobbie will go back to the way she was, to being brilliant Bobbie on her way to Harvard. I don't think so, now that I have seen Bobbie here. By the time she gets out of the hospital she will have seen and done things that will make her view the world differently. The world *will* be different. And Bobbie will be different. There's a saying that our history teacher once wrote in chalk in the top left-hand corner of the blackboard: " 'You cannot step into the same river twice'—Heraclitus." Either the river changes or we change, or both.

When we come back outside, the weather has changed. The sky's lightness has gone; the air is charged, heavy. The bare branches seem made of lead. A few snowflakes begin to fall, an aberration for the New Orleans climate, a remarkable occurrence ordinarily, but today Mudie only points and says, "Look, snow," matter-of-factly, as if snow were common in New Orleans.

Max drives down the boulevard of grand old elms; the street now has the barest covering of snow. The flakes fall, huge, irregular, thudding on the hood and windshield. Max turns to Mudie, and says, "Let's not go home. Let's drive downtown and have Christmas lunch someplace. Galatoire's should be open."

"Yes, let's," Mudie says quickly.

Downtown the air is thick with snow, the streets are slippery; snow disfigures the buildings. Max wedges the old Mercedes between a Dumpster and a ruined Cadillac, and we walk three blocks to Galatoire's without speaking, our hands barely touching. I can feel the tweed of Max's overcoat brush my cheek, and smell Mudie's perfume oddly amplified in the damp air.

To our surprise the restaurant is nearly full. Men dining alone in their best blue suits, stepmothers and their disaffected nephews, mismatched collections of children, all dine under the yellow lamps. Roast goose is on the menu; the waiters wear sprigs of holly in their lapels.

When Max was four, his father took him to Galatoire's for lunch. When the meal was over and they were waiting for the bill, his father excused himself. Max thought he was going to the men's room. He waited. The bill arrived, the waiter refilled Max's father's coffee cup, but it got cold while Max sat there. He looked around the room; he was starting to get itchy in his wool suit. Finally panic began to tighten inside him and people started to stare. Eventually the head-waiter came over to the table and Max told him what the trouble was. The headwaiter laughed and said certainly they would find Max's father, but Max wasn't so sure.

Despite a thorough search, nobody could find Max's father. It was evident he had slipped the bolt and gone out the back way, leaving Max behind. Max *knew* he was being left permanently, it was that kind of gesture. Within half an hour the waiters had befriended him, given him a second dessert, and called his uncle Stanton, the famous thoracic surgeon. Uncle Stanton came to get Max in a gray Packard. "So," he said when he saw Max, "the little bastard finally abandoned you. I always knew he would. It was his way of treating people. First his college friends, then your mother. Finally you, his only son. Hadn't a faithful bone in his body."

"No, sir," Max said.

Inside Galatoire's now, we are orphaned by our own desires, our wish not to go home to memories of happier Christmases.

Max improves with a glass of house wine; Mudie sips a kir, her fingers nipped with cold, her black eyes shining. It is as if, in the middle of the worst storm of our lives, we had suddenly found shelter: thick white tablecloths, horse-faced Cajun waiters, plates of shrimp in mustardy rémoulade, small crusty loaves of delicious French bread. Max lifts his glass in a toast.

"Merry Christmas," he says.

"Merry Christmas," we echo.

"Look," Mudie points to banks of snow gathering outside. "We'll never drive home in this."

"We'll take a cab," Max says, "or we won't go home. We'll spend the night in the car, maybe drive to Florida in the morning."

"Let's do," Mudie says. "I never want to go home again."

"There's my office," Max says thoughtfully.

"And Bobbie," I say.

"Of course," Max says. "Well, Merry Christmas anyway."

four

I hear voices downstairs one morning, first Mudie's, then Kendra's. Mudie speaks in an excited whisper, Kendra in slow, measured sentences. When I come into the breakfast room, they are gone, having trailed upstairs to Mudie's studio. The sun fills the breakfast room with yellow: walls, curtains, egg yolk on a china plate, yellow chrysanthemums. It is February. Upstairs I hear talking, not Mudie banging. Hannah wears a dark look.

"What's Kendra doing here?" I ask.

Hannah snorts disapproval. "Your fool mother asked her over, I expect. Your mother's got her head buried so deep in the sand she's going to win an award for prize ostrich." By the tone of Hannah's voice I can tell she knows as much as Bobbie and I know, probably more.

I telephone Nathan. "You have to come over now."

91

"How come?"

"Kendra Hamilton is upstairs with Mudie."

"I'll be right there."

When Nathan arrives he looks disheveled. It's only taken him five minutes to ride his bike over, and Hannah gives him a big grin, showing her gold front tooth. "Gray, you got yourself a nosy boyfriend," she says with a laugh.

"I prefer to think of myself as informed," Nathan says.

Hannah laughs harder, gives Nathan and me a tray of coffee and a plate of lumpy oatmeal cookies to carry up to Mudie's studio.

"Kendra and I were just talking about the old days," Mudie says when Nathan and I are both seated on the floor of her studio. She pours each of us a cup of Hannah's rich, dark coffee.

"Not *that* old, I hope," Kendra says, giving the impression of movement, of laughter. I realize she is almost the opposite of Mudie—solid, blond, domineering, her blue eyes not faraway but right here, scrutinizing.

"Those were my wild days," Mudie says to me, "before I married your father. We were living in New York then, in a cold-water flat, and eating all our meals at the Automat. Kendra, you were writing a poem, I think it was . . ."

"The female *Pisan Cantos*," Kendra says.

"Living in New York, and writing, and—"

"Sleeping around," Kendra puts in. Then, remembering Nathan and me, she adds, "You're both old enough to know about these things, aren't you?"

"Certainly," Mudie says with a wave, "and dragging me out of my shell to all sorts of parties. One of the Marx Brothers lived in our building. Chico, I think."

"Harpo," Kendra says.

"Harpo, then. Anyway, Kendra was my corrupting influence. I followed her only long enough to marry Max."

"Even then you were a coward," Kendra says with a laugh. "Everybody loved Max."

"I was a virgin," Mudie remembers. "Max wore white at the wedding. I remember he bought two white linen suits before the wedding. He wore one of them around until it was just a little bit wrinkled, and then he had it laundered. He said it was tacky to wear a brand-new suit to your wedding."

"So like Maxwell," Kendra says.

"Well, anyway," Mudie finishes the story, "I married your father and moved back South."

"Where you reverted to Southern ways, Southern habits."

"And Kendra stayed North. Eking out a living as an editor, giving poetry readings at night. Then you came home, too, Kendra."

"I teach now," Kendra says, "instead of write. Nearly everyone does."

"Oh, but you *must* be writing," Mudie says.

Kendra shakes her head, touches my arm. "I saw your father yesterday riding the streetcar downtown to his office. He always looks so abstracted, as if the rails he's riding lead straight to heaven."

"Oh, that's rich." Mudie laughs. "Always so impeccable, Max."

"He said, 'Why don't you stop by and see Mudie? She hardly ever goes out, just holes up in her studio.' I was instantly jealous," Kendra says. "I thought of all the great things you must be accomplishing."

"Oh, nothing great," Mudie says, embarrassed.

I feel embarrassed for her. I keep kneeing Nathan in the back as a signal that I want to leave, but Nathan's insatiably curious. He wants to stay. Nathan thinks you should know everything you can about a situation; that way your judgment is more likely to be correct. Why waste time on feelings based on faulty judgment? Nathan always says.

I can't think about this now. I practically drag Nathan down the stairs with me and go into the kitchen pantry to cry. I cry a long time among the soup cans and tins of sardines and boxes of cereal. Nathan sits in the kitchen with Hannah, waiting me out.

"Poor Graycat," Hannah says, "she wants the world to shut up and be perfect, and it just ain't."

"But does it have to be so imperfect in such glaring ways?" I stop crying long enough to ask.

"Your daddy is just a man. Nobody ever said men was perfect," Hannah says. "You want a sandwich?"

"No," I say.

"I do," Nathan says.

"Nathan."

"Sorry. I don't mean to be insensitive, but these are Portuguese sardines. In olive oil. Do you have an onion?" Nathan asks Hannah.

"Got a bowlful."

They busy themselves with Nathan's lunch. I know Hannah isn't shocked by any of Max and Mudie's behavior; since I was a child she's had this way of accepting everything they do with a nod of her head, sometimes in a sad and final way, as if this is merely life on earth and how it is generally lived. Hannah never seems stunned by any of us, not Max and Mudie, not even Bobbie, least of all myself.

After lunch Kendra drives off in a tight black car; Mudie waves from the window like a child. "I had such fun today," she tells me, "God, I was just thinking about Kendra and then, here, out of the blue, she calls."

"Is she a very good writer?" I ask.

"What do you think?" Mudie asks Nathan. Nathan's read everything.

He frowns. "Big long books with lots of characters, in European countries, right? Pretentious."

Mudie laughs, a long trill going all the way down her throat. Perhaps her preoccupation with Bobbie's illness makes her sudden happiness seem more rare. She draws Nathan and me to a corner of the library, extracts an old scrapbook jammed with photographs and telegrams of congratulations on Bobbie's and my births, and there, amidst it all is a picture of Kendra, her hair then genuinely blond.

"She was a kind of H.D. figure," Mudie says, "Max was crazy about her for a while—all the men were. She was an intellectual kind of woman you didn't find much then. Not in the South, anyway."

"Did Kendra ever get married?" Nathan asks.

"Once. I don't know what went wrong. Her husband was a marvelous writer, an alcoholic. He threw himself off of a bridge and killed himself."

"The Huey P. Long Bridge?"

Mudie nods. We are all quiet. I am thinking about Kendra's husband's leap, about Bobbie's scars. What if Bobbie had really killed herself? That possibility makes Bobbie's story about Max having a double life seem minor, a storybook tale. I may never know if it is true, particularly after seeing Kendra here today. I certainly can't count on Mudie to tell me the truth. Mudie is strong in some ways but frail where being loved is concerned. And I am too. Everybody is, I suppose, only some people, particularly Nathan, prefer to follow the real story, no matter where it leads.

Hannah leaves to catch the streetcar home; Mudie tries to cover up her feelings of awkwardness by clearing the dishes. She breaks a wineglass on the floor, then cuts her bare foot on a sliver. The afternoon becomes empty, stale. I am left with traces of Kendra's perfume, her memories of Mudie at twenty-one, and an image, disturbing somehow, of Max holding on to an imaginary tether while the streetcar careens and sways.

five

athan takes me out to Mid-City. From the overpass we can see the giant neon MAGIKIST sign, a pair of red lips outlined in the darkness. Nathan pulls over. "We're out of gas."

"Here?"

"Not exactly the eyes of Dr. T. J. Eckleberg, but close," he says, gazing at the tacky sign. He puts his arm around me. We are standing on the shoulder of the overpass; a few cars go by.

"See those lips?" Nathan says. "They remind me of the eyes of Dr. T. J. Eckleberg. A commercial symbol that eerily takes on a larger meaning."

Nathan is lost in one of his reveries; I'm wondering how we are going to get home. Nathan is always doing things like this, dragging me to strange places so he can ruminate.

"I suppose this is part of the project."

"Definitely." Nathan kisses me, immediately lets go. "I don't have federal monies but I'm resourceful. The idea, in case you haven't noticed, is to take you out of yourself. Extend the borders of your personality."

"I hope we're on a bus route."

"Don't worry," Nathan says, "you worry too much. It's going to limit your character."

"You're right. Max says I have an old head on young shoulders."

Max has lunch with Darwin Kentor once a week. They go to the Acme Oyster Bar and eat raw oysters. Darwin eats raw oysters every day. He has a little black book he carries around and whenever he has a dozen oysters, he makes a note of the date and place he had them and how they tasted. Nathan shows me the book, which he snitched from his father's pocket. One entry reads: *Brackish. Flabby. Redolent of tar.*

"Jesus, Nathan. He must be kidding."

"I don't think so. He has an obsessive nature."

"In a way, Max does too. He has these impossible ideas. He doesn't believe in wrong, for one thing. He says people pursue the good and beautiful. He believes we are all basically good. When we were little he didn't think Bobbie could do anything wrong. Bobbie was always doing crazy things, and Max would twist himself into all sorts of positions to defend her."

"Why?" Nathan asks.

I tell him some more about Max, how his own father left him at Galatoire's when he was four years old, and how Max somehow knew Charles Osgood Maubry was gone for good. Then, when his uncle Stanton came and got Max and took him home, Max understood what was required of him: to deny the pain of his abandonment and act grateful for the opportunity. Max is always saying that it was the best thing that ever happened to him, that Uncle Stanton was a much better father than Charles Osgood had ever been, more attentive and not an alcoholic.

"So," Nathan says when I've finished, "there's your theme."

"What?"

"The redeemed orphan."

"Max?"

"Sure. First he's left all alone, then his famous uncle comes to the rescue, gives him a good education, and does his best to erase the scars of neglect. Who wouldn't grow up believing in the tendency of things to work out for the good?"

"I wish I thought so. I just keep thinking our lives have taken a big turn for the worse."

"I know you do," Nathan says. "That's where the project comes in. I want to show you another way of looking at life."

We catch the bus, head downtown. "Where to now?" Nathan says. "It's your turn to pick a spot."

"How about the Quarter?"

Nathan makes a face; he hates the French Quarter. "All right, if you think peep shows and fat Iowa sausage salesmen are significant."

"There's noplace else to go."

"Every place is another place," Nathan says with mock solemnity.

"Is fake profundity also part of the project?"

Nathan nods. "Fake profundity is definitely part of the project. Ditto poignancy. In fifth grade I wrote an essay using the word *poignant* fourteen times. The teacher loved it. *Poignant* is a nonword. When somebody says something is *poignant*, it shows they haven't experienced real emotion."

It's too early for the Quarter to be in full swing, so we walk around until it gets late. We go behind the fish market, where Nathan finds an iron-claw machine and spends a half hour trying to catch a prize with the metal claw. It's frustrating because once you spot your prize and put a quarter in, the machine grunts and groans and the claw lunges once in the direction of the prize and then gives up. "Just like sex," Nathan jokes. "Just like life. Heartrendingly pointless. More trouble than it's worth."

It's past midnight when we get home. Mudie's light is still on; she's probably been waiting up for me. As soon as she hears my key in the lock, she turns the light off. Max and Mudie like to make a point of trusting me. Max's philosophy is that if they let me know how much they trust me, I won't do anything wrong.

"It's time," Nathan says at the door.

"Time for what?"

"Sex."

Nathan climbs up and sits on the hood of Max's Mercedes, and I follow suit. Nathan wears a serious expression, with only a hint of jest.

"You mean, real sex?"

"Gray, is there any other kind?"

The idea of doing anything more than kissing seems monumental. I worry that if we use up our affection for each other too quickly, there won't be any left for our adult life.

"Don't look so glum about it," Nathan says. "I only want to make us happy."

"And you think having sex will."

"The troubadour poets thought so."

"I'm afraid, Nathan. It would be like leaving childhood behind."

"I thought that was what you wanted to do."

He's right, I do want to leave childhood behind, to grow up and gain some measure of control over my life, but I'm not sure if this is how to do it. Having sex with Nathan seems an awfully abrupt entry into adulthood, so irrevocable, like a final action instead of a beginning one.

"All right," I say, "where?"

"My house," Nathan says. "My mother and father are less vigilant than yours. Negligent, you might say. My father is so preoccupied with his latest invention he barely knows I'm there."

"What time?"

Nathan looks at his watch. "How about now?"

"*Now?*"

"What do you want, a dress rehearsal? Come on, Gray, these things are supposed to be natural, spontaneous."

We get to Nathan's house and nobody's home. Nathan goes through this ritual of checking all the rooms, closets even, to make sure. The whole time he's nervous, shredding things. He shreds a crossword puzzle his mother's working on in the kitchen, and two matchbooks. It's a habit he can't help.

Then we're on the sun porch lying on Nathan's mother's faded old chintz sofa and through the big double windows I can see the sky and parts of the street. We're all tangled up somehow. Nathan gets one of my arms pinned between two cushions and accidentally breaks his glasses. We start to laugh.

"Technical difficulties here," Nathan says, "please stand by."

The fact is, we're both embarrassed and eventually we give up and get dressed. Nathan lights a cigarette. "I don't understand," he says. "I thought biological processes happened naturally."

"Not to me."

"Thought police," Nathan says, "they're going to pick you up for negative thoughts. Of course, they might nab *me* for negative capability. Like Keats."

"It doesn't matter, Nathan. Maybe we should stick to memorizing the periodic table."

Nathan looks thoughtful. Then, to my amazement, he digs into the pocket of his khakis and takes out a little spiral notebook, the kind we're supposed to write our homework assignments in. He makes a quick notation.

"What are you doing?"

"Keeping track, like my father does. He's always telling me my trouble is I don't make a note of things. Here, on October thirtieth, we drove to Gentilly and smoked marijuana. Now it's January twenty-sixth."

"Give me that."

In the notebook, scribbled in Nathan's crabbed handwriting is the note "January 26. Sex with Gray. Not successful. My fault or hers?"

"I don't know." I hand Nathan back the notebook and gather up the rest of my rumpled clothes. "Maybe this project isn't working out."

"I'll put us down for February first," Nathan says, consulting his notebook. He looks up with a professorial squint. "Can you wait that long?"

Max is quiet these days; Mudie seems distracted. I'm sure they haven't noticed any changes taking place in my life, other than all the time I spend with Nathan. Max approves; he thinks the Kentors are a good influence. They don't drive flashy cars or spend money in conspicuous ways. The only extravagance they allow Nathan is an unlimited charge account at the bookstore. Their house, though large, is unadorned except for a marvelous green-tiled swimming pool in the backyard.

To Nathan's horror, the Kentors invite all of us to dinner. Nathan is always worried about his parents appearing too eccentric. "Relax," I tell him, "consider it part of the project. Anyway, Max eats oysters every week with your father."

"And eating oysters together signifies *some* common ground."

"You said it."

Our two families seem made for each other: just the right blend of eccentricity and seriousness. Before dinner Alice takes Mudie into the kitchen to help with the hors d'oeuvre. "It's called saganaki," she explains. "Darwin and I had it in Greece. It's a kind of flaming cheese with sherry and lemon juice."

"Sounds beyond me," Mudie says. "I usually just open a can of olives."

The two women go into the kitchen. After about ten minutes we hear shrieks. Nathan races in to see what the matter is; Mudie and Alice are at the stove laughing, with tears streaming down their faces. The ceiling is scorched but otherwise undamaged.

"A little too much flambé," Alice decides.

"Just a bit."

After supper Max and Mudie have coffee and brandy in the library with the Kentors. Nathan and I sneak upstairs to Nathan's room. He locks the door and starts trying to make love to me. I can't relax. I keep getting the feeling that Nathan is trying to achieve mastery over me. "It's no use," I finally tell him.

"You might try relaxing."

"Here? In your parents' house?"

"They're oblivious," Nathan says.

"But I'm not. I'm sorry, Nathan."

"It's okay." Nathan reaches for his clothes. "I imagine after flaming cheese any fireworks we might produce would be anticlimactic."

"Another time, maybe."

"Definitely," Nathan says.

Back home Max and Mudie seem lighthearted. They kiss in the foyer. I go upstairs and feel like hiding in bed except that alone in bed is where I run into myself most. Instead I sit up in the library reading. Reading, it's possible to go an hour or two without running into myself.

Nathan calls me on the phone, asks if he can come over.

"I don't think so," I tell him. "I need to be alone."

"You said that yesterday."

"It was true yesterday."

"And the day before."

"Look, Nathan, I just don't feel like it."

"How do you know until I get there?"

"I know you."

"I thought we'd been over that and agreed upon the mutual impossibility of ever knowing one another."

"Cut it out, Nathan."

"Admit it, you smiled."

"All right. I smiled. Listen," I tell him, "I'm going to meet you at K & B by the paperbacks. But I'm not in the mood for anything."

"All right," Nathan says quietly, "we won't do anything. I'll just watch you emerge from amidst the paperbacks. Our Lady of the Pulp."

"I told you," I say, "cut it out."

We sit in a booth and talk. There's something about the tacky and familiar surroundings of the soda fountain that jars loose my sadness. Nathan shreds half a dozen paper-straw covers and looks uncertain. "How's home?" he asks.

"On the surface, everything is normal. We go about everything in the same way. But there's something off in the rhythm. I can't explain it. With Bobbie gone, we're like those light isotopes they talk about in chemistry class."

"How's your father?"

"Oh, you know Max. Tries to be so disciplined. To look valiant in the face of catastrophe. I think he feels guilty. He wanted Bobbie to go away to school in the first place. It was his idea."

"Says who?"

"Bobbie. She told me over the phone Max wanted her to go away because she knew about his affair with Kendra Hamilton."

"Bobbie's a cynic," Nathan says.

"I never thought of it that way. Here the whole time I'd been thinking Max just wanted Bobbie to have a better education. You think Bobbie's story is true?"

"Could be." Nathan looks at me pointedly. "Sometimes I get the feeling you let your father exaggerate Bobbie's talents so you can avoid yourself. You spend a lot of time worrying over this stuff, Gray. Meanwhile, where are you?"

"I just don't feel that significant, Nathan. Sometimes I try to change that, but it's very hard to maintain. I grew up thinking I wasn't very important. Sure, there are times now I feel otherwise, but it doesn't last. All it takes is some family crisis or a phone call from Bobbie and I feel my own self shrinking."

Nathan looks rueful. We let the waitress between us clear the table, then Nathan orders coffee. We smoke a cigarette apiece, looking out the plate-glass window. A streetcar clatters by going up St. Charles Avenue.

"My impression of your father is that he tries very hard to be correct, to do the right thing, but underneath he's pulled in a wayward direction. A part of him rebels against having to be so excellent."

"Sounds like me."

"You mean staying up all night to work on your science project so you can get an A and the next day smoking grass with me and getting detention at school?"

"Sort of."

Nathan nods understanding. "Since Bobbie left, you've been working harder than you usually do. Is there any reason?"

"I'm depressed. It passes the time."

"You want to go to Harvard yourself."

"I've thought about it."

"Study psychology."

"No, biology."

"Theories of personality? Dreams?"

"Enzymes."

Nathan sighs. "Harvard, then Johns Hopkins. We could do both. Get married. Our lives would be one unbroken line running back to childhood."

"We haven't even slept together yet. Maybe we're incompatible."

"Antibodies," Nathan muses.

"Maybe."

"Think about it," Nathan says. "The endless possibilities."

I stay up late drawing a cross section of the heart. In Bobbie's room I find a cache of markers, expensive, fine-line drawing tools slim enough for detailing the insides of arteries, the sleeves of veins.

Nathan's right: Since Bobbie left I've been pulled in two directions. Part of me wants to go to Harvard to fill Bobbie's place, to make up to Max and Mudie for her loss; the other part wants—what? Harvard. And not for Max and Mudie or Bobbie, but for me. I hold the finished drawing under the light; my heart is perfect, it seems almost to have a life of its own. In Bobbie's drawer I find a sheet of tracing paper and cardboard, tape the paper to the board, and slide the drawing inside to protect it. *Human heart   Gray Maubry   December, 1966.*

six

arnival is late this year. For weeks Max has been going to lunches and secret meetings; the Maubrys have been members of the city's oldest Carnival organization, Comus, since its formation. Max takes Mardi Gras seriously. He is the head of Comus now, and on Mardi Gras night he will appear at the Comus ball in a black knight's costume, masked and shiny with sequins.

Mudie, on the other hand, makes fun of Mardi Gras. She calls it a "quaint folk festival" and pokes fun at Max's meetings and the archaic protocol of the Carnival krewes.

"When I was a little girl I watched Carnival from a balcony in the Quarter; my father, Raphael Abunza, was once invited to toast the king of Rex, but otherwise my family didn't hold important positions in Carnival. It was a good thing, too," Mudie tells me, "because by then Mother and Daddy were broke. If I had been queen of Comus,

Daddy would have sold every stick of furniture in the house to buy my dress. As it was, he sold the dining-room table the year I got invited to Twelfth Night. Mother had the dress made with the money from the table. God, it was gorgeous, all that beading. Daddy cried when he saw me. But he was furious the next day when he had to eat supper on a card table. New Orleanians are crazy—they'll do anything for Mardi Gras."

The last week of February Max comes home from one of his luncheons; he hangs his knight's costume in the dressing room in front of the mirror. "I'd like to take Bobbie to Comus this year," he says.

Mudie looks amazed. "Max, Bobbie's in the hospital."

"I know, but St. Vincent's isn't a *real* hospital."

"You don't think of a psychiatric hospital as being real? I do."

"I'm sure they have special dispensation for things like this, don't they, Gray?"

"Don't ask me."

"God," Mudie says, "you're serious, Max. You honestly think it would be helpful to Bobbie to leave the hospital and parade around on your arm with a bunch of drunk men in ridiculous costumes."

"Of course I'm serious. It couldn't hurt to let Bobbie out of that place for one night of fun. What girl's state of mind wouldn't be enhanced by putting on a pretty gown and dancing with her old man? What do you think, Gray?"

"I think it's obscene."

Max puts on his wounded look. He rubs his hair in this deeply thoughtful way he has which usually means he's not thinking at all but feeling stubborn. "I'm going to call Bobbie's doctor anyway," he says, "despite what you two think. Spoilsports."

A few days later Bobbie calls me. "Max got me a pass to go to the Comus ball. Wouldn't you say his priorities are a little askew?"

"Mudie and I tried to talk him out of it, but he has this romantic notion it will do you good," I tell her.

"Getting out of *here* will do me good," Bobbie says, "you have no idea what it's like to have every move you make supervised by the nuns. And bath time—what a horror show. Imagine being herded in with thirty naked women all at once. They dole out the soap and shampoo in minute quantities so you don't try to kill yourself by swallowing it. The thing is, after a while it makes you want to *try*. Billy Fitzsimmons stole a dinner plate and smashed it and tried to eat it. Now they give us paper plates."

"Mudie says you can have a dress made."

"Where was *she* when Max came up with his brilliant idea?"

"Oh, you know Mudie. She tried to point out how absurd it is for you to go on pass from St. Vincent's Hospital just to go to a Mardi Gras ball but Max wouldn't listen. I wonder if there's ever an instance where they argue and Mudie wins."

"She doesn't want to win," Bobbie says, "she wants to be Max's darling, his child, his charming plaything. Krewe of Dementia Praecox, if you ask me. Who's crazy, them or me?" Bobbie sounds crestfallen, the way she sometimes does when she compares her life to the life she wished she had. "Don't worry, Graycat," she says, "I'll think of something to get back at them. 'If it be not now, yet it will come.' "

Bobbie has three fittings for her ball dress. The only good part is that afterward she comes back home to Harmony Street and we sit together on the balcony that runs behind our two rooms, connecting them. We sit on the floor and admire the massive twisted oak in the middle of the gravel driveway.

"This whole thing is repulsive," I say.

Bobbie smiles. "You mean my being in this ball."

"It's barbaric. As if you haven't got enough to feel bad about without being paraded about like a hunk of meat."

"Not exactly my idea of a civilized society," Bobbie says, "but then the Greeks were considered civilized and look what they did to one another in those tragedies. Can being in a Carnival ball be worse?"

"Possibly."

"Look, if it puts me back in Max's good graces, I'd swallow a giraffe."

After that Bobbie doesn't have any more fittings so I don't see her for a while. I'm busy spending time with Nathan, working on the project. I'm not sure whether the project really is what Nathan claims, to extend the boundaries of my personality, or whether he just wants to have sex with me. We spend a lot of time kissing and groping on his mother's sofa.

When Carnival starts, Nathan and I go to as many parades as we can. We prefer the neighborhood parades like Thoth and Freret to the grander, old society ones: Momus, Comus and Proteus. On Sunday before Mardi Gras there's an all-woman parade called Iris which is Nathan's personal favorite. The other parades are dominated by men and Iris manages to convey an undertone of mockery toward them. "I heard a rumor the queen of Iris this year weighs over three hundred pounds," Nathan tells me. "So much for nubile young flesh."

Bobbie calls, and in this mysterious voice she says, "I have something to show you, Graycat. Can you come over?"

"Now?"

"Visiting hours last until four-thirty. I promise it will be worth your while." Then she laughs in this odd way.

"What is it, Bobbie?" I ask.

More laughter. "Just come."

At the hospital Bobbie's nurse, a young black woman named Frankie, gives me a look when I sign in. "Bobbie's in the dayroom," she tells me. She sighs. "She doesn't have any hair, so don't act too amazed when you see her. She does like to amaze people."

"What do you mean, she doesn't have any hair?"

"Check it out," Frankie says.

Bobbie's in the dayroom watching *As the World Turns*. She's wearing blue jeans and a yellow buffalo-plaid shirt, and she's completely bald, just as Frankie said. This gives her face a pale, other-worldly look. "Like a Martian," Bobbie grins, "that's how I look. Don't you think so, Graycat?"

"More like a mental patient," Bobbie's friend Robin says to me. "This latest action has got 'mental patient' written all over it, Bobbie. Hell, why not write it in Magic Marker across your forehead?"

"Thanks for being so supportive," Bobbie says.

"Fuck you too," Robin replies.

I look at Bobbie. "What happened?"

"I talked Chuck in the beauty shop into letting me use his clippers. He bet me forty dollars I wouldn't shave off all my hair. So I did."

"Just like that. On a bet?"

"Yes. For the hell of it," Bobbie says.

"The hell of it."

"What's the matter, Gray? Don't look so serious."

"What are Max and Mudie going to say?"

"Who cares, it's not their hair."

"What about Comus?" I say.

"Oh, shit. I forgot," Bobbie says. She makes wild eyes and covers her mouth to stifle a loud laugh, and finally we both laugh, but not loudly or for very long.

That night Bobbie's supposed to come for dinner and to make final Mardi Gras plans. I keep expecting her to call and say she has the flu or something but she doesn't; she takes a cab over from St. Vincent's. She's wearing a long trench coat, a flowing white scarf; her head is bald. I answer the door.

"No one ever accused me of being fainthearted," Bobbie says. Her eyes look slightly bloodshot. Probably from smoking a joint in the cab on the way over. I can't stop looking at her bald head; she looks like such a completely different person.

"Max and Mudie are in the library having their usual martinis," I say.

"Promise me if Max kills me you'll come to my funeral," Bobbie says. "I wouldn't want to be the only one there."

We go into the library. Every day at cocktail time Max has this ritual of making martinis in the silver cocktail shaker he and Mudie got as a wedding present from Uncle Stanton. The gift was an insult really, since Uncle Stanton left thirty million dollars to Tulane Medical School and a cocktail shaker to Max. Max never let on that he felt insulted by such a stingy gift; acting gracious is his form of denial. Now, though, there is nothing gracious about the way he greets Bobbie.

"Bobbie! My God! What happened to you?"

"Cheers, everyone," Bobbie says. "Drink up, Max."

"Oh no," Mudie says.

"What the—"

"Max," Mudie says, "easy."

"I forgot to tell you," Bobbie says, "they ordered these electroshock treatments, and they forgot to warn me about the side effects."

"It's a joke," I say.

"There isn't a single hair left on your head," Max says. "Not even one."

"It's minimalist," Bobbie says. Mudie stifles a laugh.

"How can you go to Comus tomorrow night?" Max says.

"Beats me," Bobbie says.

Now I understand; this is Bobbie's retaliation at Max for making her appear at Comus. A low blow, but I don't entirely blame her.

Max stares at the olive in his martini glass. He's trying to regain his equilibrium. He sets his glass down. "I don't ask much," he says, quietly, finally. "I support this family in the manner to which it is accustomed. And what do I ask in return? That my daughters treat me with a little decency."

"Max," Mudie says, "this isn't *King Lear*. Bobbie's hair will grow back. In a strange way, she looks kind of beautiful."

"Not at Comus she won't."

"Well, obviously. She can't go to Comus."

"Well, *obviously*."

Max sets his glass down. "That lovely dress," he muses, looking at Mudie. Mudie shakes her head no.

"I'll go in Bobbie's place." As soon as the words are out of my mouth, I regret them.

"Excellent idea," Max says.

"Bobbie and I wear the same size."

"Do you really want to?" Mudie asks.

"I'll make it part of the project," I say, evasive.

"What project?" Mudie asks. "Something you're working on at school?"

"Not exactly. It has to do with Nathan. With changing the way I see things."

I don't think Max and Mudie understand but they are both so relieved Max makes another shaker of martinis.

Bobbie treats me coolly during dinner; I can't tell whether she feels let off the hook by my offer, or betrayed. In any case, I have shifted the focus away from her and onto me; I realize she's peeved. At dinner, Mudie goes on about how Nathan can drive me to the ball and pick me up, how she thinks she remembers how to do hair in a French braid, how good Bobbie's dress is going to look on me. She's just glad she doesn't have to go herself.

When Nathan calls I tell him the new development. "Bobbie's not so crazy after all," he says. "What a clever way to get out of social engagements."

"It's not funny, Nathan," I say. What Bobbie did, and our reactions to it, encapsulate the way our family works. Bobbie does something outrageous; Max is outraged, Mudie stunned; and I step in to save us, trying to think of some way to make everybody happy. Everyone except myself.

"You have to drive me to Comus tomorrow night," I tell Nathan, "so we can't get too drunk. And I need you to pick me up afterwards."

"I'm good enough to drive you there and pick you up, but I'm not good enough to be invited," Nathan says mildly. "How do you feel about that?"

"Oh, Nathan, this not a Jewish issue."

"Jews aren't asked to Carnival balls," Nathan says. "That makes it a Jewish issue."

"All right. Now, will you please drive me?"

"I'll drive," Nathan says, "but I'm not going to drive blindfolded."

On Carnival day Max wakes up early. I can smell the coffee from my bedroom, and when I go down he's made this elaborate breakfast and brought out the silver coffee service. There's a box of long-stemmed roses for me in the refrigerator, and a corsage for the ball this evening. Mardi Gras turns Max into a child; he so relishes all these preparations that it seems mean-spirited to disappoint him.

Mudie sleeps late. Finally, when Max can't stand it anymore, he wakes her up and makes her breakfast. "Are you going to Rex today?" he asks, meaning the Rex parade.

"I hadn't decided," Mudie says. She lingers over her coffee so long that Max gets fidgety and starts loading his costume and box of carnival beads, his "throws," into the trunk of the car. Mudie watches him through the window. His movements are precise, charged.

"I guess Mardi Gras means so much to Max because it's really a giant family. A family with peculiar rituals and customs and certain orders to be obeyed. A family with secrets mingled with hilarity. Max never had a real family. Personally, I think Carnival time's a mess—all those people drunk and falling down and having accidents—but everyone else seems to like it."

"You can stay here," I say. "I'll go to the parade with Nathan."

Mudie looks grateful. "Thanks. Be careful. And be home early, say no later than three. We have to get you ready for the ball."

"Don't worry, Mudie."

"Gray"—Mudie hesitates—"it was good of you to offer to go in Bobbie's place. You didn't have to, you know."

"I know."

"Don't feel you have to make up for Bobbie."

"I couldn't begin to."

"But you try sometimes, don't you?"

Embarrassed, I leave the room to go get dressed for the parade. Nathan and I are going as gypsies. I put on my purple gypsy skirt, peasant blouse, purple satin mask. Nathan arrives dressed in his gypsy trousers, sash, green satin mask. We giggle and kiss each other. Nathan's mouth tastes like cigarettes, mine like coffee.

The streets are full of people in costume. Maskers call out to one another—"Hey, Mardi Gras!"—and swill beer or nip from flasks. Nearly everyone wears a costume and mask. I find myself feeling there's something different even about Nathan, a slightly altered mood.

On St. Charles Avenue we buy two beers from a vendor. My reflection in the window of a flower shop makes me flinch. There's something both comforting and frightening about wearing a mask, about being myself yet someone else. I try to take my mask off but Nathan won't let me. "It's part of the project," he says, and fits it back onto my face. "Don't spoil the experience."

Nathan and I have both seen the Rex parade since we were babies on our fathers' shoulders. I have a picture in my room of Nathan and me at Mardi Gras when we were six months old; I was dressed as a carrot and Nathan as a grinning, toothless gladiator. In the background of the picture is the huge papier-mâché *boeuf gras*, the fatted calf, symbol of pre-Lenten excess and gaiety.

After the parade we go back to Harmony Street. Mudie is waiting for us with mugs of hot tomato bisque and crawfish étouffé. There's a box of petits fours from Gambino's Bakery, decorated in Mardi Gras colors: gold, green, purple.

Nathan goes home to sleep, and Mudie and I go upstairs to get me ready for the ball. She draws me a hot bath with gardenia-scented bath milk. "I can tell Max really appreciates your going to Comus tonight. If Bobbie really didn't want to go, she could have chosen a less drastic way of communicating it than shaving all her hair off. It's typical, I guess. Bobbie is always so extreme."

"Maybe she didn't feel she had a say. Max was so imperative about the whole thing."

Mudie darkens momentarily, then brightens. Whenever I am critical of Max, Mudie flinches, but she doesn't say much. She's attached to him in such a delicate way, maybe she's afraid any little wind will shake the two of them loose. "You're going to look scrumptious tonight"—Mudie turns her attention to my ball gown, made for Bobbie, hanging from the door—"like a fairy princess."

"I don't feel like one."

"I suppose not. I'm sorry you have to be growing up this way, Gray. So fast, so much going on. Having to face such hard things, like Bobbie getting sick just when your view of the world is being formed. When I was your age I had no idea how varied experience can be. But I've always tried to be honest with you, Gray. What can I do? Either lie to you and keep you a child or tell you the truth and watch your childhood end too quickly."

"You've already chosen," I say. "We both have."

What I mean is that we've chosen to let my childhood end, but Mudie still hangs on to the idea that she can create for herself a private world where nothing can touch or harm her. I'd like to create such a world for myself, too, but I don't believe in my ability to accomplish that. I see that being an artist helps Mudie in this respect.

"You know," I say, as I slip into the silver princess dress, "I never liked being a child. I couldn't understand what the big deal was about. Grown-ups had all the power, made all the decisions. Even down to what kind of sandwich you got for lunch or the color of your bathing suit. Or getting sent to bed early or being punished for things I hadn't done."

"Don't say that!" Mudie cries. "I want to believe you were happy."

"I hated being a child."

"Oh, to stay young," Mudie says, "that's the great thing."

"Maybe for some people. Not me."

She leaves the room a moment to find a hairbrush. I think about Bobbie's and my childhood, about the lovelier aspects of that time, and how important the feeling was then between Max and Mudie. Those early days, when we lived on Marengo Street and Max was dreaming about building a new house because the hallway was jammed with Mudie's sculptures. On Saturdays we'd put on the phonograph and dance, Max in an old but impeccable white shirt, Mudie's eyes intelligent and lovely, a tear in her stocking. The light fell just so across the floorboards, and there were pink shrimp and green bottles of wine in the old Kelvinator. At night Bobbie and I read to one another, nestled together in one bed, our arms around each other so it was hard to tell whether we were one sister or two. Bobbie would laugh at the story and I would cry, although it was the same story. Snow White and Rose Red, light sister, dark sister, we called ourselves.

Now there are other memories. The telephone ringing at strange times, Max's unexplained disappearance one weekend, Mudie's muffled crying, a book thrown from a second-story window, a single, premonitory visit Mudie made to a psychiatrist. Bobbie and I knew something was wrong but when we asked, they never told us. Max and Kendra Hamilton, did they go back that far? Nine years? Most likely. Parents' lies are worse than whatever truth is being hidden. Not telling children the truth is leading Hansel and Gretel into the woods and telling them, "Find your own way back home." What saves them? Crumbs, like memories, fragments of truth. So there are parts of Bobbie's and my childhood that are true and parts that lie. I want to know what was real. We can't live on gingerbread forever.

Mudie comes back into the room carrying a silver brush and begins brushing my long dark hair. Bobbie's is blond, or was. "She would have looked better in this dress," I say.

"Not better. Different," Mudie replies. She hugs me to her, then turns me loose to look at myself in the mirror. At first I don't recognize myself; then I do.

. . .

Nathan comes for me at eight-thirty. We drive together through the languid streets still ruined with Carnival debris. Nathan scowls; he hates the idea of Carnival balls and is here both to please and to criticize me. I try to block him out and concentrate on the idea that I am doing something for Max that Bobbie can't and Mudie won't. It's weird to be sitting in my princess dress next to Nathan, and I wonder what Bobbie is doing back in the hospital. Cursing me? Laughing?

"Remember everything," Nathan says at the door to the auditorium. "Do you have a notebook and pencil?"

"Cut it out."

We kiss at the auditorium door. For some reason Nathan's kisses always catch me by surprise; there's something funny about his timing that endears him to me.

"In a perverse way I wish I could stay for the ball. I feel like I'm throwing you to the wolves," he says.

"What wolves?"

"There's Kendra Hamilton." Nathan nods toward a tight black Porsche blocking the fire lane. I can't see who's driving, but sure enough, Kendra gets out and the Porsche speeds away. Blond Kendra in a purple gown and black cape eyes the entrance bravely and goes in right past me without acknowledging my existence.

"What time should I pick you up?" Nathan asks. "Midnight? One? Or do you have to go to the queen's supper afterwards?"

"God, Nathan, I don't know. Max will probably take me home."

"Don't count on it. I'll be back here at midnight. And, Cinderella, don't lose sight of the project."

Inside the auditorium I am immediately overwhelmed. Women, women everywhere. Smoke, the smell of perfume, the rustle of silk, chiffon, organdy. I make a beeline for the ladies' room to smoke a joint; everyone else is drinking from flasks and fixing their makeup. There's so much smoke and perfume and talk in the air, I hope nobody will notice the pungent smell of grass coming from my stall.

When the ball begins I am escorted to the call-out section, where the women sit who have formal invitations to dance. The stodginess, the dullness, the inane ritual of it all make me feel like I'm living a cross between a bad Jane Austen novel and a Fellini movie. Then Kendra sits down next to me; her bare shoulders rub up against mine. "Hello, Gray," she says. "I didn't expect to see you."

"I know. You expected Bobbie. Unless Max told you . . . Bobbie shaved all her hair off."

"Maxwell didn't tell me anything."

"I'm surprised Max didn't buy Bobbie a wig rather than let me take her place."

"You don't think very highly of yourself, do you?"

"Should I?"

Kendra smiles, ambiguously it seems to me, and at this point the tableau begins. One at a time the debutantes are presented to the court. Kendra yawns and whispers, "I'm dying for a drink."

"Are you and Max having an affair?" I blurt out.

"You're not as shy as you look," she says, after a pause.

"*Are* you?"

"No."

Kendra closes her eyes and opens them again as if she expects the scene to have changed in the meantime. "Young people are so precocious nowadays," she says. "At your age I never would have had the guts to ask my mother's best friend if she was sleeping with *my* father."

Kendra's whole statement sounds false. I look at her: blond hair done in a perfect chignon; smooth, ample body; eyes the color of tobacco; purple velvet gown; breasts; the aura of artiness and worldly experience, and I know the truth. She is Max's lover. I know it only because Max would have no reason to abstain from loving her; his needs are always satisfied. And because he would have for himself a believable excuse: Mudie's unpredictable ability to leave the house, to act for herself, to follow through, to stand up and insist on fidelity.

"Ah," Kendra says, "there's Max now. I can't think of anything more fitting than Max as the black knight. He *so* wants to be the white knight."

"So it's true, then. Being lied to is worse than whatever the truth is, you know."

"Exactly," Kendra says, looking contrite. "I think Henry James said that the inconvenience is not that you mind what is false but that you miss what is true. Something like that. James is hard to paraphrase."

"Are you going to stop?"

"Stop what? Quoting James?"

"Fucking Max."

Kendra laughs, and she gets a few dirty looks from the old ladies sitting in front of us; to them the presentation of the court is a sacred occasion. "I think it would be better if you left yourself out of your father's business," Kendra says as she reaches over and smooths a stray strand of my hair back into place. "I imagine your own plate is full enough."

"There's my mother to consider."

"Oh, well. Mudie. She's tougher than she looks."

"Aren't you her friend?"

"Gray, adult life isn't that cut-and-dried."

"People only say that when they want to get away with something."

"Look," Kendra says, "your father and I go back a long way. I think he's absolutely grand. Always have. He's good-looking, witty, smart, original, charming—completely divine. Don't spoil him for yourself, Gray. You're lucky to have Max for a father."

What Kendra means is, she's lucky to have him for a lover. I hate it that the same qualities in Max I loved as a child are being used to separate him from us.

A page appears and escorts Kendra to the dance floor for her dance with Max, the black knight. The entire floor is covered in white canvas, to protect the ermine mantles of the Comus court. I watch Max dancing with Kendra, blond Kendra in her purple gown, but there's nothing inappropriate about the way he behaves. Kendra has a beautiful back. Max is a lousy dancer.

Then it's my turn to dance with him. It's disconcerting to dance with your father while he's wearing a mask; it reminds me that I know only those aspects of him that he wishes to present. I'm not feeling well. Maybe I smoked one too many joints in the ladies' room. Maybe Kendra makes me sick.

"Second daughter," Max says fondly, "you look lovely."

"I wish you wouldn't call me that. It makes me feel like one of a number of signed lithographs."

Max laughs. "Well, I only have two daughters. Both originals."

"Bobbie's a lot more original than I am."

"Originality isn't everything," Max says. "I could do without shaved heads, for one thing."

"Bobbie doesn't want to be what you want her to be," I say to Max, finally taking the chance. "That's part of the problem."

"All I asked was that she come to one Carnival ball with me. It would have restored her name in the community."

"What's wrong with her name?"

"Don't be silly, Gray. You know as well as I do she's got the label 'mental patient' as long as she's in that hospital. I only wanted to help her restore her image."

"It looks like Bobbie's got her own idea of what her image is."

"Unfortunately," Max says. The dance is almost over; I can feel Max loosening his hold on me, and for a moment I have the sensation that I am dancing alone. "Do you want to ride home with me afterward? Or is Nathan coming to get you?" Max asks.

"Nathan's coming. I didn't know if you were coming straight home after the ball."

Max winks, opens the silk favor pouch, and gives me a small present, the custom among members of Carnival krewes when a dance is finished. "Thanks," I say.

"Thank you, Gray. For being here. I can't imagine that you really wanted to be."

I open the box. Inside is a lovely green enameled pendant watch inlaid with tiny pearls and diamonds. For a moment I am overwhelmed with love for Max, ashamed that I could ever have felt shortchanged by him, guilty for not loving him more. Then I realize the watch is too sophisticated for someone my age. Max must have bought it for Kendra, and something made him change his mind at the last minute and give it to me. I stare at the watch a moment, then put it around my neck, over my princess dress, stunned with love and fury.

seven

"Graycat," Bobbie says, "how's tricks? How's the vast ruinous empire?"

"Depressing. I never realized until now just how much energy you generated for Max and Mudie."

"I saw you on television dancing with Max. My, my, the fairy princess. I really missed going to Comus."

"I bet," I say.

Bobbie lights us both a cigarette from the one she has going, inhales rapidly. Speaks rapidly. "Here on the ward they elected yours truly queen. Crazy people have such an instinct for nobility. Know what they call me around here? 'Noblesse Oblige.' Guess it comes from Max and all that Carnival crap."

"Kendra was there. Beautiful in her too, too solid flesh. She came and sat next to me. Max danced with her."

"Did you pry a confession out of her?"

"Yes. At least it sounded that way to me. But you know something, I don't think I really care now. I care about me now. I care about doing well in school, and Nathan, and going away from here as soon as possible. And you. I still care about you, Bobbie. Although in some ways I ought to hate your guts."

Bobbie laughs. "You can hate my guts if you want to, Gray. It's a free country."

"Not for me. For me, everything costs. And if I start hating you, I lose the most vital connection of my childhood. I can't see doing that. But I can see turning down the volume. When we were children you were always so *noisy*; I could hardly hear myself."

"God, Graycat. I didn't mean to drown you out," Bobbie says.

"I know. And anyway, it was drowning Max and Mudie out you wanted. The childish operetta. Max in white pajamas and Mudie in one of her torn dresses, waltzing across our childhood."

"God, you've got it exactly right," Bobbie says.

I'm struck by the dramatic change in Bobbie since Christmas; she's wearing a bright green silk kimono and socks with sandals—part costume, part hospital gown. Her pale skin looks faded, and her hair is beginning to grow back in small blond burrs. I try not to look at her eyes, which reflect a kind of frozen pain, but beyond her, at the room.

"This hospital is a tacky place, don't you think?" Bobbie says. "It's a problem with the genre. Mustard-yellow walls, dayrooms, the hostile glare of the night dormitory, toilets without lids so you don't drown yourself . . . Doesn't leave much room for aesthetic grandeur."

"You never should have had to come here."

"You think not?" Bobbie narrows her eyes, taps her cigarette ash into the sand-filled ashtray. "Easy for you to say, living over on Harmony Street with Max and Mudie. Incidentally, Max told me about last semester's grades. All A's. Quite the scholar, now that Bobbie's out of the way."

"I miss you, Bobbie. I'm only studying so hard out of loneliness. And to shut out my anxiety over Max and Mudie."

"You forgot something," Bobbie says.

"What?"

"You forgot that you have talents too. Botany, literature, anatomy. Talents from the dark and luminous side. Oh, and poetry. You still write poetry, don't you?"

"How did you know about that?"

Bobbie taps the side of her head. "Clair-de-lunacy."

I can hardly bear to be here, to see her like this; underneath I know that whatever pain I'm feeling must be a fraction of what she feels, pain and disorder. When Max, Mudie, and I came to visit at Christmas Bobbie seemed lost to us, and that was bad enough. Now she seems lost to herself.

"Remember Billy Fitzsimmons?" Bobbie says. "The boy who set his hair on fire for me? He shot himself in the head the day after Christmas. Boxing Day. He didn't even do that right; he blew off a third of his face and managed to live a day or two before he finally died. Poor Billy. All that's left of him is a blood spot on his mother's good Aubusson."

"I'm sorry, Bobbie."

"Why be? He wasn't going to get better anyway. Just fall in love with hopeless crazy girls and set his hair on fire and blow his brains out, over and over. The same old gay and empty journey. Kafka."

"Good-bye, Bobbie. I'll come back soon."

"No, you won't," Bobbie says. "You're going to walk out of this place and every step is going to take you farther and farther away. And it should. It's good."

● ● ●

At the elevator doors I hug her to me; her bones feel light and filled with air like the bones of a bird. The large doors open slowly, and slowly we let each other go.

I'm walking down St. Charles Avenue toward K & B Drugstore when Nathan rides up on his bike.

"I looked up sex in the *Encyclopaedia Britannica.* It's under 'Coitus.' The entry was really quite detailed. We have the thirteenth edition. My father says it's the best, a classic. I probably owe my very existence to the thirteenth edition."

"Look, Nathan, I'm not in the mood."

"Of course there might be information in later editions that we could use. New positions, more elaborate foreplay . . ."

"Nathan."

"It all depends on whether you're a classicist. Being Maxwell Maubry's daughter, you probably are."

I can't help smiling.

"There"—Nathan sits straighter on his bicycle, pedaling backward—"I told you the natural tendency of things in the universe is toward hilarity. Moroseness is an unstable state."

"It *feels* permanent."

"An illusion," Nathan says. "Tonight is Saturday. I'll pick you up at eight. We'll go to the Huey P. Long Bridge, contemplate suicide, get that out of our systems, and then we'll go have sex."

"That's not funny."

"You smiled," Nathan says. "I saw you."

We have a nine-thirty curfew and it's already eight but I don't care. I get in the car and we drive down to a deserted wharf on the river. We stand for a while listening to the distant mad hooting of the barges; black water laps against the pilings.

Nathan takes his glasses off, kisses me, removes my jacket. I unzip his pants. We make love standing up against his car, cold and astonished.

eight

ax, Mudie, and Kendra in the library, dancing. There are two empty bottles of champagne on the kitchen counter; a third bottle is open on the library table. Louis Armstrong is playing, the two women have taken their shoes off, Max has unbuttoned his vest. He hears me come in the back door and comes out to ask me to join them in the library.

"No, Max," I say. "I think I'll go up to bed."

"You're turning into such a recluse. I don't ever see you having fun." He reaches out and takes one of my hands and kisses it.

"No thanks, Max."

A box of cigarettes is within reach. I reach for one and light it, studying Max's face. He looks flushed and exultant; he starts taking cigarettes out of the box and sticking them in my hair, behind my ears. I hold my head down and to my amazement, start to cry; I'm right there in the kitchen with seven or eight cigarettes stuck in my hair, crying without being able to stop.

Mudie comes into the kitchen looking for Max. When she sees me, she freezes.

"Max, Kendra and I just had the most marvelous idea. Why not go to the Allgood for waffles? Gray, you could join us."

"No thanks."

"You're crying," Mudie says. "Why?"

This only makes me cry harder.

"Does it involve Nathan?" Mudie asks.

"I don't know."

"What are all those cigarettes doing in your hair?"

"I put them there. To cheer her up," Max says.

"Max, really."

I leave the three grown-ups and run upstairs to my room. Occasionally I hear snatches of Armstrong, or Mudie's infectious laugh; they must have abandoned the trip to the Allgood and decided to stay at home.

I call Nathan. He offers to come over but I tell him it isn't necessary. I'm just suffering from postcoital *tristesse*, I tell him, plus I'm unnerved by the presence of Kendra in our house. What are the three of them doing, playing some stupid game because none of them can face what's really going on?

I've started reading poetry. At first, it frightened me because my responses are so unpredictable. Each poem seems like a steep climb into another country, and, while this is exactly what I want, I am never sure where I will end up, what I will learn. Writing my own poetry is a frustration that often makes me cry out loud. But I keep filling notebooks to guard against the chaos in my family.

I wake up around two A.M. and the simple thought comes to me: I don't have to live this way. Other people don't. Other children don't. My mind races, and without much thought I devise a plan so simple it is bound to work: I will go to school and never return. Take a backpack, as much money as I can find in Max's desk, my notebooks, the photograph of Max and Mudie in New York, a carton of cigarettes, a change of clothes, an old Indian blanket. I will disappear into another life the way people on television or in the movies do. Of course I'll miss Nathan—for a moment I stop, stymied in my plan for love of Nathan—but I have to leave him, too. I'm sad now, but determined. Downstairs, a champagne glass shatters on the kitchen tile. On the phonograph is Cole Porter. Mudie and Kendra are singing along.

In Mudie's medicine cabinet I find a Seconal and swallow it. I sleep an unfamiliar, dreamless sleep.

On Friday I go to school. The lessons float past; I can't seem to catch hold of anything my teachers say.

"What are the classical unities?"

"Unity of time, place, action. Unlike in our society, no violence happens directly onstage to traumatize the audience."

"The pathetic fallacy. Anyone. How about you, Gray?"

Nathan nudges me. "I don't know."

"The fallacy that human beings aren't pathetic," Nathan says, and the class laughs. The teacher goes red in the face.

After class Nathan stops by my locker. "Are you okay?"

"No."

"I have the car this afternoon. We can go for a drive, maybe it would cheer you up."

I go with him but without much heart. I want to share with Nathan my plan to run away, but telling would spoil the whole thing so I don't mention it. The silence between us hurts me more than almost anything else. I postpone the plan a day or two.

Sunday afternoon it rains. Rain comes down in heavy waves, blackening the streets, the sky, darkening the houses. I go to Nathan's to escape the quiet on Harmony Street, and to give him a surreptitious good-bye.

I hitchhike to the airport. When I get there, drenched and mud-spattered, I come up against a simple fact: I have neither enough money to buy a ticket nor the gall to forge a check, as Bobbie would do. I sit in the bar forcing down drinks. Men are willing to pay for them as long as I let them fondle me. I put up with a little of this and then go to the washroom and throw up in the toilet.

I have some more drinks and then stumble out onto the Airline Highway. All my plans coalesce into one goal: to walk somewhere so I can dry out. It's too far and the drinks have made me dizzy. Planes overhead on takeoff make deafening noise. Rain spatters me, my face, my clothes. I know why I left, but the reasons now seem nonsensical to me. Still, I don't want to go home. Finally I find a spot along the highway and lie down and cover myself with the blanket.

I drift in and out. I don't know how many drinks I had, but enough to disorient me. Each car that goes by I hope will see me, and when it drives by I am glad because being seen is just one step closer to going back home.

I hear the crunch of soggy shoes on the gravel before I see anything.

"Hello there, Gray?"

It's Dr. Cavendish.

"Everyone's out looking for you. Are you all right?"

"Please, Alan, don't find me. I don't want to go home."

"We can discuss that later. I can't leave you here."

He helps me into his car. I am completely filled with shame.

Max and Mudie stand on the grass, still and unnatural as lawn ornaments. When Alan's car stops they rush at me.

"Thank God you're safe," Mudie says.

"Running away is not like you, Gray," Max says.

"What could you possibly want that we don't give you?" Max says.

"Bobbie didn't put you up to this, did she?" Mudie asks.

I shake my head, no. The only thing I can manage to say is "I want to talk to Alan privately."

"In his office?"

"A regular appointment?"

"It would be a good idea," Alan says.

"But Gray doesn't need a psychiatrist," Mudie says.

"There's nothing wrong with her," Max says.

"There doesn't have to be," Alan says quietly.

"We'll talk it over," Max says.

"Yes," says Mudie.

I follow them inside, wrapped in my muddy blanket. I know neither one of them wants me to talk to Alan again, not as a psychiatrist. Both Max and Mudie need me to be fine, need desperately to have a daughter who will represent their wholesomeness in public, so that they can continue with their sickness in private. The selfishness of this infuriates me. Even Bobbie was probably acting in some twisted way to alert other people to our parents' destructive marriage, only nobody saw it.

In the week following my runaway attempt, Mudie keeps saying how unlike me it was. Max hints that I'm ungrateful, that I'm just trying to get attention.

"Don't we give you enough? Don't we do enough for you, Gray?" he asks at dinner.

"What?" I say.

"Then what got into you?" he says.

"Oh, Max. I just felt so unhappy."

Max looks surprised; he can't imagine that I would have character enough to be unhappy, moreover that I could be unhappy enough to run away. I find myself genuinely regretting that my attempt failed; if I'd succeeded I might be miles away from Harmony Street and the pain of losing Bobbie, then seeing Max and Mudie's marriage exposed. Marriages like theirs are only good as long as the charm comes from real innocence; defile that, and nothing remains.

Nathan understands. "Gray, you look so depressed, I figured you needed a second opinion."

"Well, give me yours."

"Someday you won't care so much about your family. I hope it will be me you care about. Me, and yourself. I know it's hard to imagine, but there will come a time when all this will be background noise."

"Nathan, I do care about you. I'm almost glad I didn't get away, because of you."

Nathan takes me out as much as possible. He has sworn to Max he'll keep an eye on me. We go to the Fatted Calf and eat enormous fresh cheeseburgers and drink beer. On the way home I make Nathan drive through the park. We stop at the large green lagoon and get out. It's early March and still cold. The cold makes the abundance of leaves on the trees seem unnatural.

"What are you doing?" Nathan asks.

I fish around in my purse for the little box Max gave me at Mardi Gras with the jeweled watch inside. I hold it in my hands, blowing on them because it's so cold.

We're standing by the lagoon. "Max and Mudie said it was unlike me to run away. Well, here's another thing that's unlike me."

"I'm a captive audience," Nathan says.

I reach out and hurl the box with the watch inside into the lagoon.

"*Gray*," Nathan says, shocked.

"Come on, Nathan. You're always talking about changing the way I do things."

Nathan touches my arm. "Are you all right?" he asks.

"Not really. But Max and Mudie won't let me go to a psychiatrist. It would mean admitting they had *two* daughters with problems. Which would mean admitting *they* had problems."

"Gray," Nathan says, "does this have anything to do with us?"

"You mean because we had sex?"

"Well, yes."

"No, Nathan. The sex was wonderful. You didn't hurt me at all."

"Well, that's good."

"I've just outgrown myself. And my family. It's not easy."

"It was meant to happen, Gray. Sooner or later."

"The project, you mean."

"Yes. But I didn't want it to *hurt* you," Nathan says.

"It's okay that I hurt. It would be nicer if I didn't, but what can I do? My whole life has been spent trying to avoid the pain, and the pleasure, of being myself. Well, that's over. I'm not sure what's next, but it isn't sleepwalking. I'm absolutely sure I want to go to Harvard, Nathan."

"Great."

"But listen. It's not just because Bobbie was supposed to go there and I want to make it up to Max. Now I want to go there for me. Just me. Do you think I have a chance?"

"Do you?" Nathan asks, smiling.

nine

obbie comes for dinner on Harmony Street. Her hair has pretty much grown in; she's wearing a blue silk shirt I recognize as belonging to Mudie. Mudie doesn't say anything, though. "You're looking well, Bobbie," she says.

"I don't *feel* well. I hate that place. The television's going all the time, they never turn the lights off, the food stinks. Does anybody have an idea how long I have to stay there?"

Max puts down his knife. "Bobbie, you have no idea how lucky you are. In the past few years the whole basic theory of schizophrenia has changed."

"Lucky me," Bobbie says.

"It used to be thought that parents caused schizophrenia. Now scientists are saying it's a brain disease. A chemical imbalance of some kind. No more psychotherapy. Exit Oedipus and Electra. Enter neuro-transmitters."

"I'm thrilled, Max," Bobbie says.

Max lifts the twin arches of his eyebrows. He looks genuinely happy. "In fifty years they'll be able to prevent diseases like schizophrenia at birth."

"Too late for me," Bobbie says.

"Can we change the subject?" I say.

Max looks surprised, Mudie less so. "Gray feels left out of the conversation," Mudie says.

"No, Gray feels horrified by the conversation," I say. Bobbie sniggers, Max looks offended. "This is an important subject," he tells me.

"Max is right," Mudie says. "I think it's good to have this discussion."

Bobbie gives me this look, a look that goes way back to our childhood; it usually meant Bobbie was about to steal something, or run away, or set something on fire.

"Go ahead, Max," Bobbie says, "about schizophrenia. What is it you were saying?"

"I hope you take these developments as good news," Max says.

"Why not?" Bobbie says.

My cigarette's glowing in the crystal ashtray, next to my glass of cabernet. I down my glass of wine and pick up the cigarette. Nobody sees me reach down and begin to set the corner of Mudie's good damask tablecloth on fire. Even I can't believe I'm doing it. It takes a while to get the fire burning through such good, creamy fabric. Bobbie is the first to notice, of course: She gives me a sly smile.

"What the hell"—Max breaks off his conversation—"the damn dining room's going up in flames. Call somebody, Mudie."

"I don't think that's necessary," Mudie says.

"Why not? Don't just sit there, everybody and let my house burn down."

At that moment the sprinkler system in the house Max designed turns on. Max jumps up from the table. He pulls the tablecloth off the table with the dishes still upright, as in a movie stunt, but the dishes all crash on the floor. Mudie gets up and races to the window; when cornered, Mudie always looks for a way out, but seldom takes it. Bobbie and I sit there calmly under the sprinklers, getting drenched. Bobbie looks at me. "Way to go," she says.

I go to Nathan's house. We make love on the faded chintz sofa on the Kentors' sun porch, and afterward go for a swim in the Kentors' green-tiled pool. The only times I am happy are when I'm with Nathan; he teases me about my behavior and calls me "torch." I think Nathan understands the real reasons why I've done these things: that it angers me to hear Max go on and on about Bobbie's problem while his own behavior goes unchallenged. Also, that I'm expected to pick up the slack for everyone else in my family.

"Bobbie's not crazy," Nathan says, "and neither are you. But I'm worried about you, Gray."

"How so?"

"Your behavior is becoming very excessive. You stay up all night studying so you can get good grades, spend all your time after school writing poetry, do bizarre things at home, like set tablecloths on fire. Where will it end?"

"I don't know, Nathan."

"Be careful."

"I can't."

At home Mudie is standing in the kitchen. Her eyes are red from crying; she's waiting to accost me.

"Gray," she says, "remember when you asked me if Max and Kendra were lovers?"

"I remember."

"I didn't believe you. I laughed at the possibility. Well, today Max told me the truth. And here I've been going around with her in public."

I take the silverware out and set the table in the kitchen. The dining room is still being repainted. I put crystal out, and candles. Mudie is still standing there, raking her hand through her hair.

"So all this time you knew?"

"Yes."

"And Bobbie knew?"

"Yes."

"God, what an idiot I am." Mudie sits down and puts her head on the table like a tired child. She fingers the saltshaker, spilling some salt. "All this time I assumed *I* was the weaker half of this marriage. With my peculiarities, my work, not leaving the house, my disliking parties and the world Max likes. I just assumed Max would never do anything like this, and now that it's common knowledge, I don't really know what to think. Should I care? Not care? Part of me is appalled and some of me wants to laugh. Adultery, it's so *unlike* Max, so trivial. Not to mention tacky and mean."

"I tried to tell you, Mudie," I say.

"I know, heart. But it shouldn't be up to you to keep this family together. Max and I are not yours to save."

Max comes in the front door. We hear him whistling softly as he crosses the polished floor to the library. "Mudie?" he calls softly. "Gray?"

"In the kitchen," Mudie says.

When he sees me he looks bewildered. He doesn't sit down.

"Gray and I have been having a talk," Mudie says. "She knows all about your screwing Kendra."

"Mudie, your language."

"Your fornicating, then," Mudie says. "How can you be so concerned about language?"

"There's Gray to think of."

"Since when? Since when have you been concerned about Gray?"

"Mudie," Max says, "I think you should calm down."

"Don't tell me how to be, what to think. Have your stupid affair if you want, but don't orchestrate my reactions."

Mudie opens the kitchen closet and takes out an old raincoat of Max's. They are nearly the same height, but Max's coat swallows Mudie.

"What are you doing?" Max asks.

"I'm going out."

"Now?"

"If I can't have my own feelings in my own house I won't stay."

Max frowns; Mudie's unpredictable behavior is sometimes too much for him.

"Not one word," Mudie says. "I'm getting my purse and then Gray and I are going out."

"But why?" Max says.

"For the hell of it. There doesn't always have to be a reason. Come on, Gray."

"She can stay here with me," Max says quietly. "She doesn't have to go."

I stand there without moving. Max loosens his tie and pours himself a drink in the good crystal usually reserved for company. Mudie fumbles with a lipstick. I hate being part of their conflict; I'm sure whichever side I take will be the wrong one. I will lose either way. I lean back against the wall and try to imagine going back in time to the day when everything started to go wrong, but I can't seem to pinpoint the exact moment. I am too old to believe any longer in happy childhoods, mine or anyone else's.

Part 3

one

ax moves out, into his French Quarter apartment. This is what Mudie calls a "trial separation," necessary in Louisiana before getting a divorce. The separation is supposed to last a year. Max goes out and buys himself a new sound system and a beautiful leafy ficus. His clothes are conspicuously absent from the bedroom closet.

I feel awkward, alone in the house with Mudie. Her loneliness, her neediness, her fear frighten me. I try to avoid running into her, then feel guilty for my avoidance. I can't seem to get comfortable anywhere.

Mudie spends more time than usual in her studio, but whether she is working or just standing at the window looking out, I can't tell. She cries a lot and has emotional conversations with old friends, people she hasn't seen for a year or two because of her tendency toward isolation. She has lunch with Alice, Nathan's mother, and takes the streetcar downtown to see her lawyer. Despite this activity, there's a scattered feeling to Mudie's way of going about things, as if she isn't entirely serious. Wounded, yes. I think the thing she's maddest about is that everyone else knew about Max and Kendra before she did. As if she could have changed anything by knowing first. I feel sad for her. And then I realize that feeling sad for Mudie is a way of not feeling sad for myself.

Nathan keeps me busy. He knows there's nothing he can do to make Bobbie get well faster or to bring Max home; he doubts the wisdom of wishing for these things. It's been Nathan's experience that if you wish too hard for something, you miss what might be more valuable to you.

Part of our project for the summer is working for a doomed mayoral candidate. The more hopeless the candidate's chances, the harder Nathan works. We work every day in an office above a dry cleaner's, with no air-conditioning. We make phone calls to solicit contributions, we stuff envelopes. Then we go to Nathan's house and swim naked in his swimming pool. We order oyster loaves from Casamento's and have them delivered by taxi.

Mudie sleeps a lot or holes up in her studio. When I ask her if she wants me to stay home more, she shakes her head absently and says, "Do what you feel like doing. You don't have to stay in for me." Only once do I go up and take a peek at her alone in her studio. She is wearing a white bathrobe stained with clay and has her head down on her worktable like a tired child. I want to go in to her and stroke her long dark hair but I resist the impulse. I feel like I'm already parent enough.

Nathan brings me news of Max. Apparently Darwin Kentor went to lunch at Galatoire's with Max and said, "Look here, old man. This is pretty silly. Go home to your wife and children."

So far, he hasn't. And would Mudie take him back? Maybe she would tell him no. I'm not sure if this is because Mudie really wants to live apart or because she thinks she ought to make a show of strength. I'm not even sure Mudie really *knows* what she wants. Either way, with Bobbie in St. Vincent's and Max in the Quarter, we don't feel much like a family.

Then Max invites me to lunch. I don't really want to go but Mudie convinces me it would be a "good idea." For her, probably, not for me. I agree to go anyway, despite my misgivings. What can happen? I ask myself. How bad can it be?

Max picks me up at eleven on a Sunday morning. I am already tense with apprehension, but I try not to show how I'm feeling. Max looks wonderful; he's wearing a white linen suit and a Liberty of London bow tie. He greets Mudie with restraint, managing to convey the impression that all this trouble is somehow her fault. We leave, and Mudie turns away crying, her hand over her mouth.

Max wants to go to a French country restaurant across Lake Pontchartrain. On the way over his talk is mild, noncommittal, as if this were an ordinary outing. I know he is only trying to make up to me for having splintered our family, and I am angered by his effort. At the restaurant we order Sazerac cocktails; Max sketches two of his latest buildings on a cocktail napkin.

The restaurant grounds are beautiful; peacocks wander among the pine trees. I find myself watching them instead of listening to Max. He orders me a second cocktail. He takes my hand.

Our drinks arrive, and though I don't really want mine, I don't want to hurt Max's feelings. Max looks up from his drink with a serious expression and says, abruptly, "I had to leave your mother for Kendra, you understand. Kendra is a superlative lover. Your mother is romantic, that I can't quarrel with, but Kendra is really knowledge-able."

Max begins to describe Kendra's lovemaking to me. His language gradually becomes more explicit, even obscene. While he talks, Max has my hand in his and strokes my fingers. I pull my hand away but I feel compelled to stay and listen. I don't want Max to know how unnerved I am.

The food arrives, Max's trout and my veal; Max orders a bottle of wine. His face is flushed. When the waiter brings our bottle and uncorks it, Max takes a sip and nods approval at the waiter, who fills both our glasses.

"I'd like to leave Mudie and marry Kendra, but I really can't," Max says. "Mudie is too dependent and Kendra too independent."

I excuse myself and go around the veranda and inside the restaurant building to the washroom. I lean my head against the cool tiles but I can't make myself feel any better. Eventually, I return to the table and tell Max, "I feel sick. I want to go home now."

Then Max is all contriteness and concern. He apologizes. He says he's afraid he became "too intense"; he pays the bill. He escorts me back to the car, all the while apologizing; it's hard to believe he's the same man who told me sexual details about Kendra. But he is.

On the way back over the bridge neither of us says anything.

I think about the fact that Max is gone, and I don't just mean in this instance, today; I mean forever, irretrievably. Children long to grow up, to become their parents' equals, but the moment Max treated me like an adult, he took away the sense I have of *father.* I wish he hadn't shared with me the details of sex with Kendra; not that I didn't know about his other life, but I didn't want to hear about it from him. I feel cheated, the good and beautiful spirited away just like that, and in their place perversity.

What is the meaning of the word *charming*? I am reminded of a collection of bright cheap objects, with something dear and sentimental about them—and, yes, attractive—but nonetheless cheap. Is that what people mean when they say Henry Maxwell Maubry is a charming man? Or do they mean something else?

He has the ability to charm, captivate, delight, the power of giving delight. Yes, that's it, delight. Every memory I have of Max, even the dark ones, has this quality. I think of when Bobbie and I were babies and Max would play Brahms in the nursery and read to us from Shakespeare. Or when, later on, he went to London for a few weeks and brought us back kilts he'd had made especially for us and a box of beautiful soldiers made of lead. What other father, having no sons, would have dreamed his two daughters would love those toy soldiers, not for themselves, but because *he'd* brought them home for us? It was Max he gave, not the gift itself.

I think of him sitting in the library, on the buttery-soft leather sofa, dreaming of buildings. His eyes are open, focused behind his tortoiseshell glasses, his body both intense and dreaming. He is creating; we are quiet, respectful, we don't disturb him.

Later on, he rises, shakes off the daydream, accompanies us to the park. He has a bag of popcorn to feed the ducks. Bobbie laughs in the sunshine; my long brown hair is caught in Max's watch chain. Tenderly, tenderly, he untangles it. At the park he buys us Sno-Kones and shows us the botanical garden. He describes the different ways specimens are planted, in what arrangements, compares formal English gardens to tropical gardens such as we are used to. Bobbie and I on either side, holding his hand. He is ours, ours.

I know now that many children have contradictory childhoods. I have sacred memories, such a tumble of bright dear images of Max and Mudie when they were young and hopeful. I can see the new grass in the yard, our Easter bunny nibbling the edge of a caladium leaf. I can smell the startling masculine odor of Max's dressing room. I can, wherever I go, hear his incredibly deep voice discussing Shakespeare with Bobbie and expounding the need of formal education, even for actresses.

When I was a child I longed to be treated like an adult, and now that I am almost an adult, I want Max to protect me like a child.

Bobbie pretends not to mind, or if she does, it's because long ago she traded off her innocence for various kinds of intimacy with Max. Sometimes it was plain friendship, camaraderie; sometimes it was tinged with sexuality. Often he was her mentor, although with an intensity borrowed from the other roles. And sometimes they were playmates, charmed people with bright ideas and laughter.

Bobbie never had a choice. Now I understand it: what was between them and why I always wanted him just for myself. We both got the short end of the stick, since what can replace the days of childhood? Fantasy? Delusion? The delighted ravings Bobbie often fell into when she suddenly turned manic?

When Bobbie got sick I planned to take her place with Max, but never in this way. I steal a sidelong glance at him now, but he seems absorbed in driving; his eyes are on the horizon. Nothing happened, I tell myself, and my words get repeated in the whine of the engine, the rotation of the wheels, the endless repetition of the bridge railing. Nothing happened.

I see Bobbie's face at seven, Mudie's at thirty, my own when I was five, Max's at twenty-nine, all images from photographs in Mudie's drawer that have become, to me, more real than the lives they depict. Nothing happened. No one is lost or changed. Yet no one is ever the same.

Max lets me out in the gravel driveway without offering to come inside. All he says is, "Gray, I wouldn't tell your mother about this if I were you. She's got enough problems of her own."

I listen to the crunch of the gravel as he walks toward his car.

I find myself calling after him; I'm amazed. He turns toward me. I say, "Do you think you can treat me like that, and have it make no difference? 'Don't tell Mudie,' you say. Why not? Does Mudie really matter to you? What about me?" I say. "Do I matter to you at all?"

"Gray, please," he says, turning back. "Don't. I said I was sorry."

"Do you think a simple apology cancels out how dirty I feel? 'I'm sorry'?"

"I don't have to listen to this," Max says.

"I'm the only person in this family who doesn't have feelings," I say. "Everyone treats me as if I were some kind of dummy, some cigar-store Indian. Have something awful on your mind? Tell it to Gray."

Max says, "You're drunk."

"So what? My father got me drunk."

He gets into his car and drives the old Mercedes away. I stand there by myself on my parents' driveway, watching the car disappear down the narrow New Orleans street; then I shimmy up the big oak and onto the gallery behind my bedroom. I don't want to see Mudie; she would know right away something is wrong.

But the longer I think about it, the more it seems things are more right than wrong. I can't believe how light I feel, and it's not just from all the Sazerac cocktails. I feel light because I told Max off, a first for Gray, no longer closeted in the dark.

two

August, the worst stretch of the summer. People try to leave New Orleans; houses sit empty in a kind of fitful gloom; furniture, slipcovered in white, looks funereal. One afternoon Max shows up; the air-conditioning in his apartment is broken and he wants to stay in the guest room. Mudie just stands there while he unpacks his suitcase. Out come his two wrinkled linen suits, his blue pajamas, his good handmade English shoes. When he goes out to the car to get his shaving kit I give Mudie a disgusted look.

"I can't exactly kick him out to roast in hell, can I, Gray? After all, this is his house."

"The house that Max built?"

Mudie sighs. "I'd like to take a stronger stand but I can't. Damn it, I love the man. Which way gives me more power, saying the hell with Kendra Hamilton or letting her win and break up my marriage? I'm sorry, Gray. I shouldn't be venting this on you."

"That's right, you shouldn't."

Mudie starts, gives me a strange look. Although she is not a smoker, she helps herself to one of my cigarettes, lights it, and begins to cough. Just another way of distracting herself, I think, from the unpleasantness of her situation, and from her bad feelings about me.

Max treats both of us politely, as if he's a guest. He makes frequent trips to the kitchen for iced coffee, which he laces with rum in the privacy of his room. I am filled with a mixture of love and hate for him. All I have to do is see him standing in the atrium of the house he built himself, looking bereft, to awaken these contradictory feelings.

On the other hand, he made this ugly situation. He paid more attention to Kendra Hamilton than to Mudie, and ended up with neither one. At least, not securely. Kendra's frequently in New York. But I notice Mudie hasn't canceled her lawyer's appointments.

"I can never remember why we don't go away in August," Mudie says one night at dinner. Max is sitting at the head of the table serving vegetables.

"Because there's no place to go," he replies.

"Other people go places. North Carolina. Maine. Europe."

"Other people live in impractical houses. Here, we have an excellent cooling system. State-of-the-art," Max says.

"Too bad our lives aren't that way," Mudie replies.

"Lives can be fixed," Max says.

"Like broken windows?" says Mudie. "I don't think so."

Max and Mudie have a conference with Dr. Fergus about Bobbie. They drive to his office on Prytania Street and come home looking jubilant. Max has two dark half-moons of sweat under the arms of his suit; otherwise he looks serene and unrumpled. Bobbie is making remarkable progress, that's the news they bring. Dr. Fergus is writing an article about Bobbie, he wants permission to use her case history. Max unwraps a bottle of Mumm's, and when he starts to open it, the cork shoots up and shatters the skylight. Max proclaims this good luck.

We drink the champagne out on the patio. Heat rises from the swimming pool Max put in only last summer; the pool, one of Max's follies, is shaped like a long blue question mark. Mudie jumps in with all her clothes on; Max follows her. They swim around in the pool, heavy and affectionate as puppies. I go into the kitchen and smoke with Hannah.

From the kitchen window Hannah and I watch Max and Mudie paddling around, laughing and splashing each other. First Mudie takes her blouse off, then Max takes off his pants.

"Bobbie's leaving the hospital," I say.

Hannah says, "It looks to me like *this* is a nuthouse. Who's the craziest one here? I don't know."

"They're just happy," I say. By now, most of Max and Mudie's clothes are on the bottom of the pool.

"Those two do more hurt with their happiness than most people do with sadness," Hannah says. "Be careful, Gray."

"I'm beyond careful, Hannah."

"You beyond nothing. You'd believe anything, do anything, to get their love."

"Not anymore."

I have to admit, seeing Max and Mudie so unbridled makes me begin to hope for a reconciliation between them. I have no idea whether this truce is lasting, but something tells me they have need of each other beyond me or Bobbie or even someone like Kendra Hamilton. I don't know whether it's because they come from the same kind of queer, fractured old New Orleans family that they fit together, or for some other reason.

Max and Mudie dry off and change and the afternoon heat begins to abate. We have supper. Max puts a Louis Armstrong record on the phonograph; Mudie comes to the table in bare feet. I can't remember when they've been like this, relaxed and young, as if they were in love with each other again. The past few months they've become so serious and solemn and formal toward each other. And then there's been the separation; Max off in his own world, coming over only occasionally to check on us and on the house, or calling to invite us to Sunday lunch.

Bobbie calls to tell us her friend Robin is being discharged and that she will be next. Max and Mudie have another conference with Dr. Fergus. He can see no reason to keep Bobbie in the hospital any longer. He suggests that Bobbie find an apartment of her own. His one stipulation: that Max let Bobbie make all her own arrangements and try to live independently. It's his belief that Bobbie is too susceptible to Max's expectations.

I have lunch with Bobbie while she's on a pass. She seems fine, not sick at all, only lighter and younger than I. Where did her sickness go? Has it really disappeared or is it progressing along some secret course only to reappear later?

"This apartment business is killing Max," Bobbie says as she picks at a shrimp. "I mean, having to let me find my own apartment, get a car, something to do with my days—all without his official stamp of approval. It's torture for him."

"What will you do?"

"Theater work, but not acting. You remember meeting Quentin? He has a theater called Q, down on Rampart Street. He's hired me to design sets."

"Where will you live?"

Bobbie tells me about a mustard-colored building she's interested in on Jackson Avenue, with a vacant second-story apartment.

"Old but clean," Bobbie says, "wide cypress-board floors, ceiling fans, incredible ornate plaster medallions on all the ceilings. It's got a cozy cream-colored bedroom with brass sconces, amber light. Mudie's thinking of giving me her old brass bed."

At the mention of Mudie's brass bed, jealousy darts through me, an old nerve I thought was dead. I'm used to feeling envy when it comes to Max's attentions; after all, Bobbie and I spent our child-hoods vying to be his favorite. He was so charming then, who wouldn't have wanted to be? But with Mudie it's something else. Pure sibling rivalry or the struggle between two different ways of being? When will I get over envying Bobbie?

"When will I get over envying Bobbie?" I ask Nathan the question the next time I see him. We are at his house on Webster Street, drinking iced coffee and brandy out of paper cups.

"Never," Nathan says. He cracks ice with his teeth, spits into the burnt grass. "Sibling rivalry is one of the earliest and most persistent conflicts. Count on it until you and Bobbie are about eighty."

"If we live that long."

"Bobbie will. I'm not so sure about you," Nathan says. "You beat yourself to death over every shade of emotion. So go ahead, be jealous. All you're doing is admitting that there are parts of your parents' emotions you feel denied that your sister is privy to. There's nothing wrong with that. There's a legitimate side to every feeling."

"Not this one. It's so petty."

"Well, so, *be* petty. What do you expect from somebody your age?"

"I don't feel my age."

"Ah."

Whenever Nathan says "ah," I know I'm in for one of his lectures. He says I should lighten up, that I worry every detail of a situation, "like some rotting milk tooth." He says my relationship with Bobbie is the worst. He calls me an adolescent Thomas Aquinas and says proofs of the existence of God are better left to the professionals.

"Someday," he says, "you're going to have a life. You're going to wake up and say, 'The hell with my sister. The hell with my parents. The hell with whether or not they loved me, or to what degree.' That's the day your life will begin."

"When do you think that will be?"

Nathan squints. "Oh, I give you forty, fifty years."

"Thanks."

"Don't look so awful. Some people *never* get to that point."

I ride the streetcar home. The whole way there I think about what Nathan has said. I wonder if I will someday have a life in which Bobbie is not one of the major characters. It feels strange to imagine where I will be and what I will be doing; I play at piracy, stealing Bobbie out of my plans and considerations, setting her up far away in her own life. I think about the life I might have with Nathan, ruled by hard work and gentleness. None of the complications Max and Mudie seem to generate, the mess, the contradictory feelings.

three

School starts, my last year at St. Rita's. The building itself is like a worn, comfortable old house; Nathan and I have both been students here since kindergarten. We jokingly refer to ourselves as "the old guard," as if we belong to some venerable society on the verge of crumbling.

Even the teachers nod at me with respect; nobody hauls me in anymore to ask me how things are at home and whether I'm working too hard. Nobody questions my intention to go to Harvard. I imagine that in the teachers' lounge there used to be gossip about Bobbie Maubry; I could practically feel the cruel remarks even though I hadn't actually heard them.

I remember right after Bobbie tried to kill herself people looked at me in the halls with this mixture of pity and fear, as if by virtue of being Bobbie Maubry's sister I had crossed over into unfamiliar territory, and they were afraid. What they didn't know, because nobody asked, was that I was afraid too.

Whatever time I don't spend reading, I spend with Nathan. He's developed a taste for driving around to investigate bizarre pockets of New Orleans; we spend Saturdays at the racetrack; Sundays we drive out to Gentilly and take in old movies. Nathan likes to ride the Algiers ferry across the Mississippi River, and there are days we get up early and ride across with the commuters, pretending not to be students, pretending to belong to a world larger than the one we inhabit. Back at Nathan's house we make love a lot on the faded sofa and talk about our plans; we assume our lives from here on will be spent together.

I'm not sure what to think about my love for Nathan. There are ways in which we are a lot alike; we both have basically cautious natures that long for risk. We are both drawn to quiet pursuits: reading, drawing, driving around town for long periods, quietly talking. Part of my attraction to Nathan is that he is the only person who helps me feel at home in my own skin. Before, I always felt inadequate, not good enough, certainly not good enough for Max, less intelligent than Bobbie, not as pretty or artistic as Mudie. I pleased myself least of all. Now I think if I have any chance of freeing myself from comparisons to other people, it's through strengthening my relationship with myself.

I have lunch with Bobbie at the Fatted Calf. She's due to leave the hospital in a week; Max has deposited money in a checking account for her apartment on Jackson Avenue, and she's already begun working at the theater on Rampart street. After lunch we go by the place. Nobody's there; the stage is dark. Sometimes I think Bobbie wants to impress me because it's easier than getting to know me. She rolls a joint in the back of the theater and offers it to me.

"No thanks," I say.

"Come on, Gray. Don't be such a stiff."

"Bobbie, it's not good for you."

On the way back to the hospital Bobbie wraps an arm around my neck; we study ourselves in the car mirror. "You've got to stop worrying, Graycat," she tells me. "Come next week, I'm a free woman."

"I like to worry," I tell her. "It's what I do."

Bobbie smiles, lets me start the car. While I drive her back to the hospital she takes another joint out of her purse, lights it, and offers it to me. To be friendly, I smoke a little. "It will be good for you to get away," Bobbie says. "College will be an enlightening place for you. Away from Harmony Street and the misplaced rectitudes of Max."

"In some ways he's so concerned about doing the right thing, and in others he could care less. He's obsessed with how things look to other people, but how they feel to us is another matter. It must have to do with being an architect," I say.

"He hurt you too," Bobbie says. "I can tell. What did he do?"

I tell Bobbie about my lunch with Max and his vivid descriptions of sex with Kendra.

"Oh, Gray," Bobbie says. "Both of us know how destructive he can be, as well as creative. It would be easy if he were just a pig. Then we could defend ourselves against him. But he's more complicated than that. I'm just sorry he hurt you too."

I say, "Max's real father was a terrible alcoholic who gambled."

"That's right," Bobbie says, "he would disappear for months, send no money for his family, then show up one day with some lavish present for Max."

"Remember that old photograph of Max in a toy airplane?" I say.

"An exact replica of a World War One fighter. And there's little Max with his helmet and scarf on," Bobbie says. "Must have cost a fortune."

"Poor Max," I say. "How can he do the right thing when he doesn't even know what the right thing is?"

"He can't. But why punish us?"

I don't say anything. I know Bobbie doesn't believe I am the same person she left when she went into the hospital, stable and unadventuresome Gray. It would have given all of us a sense of security to know I would always be the same, would never change, never disappoint. But I feel, despite my pain, happy for the changes in me. In the old days, I would never have felt outraged at Max's behavior; I would simply have endured him.

I crush out the twisted paper in the ashtray and let Bobbie out in front of the hospital gate. She kisses me, waves from the walk. "Don't betray me," she says. I can't think what she means.

Bobbie has moved out of the hospital. Sometimes Nathan and I drive by her apartment on Jackson Avenue. Nathan wants to stop by and say hello, but I won't let him. Dr. Fergus wants us to let Bobbie alone for a while, allow her to develop confidence. Bobbie hasn't even invited Max and Mudie over yet.

"She will, when she feels ready," Mudie assures Max.

"Since when am I someone to be afraid of?" he says.

"She's growing up, Max."

"Don't feel bad," I tell him. "Bobbie hasn't invited me, either."

Bobbie's been living in her new apartment nearly a month and a half without asking us to come over. Mudie has phoned a few times to ask her to dinner, but there is never any answer. When she calls Bobbie at the theater, they say that Bobbie isn't in that day, or that she is out running errands. I know we're supposed to take this as a sign that Bobbie is doing well, but still I feel uneasy.

"What you should do," Nathan says, "is just go over there. Why have all this mystery?"

"Because Dr. Fergus said not to."

"She's probably not even there," Nathan says. "She's probably living some gay and accomplished life on the Riviera. —Sorry," he says when he sees the look on my face. "I just thought that if you knew—"

"—the truth, it would set me free," I finish the line for him. "Not always. The truth doesn't always set you free. Sometimes it makes things worse."

Nathan gives me a look of sympathy. We light a cigarette and sit looking at the grimy Mississippi from where we have parked to make love but, because of my bad mood, have failed to. The Huey P. Long Bridge looks like a cynical smile. Now that Nathan has raised the possibility that Bobbie might be missing, that something might have happened to her, everything looks slightly menacing.

"All right," I say. "Let's go."

"Go where?" Nathan asks.

"Bobbie's apartment."

"I thought you weren't going to . . ."

"I'm just going to ring the bell and see if she's there. Now I *have* to know. You started this."

We drive over to Jackson Avenue and I point out the building. Nathan waits in the car. When I go up on the porch, a wild, uncanny fear comes over me. I look at the names under the doorbells, but there's no Bobbie Maubry.

"Maybe she hasn't posted her name," Nathan says. "Lots of people forget details like that."

"Not Bobbie. She was proud of this apartment. Besides, Bobbie's always careful about those things. Where she is, who she is, are important to her. Let's go."

Nathan is stubborn, suggests I ask the landlord. I go back up on the porch and find the landlord's bell and ring it. Eventually the landlord answers and tells me no Bobbie Maubry lives in the building.

When I get back to the car, Nathan says, "Well?"

"There's no Bobbie Maubry here," I say.

"Are you sure you got the right address?"

"Absolutely. Bobbie even *described* it to me, for Christ's sake."

We stand a moment, thinking.

"Bobbie was never here, probably never intended to live here," I say. "Max gave her all kinds of money—he trusted her, you see. God knows where she is now."

Nathan is silent. He's never experienced anything like this before, his world is so safe and circumscribed, elegant even. He has the kindness not to say anything.

I sit down on the steps of Bobbie's fictitious apartment house, and for a solid moment I have no idea what to think or feel. Here all this time I was imagining Bobbie off and living her own life, even feeling jealous of her apartment and Mudie's brass bed, and Bobbie isn't even here.

"What are you going to do now?" Nathan says eventually.

"I don't know. What can I do?"

"Are you going to tell your parents?"

I think about this. Something in me wants more than anything to fall into whatever crack in reality Bobbie has fallen, provided no one can follow me there. But that's not like you, Mudie would say. Maybe Mudie is wrong. Maybe it's time for me to decide what is like me and what is not.

After dinner I get a call from Nathan. "So," he says, "you told them."

"No."

A mild, shocked silence. "Are you going to?"

"I don't know."

"I wouldn't either."

"Yes you would. You'd do the right thing."

"Probably."

"The trouble is, I'm tired of doing the right thing. I'm tired of these people and their problems. I'm especially tired of being Bobbie Maubry's sister."

"Can't help you there."

"I thought the whole point of our project was for me to change. Well, I've changed. I'm going to stop doing the right thing; I'm going to do what I want. Why aren't Max and Mudie on Bobbie's case?

Why aren't they out tracking her down, finding out if she's where she's supposed to be? Why don't they act like parents instead of like children? Max gives Bobbie a big check and thinks that's all he has to do. How long will it take them to *notice* she's missing?"

"Then why not tell them Bobbie's disappeared?"

"The trouble is, if I tell them Bobbie's not there, then it will all start over again. More turmoil, more running around over Bobbie. Just when we thought Bobbie was getting well."

"You think you can control whether or not she's well?"

"No, but listen, Nathan. What you don't understand is, it *feels* like it's my fault. I keep thinking that if I do the right things, follow some magic sequence, I can keep Bobbie from getting sick again."

"That's voodoo," Nathan says, "not reality."

"I don't care. I just want my family to start being a family again."

Nathan says he'll call me tomorrow, that what I need is a night to think it over. I have this feeling it's going to take more than a night.

Two days go by, and I don't say anything to Max or Mudie about Bobbie. Whenever her name comes up in conversation, which it does frequently, I freeze. I catch Mudie giving me this peculiar look, as if she senses that I know more than I'm saying, but she doesn't confront me. I take more than a night to think about the situation with Bobbie: I take three nights and four days.

During this time I think about what Bobbie once meant to me, how she represented all the light and fineness in my life. When we were children she had all the wonderful ideas for things to play; she'd organize a neighborhood circus and act as emcee and sword-swallower, using a candy cane she'd whittled down with her tongue to look like a blade. She taught me how to read when I was four so we could hide together at night under the covers, reading with a flashlight. At St. Rita's, she was very popular, even a little feared. No one dared to pick on me; I was Bobbie Maubry's sister.

I have always understood her. In some corner of myself I know how it feels to be Bobbie, on Harmony Street trying to be the perfect golden daughter Max wants, then at St. Anselm's among the snobs, flying high and crashing, then finally at the hospital, picking up the pieces. Anything to get out, away from this family, find yourself. Why not make up the story about your new apartment on Jackson Avenue, it's as true as anything is. In fact, it doesn't seem so much like a lie as like an alternate possibility.

Bobbie, I know what it means to be the hope of your family and fail them; it makes you want to slip out of your life without anybody noticing, and into some other. You don't even care what your new life is, or who you are, as long as you don't have to be Bobbie. Act carefully and with some forethought, and you can escape yourself, your fate, Antigone's stone room.

That's part of it. For so long I've had this ability to become Bobbie, if only for short periods of time, that I find it hard to tell on her. And now, when I do more daring things—run away, or light the table-cloth on fire—I can feel Bobbie coming out in me. Maybe it goes back to when we were babies napping in the same crib, or young girls vying for Max's attention. Bobbie always got to be the light one and I got to be the dark one, the one who brooded and worried and hung around windows, looking out for signs of trouble. Bobbie acted out her feelings; I buried mine.

On the fifth day there are hurricane warnings. Max shutters the house, goes out with me to buy ice and flashlight batteries. The atmosphere is tense, excited. We listen to the radio, which describes the progress of the storm up the coast of Florida; when we drive up St. Charles Avenue the swaying of the giant palm trees looks demented. At the corner of St. Charles and Jackson, Max hesitates.

"Do you suppose we should ring Bobbie's doorbell?" he asks me.

"I thought we weren't supposed to intrude."

"Ordinarily, no. But these are extraordinary circumstances. A hurricane's headed right for New Orleans. She belongs home with us."

I let him go without a word. There's nothing I can do now anyway; besides, I'm tired of protecting Max. We pull up in front of the mustard-colored façade of Bobbie's fictitious apartment, and Max tells me to wait in the car. I watch him walk, shoulders hunched against the wind, his immaculate white shirt flapping. He reminds me of the classic mime exercise in drama class, "Man Walking into the Wind," the way he seems to push against some unseen force, to buffet with all his strength without appearing to lose his balance, whatever in his mind is out there.

four

The hurricane hits, and nobody has any electricity. Max calls the police about Bobbie. "Look mister," the police say, "this city's chaos. *Everybody's* missing."

"This is Henry *Maubry* speaking."

"I don't care if it's the Queen of Sheba. We're up to our eyeballs in trouble."

Max and I drive around without saying much, surveying the downed power lines and strewn debris, the aftermath of Hurricane Camille. Together we cruise the city, trying to spot Bobbie on the street, but both of us know this is probably futile.

Mudie and Kendra drive around in Kendra's car looking for Bobbie. The irony of this wears thin after a day or two; as in many situations Bobbie has put us into, we get past irony into something more profound, more painful. For me, losing Bobbie used to feel like losing myself; now it feels more like casting a mysterious line of inquiry into heaven and giving a slight tug. Who am I, if not the dark counterpart of Bobbie Maubry? Who would I be on my own? Is Bobbie somehow irrelevant to the woman I am becoming, and to that woman's future? Or will she always be there in my background—her youthful talents, her outrageous behavior, her scorn for rules and New Orleans society, her love of books and plays, her friendships with odd characters? It is against this tapestry that I must tell my story and watch myself come into being.

Nathan offers to help in the search. We let Max go off by himself, and I ride with Nathan. He knows every back street and curlicue of New Orleans, its cul-de-sacs and blind alleys. He has an instinctive sense of direction, a feel for the city's twisted geography. He looks in places I didn't even know existed, but still we don't find Bobbie.

When we get tired of looking we end up back at Nathan's house. We make love on Nathan's bed, lying on top of all his books and papers, too tired to care. Making love with Nathan is my one refuge from all the terrible feelings I have about Max and Mudie and the situation they created. Because most painful of all is the loss of my parents, the realization that they have never really been parents to either Bobbie or me. I've done most of the parenting; that's why I sometimes feel so old.

Three days after the hurricane Bobbie shows up at the front door. She's soaking wet from all the rain we're having, and she's got what's left of her possessions in a brown grocery bag. Max and Mudie run out to greet her; they remind me of puppies with a prize bone. I'm glad to see Bobbie, but I hate all this drama. I wait a while before coming downstairs, even though I know it's Bobbie; who else could it be, with all the gleeful shouting?

In the library Max makes gin fizzes. We don't have any electricity but we have plenty of liquor and ice, which Max has stockpiled in the cooler. Mudie turns on the radio; surprisingly, Vivaldi comes through.

Neither Max nor Mudie asks Bobbie where's she's been, why she wasn't on Jackson Avenue. Maybe they think she's going to evaporate if they press her too closely for the truth.

Max offers me a cocktail. "No thanks," I tell him.

"But this is a celebration," Mudie says.

I look at them. "Not for me, it isn't. It's just more of the same."

Mudie looks at Bobbie. "Gray's been awfully temperamental lately."

Bobbie looks at me. "I understand, Gray."

That night I am already in bed when Bobbie knocks on my door. "Can we talk?" she asks.

"Why not?"

Bobbie sits cross-legged on the foot of my bed. "Max and Mudie put in a call to Dr. Fergus. Of course, we *would* be the one family on the street with a working telephone. Fergus wants to put me back in the hospital."

"You don't have to go," I say.

"Fat chance," Bobbie says. "In Louisiana the alligators have more human rights than the people. They can lock you up anytime they take it into their heads to do so."

"What about the ACLU?" I ask. "Can't they do anything?"

"In civics class, maybe," Bobbie says.

"In the hospital they'll help you," I say.

"And the company is so stimulating. My last roommate in the hospital was a real numero," Bobbie says. "She wore a pigtail on either side of her head and one on top. She liked to spread talcum powder over the whole fucking room. She had a drinking obsession. She'd line up fourteen, fifteen glasses of water in her bureau drawer and hide them from the staff. Her name was Darvonne. Her mother had named her after her favorite painkiller. When I asked her where she was from, she said, 'From? From? I'm not *from* anywhere. I'm *at* or *to* but not *from*. My parents are extraterrestrials.' "

"Well"—my tone is cautious—"I know your problems are different. Max and Mudie just want to see you get better."

Bobbie looks at me. "Is that what they want? Really? Or do they just want me away so the two of them can go at it in a frenzy of unfaithfulness and reconciliation? Some sort of high psychiatric opera? Is that it? Has it ever occurred to you that we're just props in their merrymaking and destruction?"

I don't really know what is different about Bobbie, but she is like a version of herself, rather than herself. She talks a lot in nervous, quirky sentences that loop around without leading anywhere. Otherwise, she's not all that different from her usual self, but it's the *slight* difference that disturbs me.

Bobbie goes to bed. Downstairs in the library, Max and Mudie talk about her. I stand outside the half-open library door, uncertain whether to go in. They're on their second drink and Max has already glanced down into his glass as if he's looking for a third. He seems deflated, his indefinable charm less apparent now. I can tell he isn't a man happy with himself. He looks creased, sunken in.

"You know what," Max says after a while. "I'm beginning to think even the doctors don't understand mental illness. We never get the same answer when we ask them to describe Bobbie's disorder and what her prognosis is."

"I've noticed that," Mudie says.

"Suppose her whole treatment's been wrong? Everything, from the beginning? Suppose all these thousands of dollars of psychotherapy haven't done her any good? There are new theories every day. Some doctors say it's all chemical, and can be controlled with drugs."

"The same thing has occurred to me," Mudie says. "The doctors might not know."

"Christ," Max says.

Max gets up and leaves the room to get more ice for their drinks. I duck into the dark atrium. Max goes back into the room.

They don't say anything for a long time. I begin to think neither one of them is ever going to speak again when finally Max says, "I'm sorry. I never bargained for any of this, Mudie. Here I took you out of your life, with all your prospects as an artist, only to give you confusion, hurt . . . God knows what else."

"We choose, but we don't choose," Mudie says. "I chose to leave New York and marry you, I wanted children, but neither one of us wanted it to be complicated, did we?"

"I always thought that if I tried, I could have some order, and some beauty, in my life."

"You have," Mudie says.

"But I've also got this. My firstborn child, and who knows what will happen to her?" Max says.

"At least we have Gray," Mudie says.

At Nathan's the next morning we make coffee. It's fall, or what passes for fall in New Orleans; we have two days of bright leaves and then some of the trees are bare and some green. There's a thin fall sky, though, and the air feels cool. In two weeks Mudie and I are going to Boston for my Harvard interview and then on to Vermont to see old friends of Mudie's.

I show Nathan my application essay for Harvard. He reads it, chewing the end of a pencil the whole time. Occasionally, he makes spidery notes in the margin. It takes him about twenty minutes to finish. Then he says,

"I thought you wanted to go to Harvard, Gray."

"I do."

"There's nothing real of yourself here. Anybody could have written this."

I grab the paper and tear it into shreds. He's right, of course, and I act angrier at him than I am. I realize I'm afraid to write about myself because it never seems good enough, or beautiful enough, for the goal I have set myself. Nathan says I want to be invisible.

"I don't trust my own motives. What if I really want to go to Harvard just to compensate for Bobbie?"

"Life's not that simple," Nathan says. "Just rewrite the essay. And this time use your own voice. It's bound to be better than no voice at all. Don't be so worried about having impure motives. You don't have to be heroic. Just write a good essay."

I sit up late writing. We have our electricity back and the house has lost some of its freakishness. Around eleven-thirty Max knocks on my door.

"Come in," I say.

Max looks a little nervous. "Are you doing your college applications?" he asks.

"Yes. The one for Harvard."

"I want to ask you to downplay Harvard in your talk with Bobbie," he says. "It's a bit of a rough time for her. No sense rubbing it in."

"Max, I think it hurts you more than it hurts Bobbie. She doesn't care about Harvard," I say.

"Maybe not," Max says.

"And it hurts me that I can never feel the way *I* feel about anything. Excited or otherwise. I always have to hide what I feel for somebody else's sake. It hurts," I say, "it feels false."

"That wasn't my intention," Max says.

"Well, think about it. And stop telling me how to feel or whether to show my feelings. After all, you say whatever you want, about whatever you feel, to me."

That odd, bashed look I've seen before crosses Max's face. "Well, Gray," he says, "you have a point."

five

ax doesn't move back into his apartment. He lives out of his beautiful English suitcase in what used to be his dressing room; he sleeps on a chaise lounge there, in the room next to Mudie. There's no explanation for their arrangement, which is typical of Max and Mudie, I guess.

As usual, they're in a quandary about Bobbie. Max takes her to the psychiatric clinic at Tulane Medical School for more tests. This time I'm not going to read the results; I don't want to know.

I try not to spend too much time with Bobbie. I have the feeling that if I spend too much time with her, I'll be changed. I don't really know what goes on in her mind, but on certain afternoons when the light is right, I have the feeling that the boundary between us is transparent, that we could become the same person. Nathan says I have survivor's guilt, but there's more to it. I don't tell him this, but sometimes I can feel the same things Bobbie says she feels. It's disconcerting because I don't understand why we *act* so differently.

One psychiatrist told Mudie, "Schizophrenics don't feel emotions in the normal sense." Whatever *that's* supposed to mean. Deep down I wonder if any of us really knows anything about the other. I don't seem to be able to know myself. I have a sense that I have all these aspects I've only gotten to see briefly, like a house with many lighted rooms you glimpse driving by at night.

Bobbie has been home for a month when Max comes to talk to me. It is nighttime; Mudie and Bobbie are in the kitchen making coffee.

"Gray," Max says, "it's time we talked. This can't be easy on you, having Bobbie here, not after all that's happened, but I don't think it will be for long."

"It's okay. Bobbie's my sister. It doesn't bother me."

Max smiles at my lie. He looks older than his forty-four years; his close-cropped hair is practically gray. His suits are too big for him, and Max was always careful about clothes.

"I'm going to have to make a decision about Bobbie in the next few days, a very difficult decision. I can't send her back to St. Vincent's, although that seems the obvious solution."

"Why not?"

"We can't afford it. You probably have no idea how much her last stay there cost, and insurance covers only so much. I've spent all I can on private hospitals. If I were convinced that the doctors at St. Vincent's could cure Bobbie, I'd find a way to pay them, but I'm not convinced. Very little is known about schizophrenia; some people don't even think psychoanalysis can help at all." Max laughs a tired, depressed laugh. "Now they tell me, after I've spent eighty thousand dollars."

Max has never talked to me about money before. I can appreciate how hard it is for him; he likes to think of himself as invincible, likes to show himself as having no worries. Most of all, he hates to appear vulnerable to his children, especially me. I'm amazed that he's even talking like this.

"There's my Harvard money," I say. Before I even have a chance to think, it's out of my mouth. "I don't have to go to Harvard, I can go somewhere cheaper, get a job. I don't even have to go to college." It is the first time I can remember when my own power eclipsed Max's; offering him my college money makes me feel huge, like a picture of the sun's corona taken through a telescope.

Max smiles, obviously touched. He reaches out for my hand and a tear falls between us. I realize that I have underestimated his love for me, perhaps I have concentrated on one tiny corner of love while all along there has been this vast continent of feeling.

"No," Max says and shakes his head. "I thank you for the offer, but I can't let you do it. A year ago I might have said yes, anything, anything for Bobbie, you know how much I love her. But things have changed. You have gifts too. I can't sacrifice them in the hope something can be done for Bobbie. Maybe it can, maybe not. Maybe money won't even matter—maybe there's such a thing as divine grace or, failing that, a medical cure will come along. I don't know. But I do know it would be wrong to sacrifice one daughter for another. I've already done too much of that. The answer to your offer is no. The hardest *no* of my life. Hard because I so want to help Bobbie. I feel responsible."

Max and I look at each other as if neither has ever really seen the other before, and then he collects himself and leaves the room. I sit in disbelief. Here I had been scurrying around trying to win Max's favor, and it was there all along. I lie awake watching the pattern of elm leaves against the night shade, how the leaves rustle and move and form infinite patterns among themselves. I turn over in my mind what Max said about not sacrificing me to Bobbie and about my having gifts. I think he means that I am not their surrogate Bobbie now, but that I am myself, I'm Gray.

• • •

The decision is made: Bobbie is going to Mandeville, the state mental hospital across Lake Pontchartrain in Mandeville, Louisiana. Bobbie gives me the news herself with a smile almost of satisfaction.

"Mandeville, the end of the line," she says. Her voice is a hoarse whisper; her eyes are remote and distant, the color of ice on a faraway planet. We don't talk about it anymore because there is nothing further to say; Bobbie carries her thoughts around with her like a hoard of gems. Emerald thoughts, ruby thoughts, rare sapphire thoughts: None of them are mine. From here on I'm going to concentrate on what I think and feel instead of trying to read Bobbie.

Over dinner a week later Max talks about his conversation with Dr. Fergus. The medical team at Mandeville agrees with the premise that schizophrenia has a chemical basis; Dr. Fergus concedes that the early psychiatric approach taken with Bobbie may have been essentially wrong.

"Her illness may have been caused at birth," Max says, "possibly before. At any rate, it's nothing *we* did."

"*Now* they tell us," Mudie says. "Do you remember those first visits with Dr. Cavendish, when he tried to convince me that *I* caused Bobbie's illness? He tried to beat from me a confession that I hadn't wanted children, that my artistic ambitions were thwarted because of children, and that I took it out on Bobbie."

Max says, "You aren't eating, Gray."

"I'm not hungry."

Max and Mudie exchange a glance. Max's look warns Mudie not to burden me with the truth; Mudie's says, What else is there? The two of them sit coolly, dissecting fish on their plates. After dinner Max gives me a few articles he's read about Bobbie's illness; at subsequent dinners we discuss brain chemistry, how there is a chemical disturbance in the brains of schizophrenics. It may even be possible, according to one theory, that a tendency to schizophrenia is carried in the genes.

I've always wondered if it was by some freak genetic accident that Bobbie carried the illness and I didn't. It's hard, thinking about it in this light; easier to accept that a personality is warped or wrecked, or damaged somehow by experience. But a beautiful mind randomly wrecked by a virus on a gene? It seems too diabolical.

Nathan says, "Stop thinking about her so much. It's unhealthy for a girl your age to be so preoccupied with a disease."

"You're right. But sometimes I think if I could understand the disease, then I might understand the world. Or at least the life we've been given, Bobbie and I, the set of circumstances."

Her illness changes the way I think and feel; it unsettles the view of life I was developing. It often leaves me in a cold and fogbound place, prone to depressions. I just can't be like other high school seniors, preparing for the bake sale, saving money for the senior trip to Mexico. Except that I do these things too, to make Nathan happy. But I don't believe in any of them.

I try to imagine what we will all be like in ten or twenty years, try to see Max and Mudie and whether they've worked things out between them, try to see Nathan and me, and Bobbie. The curious thing is, that in all my imagining, Bobbie is always the only one of us who doesn't age, who seems to remain exactly as she is now. An image of her waving to us from the hospital parking lot remains in my mind, almost out of reach but not quite, like a photograph of a lost child kept in a mother's wallet.

The week I get accepted to Harvard, Bobbie is home on pass. Max goes out and buys two bottles of champagne to celebrate both events. He pops the cork and fills our glasses. He proposes a toast. "To my girls," he says, "I love you both."

"Yeah," Bobbie says. "Gray got into Harvard, and I got into Mandeville."

"*Bobbie,*" Mudie says.

The bubbles burn going down; the words burn. Bobbie looks

nonchalant, fills my glass again. The color of the wine matches exactly the color of the sky outside the library windows, a light transcendent gold. I press my face to the windowpane the way we used to do as children, and wait for the awkwardness to pass.

"Sorry, I didn't mean it," Bobbie says.

"Yes, you did," I say.

"It's the medication I'm on . . . these pills . . . make me flippant. I've flipped for sanity."

Max and Mudie are at the other end of the room, and while they are only ten feet away from us, it feels much farther than that. I am brought back to the sense I used to have when Bobbie and I were younger that two separate worlds existed; there was Max and Mudie's world, and Bobbie's and mine. People were always telling me how charmed childhood was, how safe, how happy, but it was Max and Mudie's world I wanted to belong to; Bobbie's world frightened me. Bobbie looks at me as if she can read my thoughts, and lifts her glass to mine. My face is curved in an ironic smile. I have a momentary sense, fleeting but indelible, that I am not here, not in the room. This other Gray, this impostor wearing the ironic smile, is a bad copy of the true, the real Gray Maubry.

That night, after Max and Mudie are in bed, I take my letter from Harvard out of its envelope and reread it in privacy. It occurs to me that I would not be going there if it weren't for Bobbie, for my original wish to make up to Max for Bobbie's illness. I used to think of myself as saving Bobbie's place for her, but now it's clear that I've been saving it for myself. All this time I've been growing into myself, not a replacement for Bobbie; the simple thought stuns me.

I knock on Bobbie's door. "It's open," she says.

I go in; Bobbie is curled up on the bed reading.

"All I want is for you not to hate me," I say.

Bobbie looks up. "Are you sure you want to have this conversation?"

"Just don't hate me."

"You know," Bobbie says, "there are days when I think back to our childhood, to the way you were. The possibility that I could ever resent you makes me laugh out loud. You were so hazy, so unpromising, so easy to tease. It was easy to mistreat you, and because it came so easily I liked to humiliate you. I never thought someday I'd be living in an open ward of the state mental hospital while you moseyed off to Harvard."

"I thought it was what you wanted."

"What difference does that make?" Bobbie says, "It's what *you* want that counts. Sure, I got the flame started, I egged you on for a while, but you were ready and willing. You wanted Max's love for yourself, so enjoy."

"Max loves you," I say.

"Seems petty, doesn't it, two sisters vying for their charming father's affection," Bobbie says.

"He was charming, wasn't he? I forget how he was, sometimes."

Bobbie looks down at the scars on her wrists, now faded, pale and spidery. "I really thought I was going to die that time," she says. "When Ted found me on the bathroom floor I didn't want to be alive to see the expression on Max's face, the disappointment. I'm so tired of disappointing people. All the while the surgeon was sewing me up, I could see this sad smile of Max's floating isolated in my brain."

"Nathan says fathers should be banished from the universe of daughters forever."

Bobbie brightens. "Did he really say that? Maybe Nathan's not as straight as he looks."

"I love him," I say. "I like his quiet attention."

"Two Harvard brats," Bobbie says. "That's right, we were talking about Harvard."

"We don't have to."

"Tell me something," Bobbie says. "Do you think I'm ever going to get better? Or am I going to spend my whole life in places like

Mandeville? Because if I am"—she speaks softly now—"I'd just like to know."

"The ancient Greeks thought that the future was what lay behind you, not in front of you. It was the past that lay in front, where you could see."

"The Greeks were brilliant," Bobbie says. "Funny, people used to say that about me."

"You still are."

"No." Bobbie shakes her head. "Every day that I'm alive I can feel something dying in my brain. Sometimes, when I'm up, I can feel riots in my head, like flambeaux carriers at Carnival, but the next day is dark deserted streets, Ash Wednesday. The medication's doing a lot to dull these sensations, but underneath, I know. No matter what drugs they give you, you always know who you are," she says.

The next afternoon, Sunday, Max takes us for breakfast at the Pont-chartrain Hotel, a delicious breakfast that obscenely mocks my sadness, my happiness. My conversation with Bobbie the night before lingers between us like a ghost; otherwise Bobbie is distant, composed. If I didn't know what I know about my family I would say we were an ordinary, well-to-do New Orleans family out to breakfast on a Sunday; the avenue outside the hotel looks freshly rinsed with rain.

It rains again in the afternoon. Mudie is upstairs, squirreled away, working; Max stands at the long library windows, looking out. Bobbie and I go for a walk around the block, rain pelting our two umbrellas. In a few hours, Max will drive Bobbie to Mandeville, crossing the invisible boundary between us. I sneak a look across at Bobbie; in the rainy light she looks both frail and luminous. The rain on her face is tears.

"Listen," she says, "about last night. I didn't mean to make you feel guilty about going to Harvard. Forget what I said. Forget me. Do what we always wanted."

"You really mean it?"

Bobbie nods. "There's just one thing."

"What?"

"I wish you'd stop trying to make me feel better."

I go to say something, but Bobbie puts a rainy finger on my lips. "I know, I know, I know everything there is to know about your feelings. We were babies together, remember? You've always tried to save me, I've had that feeling since we were small. You know what saving is?"

"The life you save may be your own?"

"Exactly. So stop trying to make me feel better about my situation. There *is* no making me feel better. Don't you see," she says, releasing me from her grasp, into the rain, "not feeling good is all I have to go on sometimes. It's like being blind in a foreign country, somebody might come along and hit you on the head, but at least you'd know what kind of country you're in."

We laugh together. "I see what you mean."

Bobbie smiles, and the two of us start walking toward home.

The rain has let up some, steam rises from the streets and makes a light fog; the wet warm streets and the smell of roses coming from somebody's garden make me think of being in London, not the real London of course, but the London of Bobbie's and my childhood, a kind of dream London concocted partly from Max's descriptions of his travels there, partly from books, and partly from my own desire to live in a city where no harm can come. When we turn the corner, our house comes into view.

"So," Bobbie says, "here we are."

Part 4

one

athan and I book the same flight to Boston. We sit next to each other on the plane. Nathan has the window seat. It's a perfect September day. The two of us watch the plane take off over the clear blue bowl of Lake Pontchartrain. Nathan takes a flask out of his pocket.

"Nathan, don't. It's against regulations."

"What are they going to do, Gray? Throw me out?"

The two of us watch what is left of New Orleans disappear in the clouds. Nathan says, "I won't come back here after Harvard."

"I hadn't thought about it," I say.

"If we're together, you won't come back either."

"What about my family?"

Nathan shreds a matchbook. "They can visit you, Gray. You won't fall off the face of the earth."

I'm taken aback. Here, I always pictured myself going to Harvard with Nathan and then on to Johns Hopkins or someplace, and later we would come home and have children, replicas of Nathan with dark hair and tortoiseshell glasses.

"You're serious, aren't you?" I say.

"Believe me, Gray, once you get away from this city you won't be able to come back."

"Why not?"

"It's suffocating. God, the same people doing the same things for years. Wearing the same clothes. Their children come along and *they* do the same things, more or less. If I wanted, my life could be a carbon copy of my father's. St. Rita's School, Harvard, Harvard Law. There would be nothing in all that time to distinguish me from him."

"I like New Orleans," I say.

Nathan smiles. "It's up to you."

"You see, my family was more chaotic than yours. You can discern a pattern, whereas in my family there's just this series of happenings."

"No kidding," Nathan says.

The stewardess is moving up the aisle with the drinks cart. She stops in front of us; Nathan orders two gin and tonics for each of us. When she's gone, Nathan says,

"Your parents made a lot of noise about Bobbie being crazy. It covered up their deficiencies. Focusing so much on Bobbie was a great misjudgment on their part."

"I know that, Nathan."

Both of us are silent a moment. Then I say, "God, I can't wait to get to Boston. I can't wait to leave all this behind and start my own life."

"Well, start now," Nathan says. "Leave behind your old life and concerns. Begin anew."

"Another project?"

"You don't need one anymore. You're beyond that," Nathan says.

I think a minute. "I guess I am."

. . .

On campus, students swarm everywhere. Nathan and I get our room keys; studying the map, we realize we're at opposite ends of campus. "Don't worry," Nathan says, "we'll get bicycles. We have feet."

He kisses me and shoulders his bags in the direction of his room. We have plans to meet in two hours. Nathan won't come with me to my room because he believes I should have unadulterated experiences. "I don't want to hang on you all the time," he explains as he leaves. "It will stunt your growth. You're not my appendage here."

"Oh, Nathan."

"At four, then."

"At four."

Finally I find my room. The door is locked, but the hallway is crammed with three bulging suitcases, a red IBM typewriter, a box of exotic handblown wine glasses, several boxes of books, and a battered dressmaker's dummy.

"I thought you'd never get here!" a young woman shrieks. My roommate, Anna Mink. "I live in Riverdale, overlooking the Hudson. You're from New Orleans. Separate but equal states of mind."

The two of us start hauling our belongings into the room. The whole time, I can't take my eyes off Anna; there's something so fascinating yet slightly repellent about her looks. She's about as tall as I am, but stockier, and she has enormous breasts. She's wearing a loud parroty blouse with a patched-up denim skirt, purple tights, and green suede boots. She's wearing enough makeup to clog a sewer. Her jewelry is profuse and alien-looking, bracelets and rings that look as if they might have come from the planet Venus. I can't stop staring at her. Her hands are beautiful, and she has a high-pitched, melodious voice that grows hysterical when she laughs. Her hair just misses being blond; her eyes are a remarkable, reptilian green.

I keep staring at Anna, I can't seem to get enough of her. Is she pretty or awful-looking? I can't decide. Maybe some of each.

While we unpack, Anna talks about her family. Her father held a high-ranking position in the Kennedy administration. Her mother, Julia, is a lay analyst. "That means she's trained in Freudian analysis but she's not a doctor," Anna explains. "I have a younger sister who is beautiful, but angrier than hell. She's away at school. And two older brothers. They're both gorgeous, in different ways. Leon is a law student at Yale and George is a reporter for the *Miami Herald*. He absolutely thrives on violence, but vicariously.

"My parents live in this incredible house. I used to think people hated me because we were so wealthy but, thanks to analysis, I'm almost over that now. Now I think they envy my looks and intelligence.

"My first psychiatrist, Dr. Ashe, was the most stunning man I've ever known. Absolutely lovely. The last of the old men with beautiful manners. Goddamn it, he died *right* in the middle of my transference! I had to start all over with a new analyst, a Jungian this time. Mother said the variety would be therapeutic."

I don't believe this. I'm just standing in the middle of this rather dusty, empty room, I'm at Harvard, staring at this person called Anna.

"This college furniture has to go," Anna goes on. "I've got two white leather couches and some rather good paintings, and of course we could steal one of Mother's kilims."

I find my voice and say, "It's just a dorm room."

"Nothing is *just* anything. You have to create what you want life to be."

By the end of the week our suite has white leather sofas and hand-screened wallpaper on the walls. Anna works at a beautiful old cherry writing table with spindle legs; I sit at a college regulation laminate desk. Our walls are lined with bookshelves and Meissen porcelain. Anna goes out to a plant shop and buys a huge ficus; I realize Anna will never do anything small. Everything about her, including her personality, is oversized.

Nathan takes an immediate dislike to her. "Anna represents excess and pretension. She's from the kind of overfed American family that could do something with its resources to help people, but instead licks its own wounds. All that wealth and talent, put to the service of—what?" Nathan asks.

"Julia Mink's a lay analyst."

Nathan makes a face. "That's fine, if you can afford midtown Manhattan prices to lie on a couch and talk about yourself. Gray, there are *real* sick people out there. What's Anna's mother doing for them? And look at Anna. Running into Boston three times a week for analysis. Analysis of what? She's about as complicated as a gigantic tick."

"All right, Nathan, so you hate her."

" 'Hate' is a little strong. Let's just say I have a medium-sized dislike."

"You know what I think? I think you don't like sharing me with *anybody*. You want me all to yourself. And I think Anna's worldliness threatens you."

"Anna's a fake. As someone who cares about you, I wish you wouldn't fall under her spell," Nathan says.

"No one's falling. I'm a grown woman."

"That story she tells about how she was a child prodigy on the piano and one day just refused to practice anymore—the thwarted-genius story—nauseates me. She's a complete narcissist," Nathan says.

"I disagree."

"Disagree then, but come here and kiss me."

Nathan tries taking me into his arms, but I resist him. I'm not in a romantic mood. Anna cranes around the doorway with a big smile on her face. "Wait until you taste this bread I made this morning. I call it Anna bread—really rich and white."

Nathan rolls his eyes. "Anna bread," he mumbles. "Rich and white. God."

There are times when Anna annoys me too, but overall I decide she's fun. She's a totally different kind of person from anyone I've met before. She makes me go shopping for outrageous clothes; we go to strange boutiques. I go through three or four months' allowance shopping with Anna. She never even notices the price of anything, just whether or not she wants it.

Anna takes me to have my hair cut and my nails done. I've never had a manicure in my life; it seems so decadent. I used to think people who pay attention to their appearance are in some way flawed, stupid, shallow. Anna isn't any of these things; she's an excellent student, if her first few papers are an indication.

Back at my room Nathan is waiting for me. He's sitting on the floor in the hallway reading Freud's *Interpretation of Dreams*.

"What happened to your hair?" he asks.

"I got a haircut."

"That's a haircut?"

"You don't like change," I say.

"I liked your hair the way it was," Nathan says.

"Hair grows back."

"Ah," Nathan says, "but do we?"

I think maybe things with Nathan have gotten too serious. He takes my well-being to heart more than I like. Sometimes when I'm with Nathan now I feel suffocated. Maybe it's just because we've known each other so long, and he's formed an opinion of how I should be. Anytime I deviate from his idea, he gets uncomfortable.

Around Thanksgiving, Nathan and I have a real falling-out. Anna invites me home for Thanksgiving; Nathan doesn't want me to go. "The Minks are a corrupting influence," he argues. "Stay here with me and have turkey pot pie on a hot plate."

"You haven't met all the Minks," I point out. "Aren't you a little curious?"

"No," Nathan says. "I can extrapolate from Anna."

"Nathan, I want to go. We can consider the whole weekend part of the project."

"There isn't a project anymore, Gray. I don't think you should keep hanging around with Anna."

"But why?"

"She's an end in herself," Nathan says.

"What is *that* supposed to mean?"

"You came to college so you could enlarge yourself, not obliterate yourself."

"I think you're being a paranoid."

"Maybe."

My second night in Riverdale I'm sleeping in Anna's oval bedroom overlooking the Hudson. Anna's in the guest room, "just in case," she says. All day I've been making eyes at Leon, her older brother. Leon stutters but is handsome in a rough-hewn sort of way. His complexion isn't very good but his blue eyes look as if they were lit from behind. George, on the other hand, looks just like Anna, only longer and skinnier. He looks the way Anna would if she were put on a rack and pulled like taffy.

I'm lying there wondering what sort of lover Leon would make when the door opens. It's George. I let him in, and even though he's the wrong brother, I let him get into bed with me. At first he claims he just wants to talk; eventually he abandons this pretense and we have sex. I start out being mildly stimulated by having this different man on top of me, but the sensation wears thin pretty fast. I can hardly wait to get it over with. George, who seems to be having a good time, goes on for a long while. He doesn't even fall asleep immediately after, the way Nathan tells me most men do, but lies on his back and has a cigarette and talks about himself and his accomplishments. *I'm* the one who falls asleep.

It was a dumb gesture, a gratuitous thing to do. I know it's going to come between Nathan and me even though I don't care about George. Mudie would say, "I don't care a fig about George." Suddenly I'm lonesome for Mudie, and for the days of my childhood before I realized how strange and puzzling life could become.

Anna and I discuss the problem driving back to Cambridge. Anna says, "What you don't seem to understand is, that's the whole purpose of life. To have experiences. To make mistakes. To be with all kinds of people. Life is one set of people crossed with another."

"Like fruit flies?"

Anna laughs.

"I could at least have gotten the right brother," I say.

"Well, that's too bad, but it can't be helped. Are you going to see George at Christmas?" Anna asks.

"Of course not."

I pay all the tolls on the way back to Cambridge. For somebody so wealthy, Anna is tight with money. I always end up paying for things when she has four times the money I do.

Back in Cambridge Nathan takes one look at me and says, "What happened?"

"Nathan, I didn't really mean to, but I slept with George Mink."

Nathan looks stricken. "I didn't realize you were so untrust-worthy."

Untrustworthy!—such an old-fashioned word. I remember once when I was visiting Aunt Byrd, she said the Maubry family was characterized by great charm and faithlessness. Maybe she was right, except I get to be faithless but not charming.

Anna goes in to take a shower; we can hear her singing and smell the overpowering scented soap she uses. Nathan sits on the edge of my bed, shredding *The Boston Globe*.

"Maybe we should put our relationship on hold for a while," I say.

Nathan stares at me. "In the first place, ours is not a relationship. I hate that word, *relationship*. In the second place, people don't put their feelings for one another 'on hold.' You can do it with a telephone call or some other disembodied thing, but not with human beings. Not with love."

"I'm sorry if my terminology isn't to your liking. I'm not as eloquent as you are. But then, what do you expect from somebody so untrustworthy?" I say.

"The two are entirely unrelated," Nathan says. In the living room the phone begins to ring.

"Sometimes I get the feeling you're just waiting for me to fuck up so you can feel superior," I say.

"The phone is ringing," Nathan says.

I go in to answer. It's Max, calling long distance from New Orleans. Bobbie was discharged from Mandeville yesterday and moved back to the house on Harmony Street. "She dropped by yesterday to issue an edict," Max says. "She doesn't want us to spy on her. Just treat her like an ordinary person."

"That's good news, Max," I say, although I wonder if it really is. Will Bobbie be able to live with Max and Mudie after all she's been through?

Max sends me a check so I can buy a new bicycle. I go out and select a bright yellow Raleigh touring bike with ten speeds and a book rack on the back. I keep it inside, in our room. Nathan hangs some hooks to hold the bike in place on the wall like a piece of modern sculpture. We know things have changed between us but we aren't sure yet what the changes mean. Sometimes we make love on the white leather sofa underneath the bicycle, staring at the wheels and brand-new spokes. There's a sad, querulous tone to our lovemaking now.

I don't hear much from Bobbie. The occasional cards I get in the mail are cryptic. "Having a wonderful time. Wish you were here, or I were there. Or almost anything. Love, Bobbie."

"Typical Bobbie," Nathan says, "maddening but not mad."

During Christmas break Nathan and I fly home to New Orleans. Anna drives back to New York, having promised to call, write, send gifts. I don't take her promises seriously; after a term of living with Anna I know she never does what she promises. At first, I was disappointed in her, then I told myself what Anna had told me: Life is one set of people crossed with another. I like the variety she gives to my life, even if she isn't careful, or thoughtful, or considerate of other people. I am those things; Anna is outrageous, excessive, inconsistent, colorful.

The minute I open the front door something feels different to me; Max and Mudie must have reconciled. Or else, with both Bobbie and me gone they've wandered back into familiarity with each other.

Max and Mudie and Bobbie and I hug, and for a moment I feel as close to them as I ever did, except that the knowledge of what has happened between us and to us comes creeping in.

The next day Bobbie and I borrow Mudie's car and drive out to City Park. We bring a picnic basket filled with cold chicken, a bottle of Riesling, and these tiny mushroom sandwiches I made from a recipe in the *Alice B. Toklas Cookbook.* On the seat beside me is a white box filled with lemon doberge petits fours. There's a joint in my pocket.

Bobbie talks about all sorts of things without really making contact with me. Finally, when we get to the park, she opens my door for me.

"Graycat"—she hugs me with a child's enthusiasm—"it's really you."

"Did you think I'd forget you?" I ask.

"You never know," Bobbie says.

I set down the picnic basket and take hold of her by both shoulders. "We belong to each other. I may go away, or you might, but that doesn't mean I forget you."

"Forget me and my problems," Bobbie says. "I'm a nest of baby scorpions."

"You have good descriptive powers, that's all. I love you."

"You do?" Bobbie says wistfully. "I was a mental patient."

"So?"

"So you're not," Bobbie says.

"So far," I say.

"You'll never be. You're eminently sane. Tied to the earth."

We go out into the December sunshine, smelling the sun-warmed winter earth. I want to explain to Bobbie that my groundedness is only a response to her flightiness, as one note is played in response to another. I've come to see, in the few months I've been away, just how far my personality has bent in response to hers; how, in a sense, my real nature is just beginning to form.

"Let's go over here, under these trees," Bobbie says.

We uncork the wine and smoke the joint. I want to make this a good day for Bobbie, a day she might remember as having helped her through a difficult time.

"What are you studying?" Bobbie asks.

"Oh, biology and psychology and a humanities course and chemistry, which I'm flunking. And English."

"Still planning to be a doctor?" Bobbie says. "You could be a psychiatrist with all the training you've already had."

"Maybe," I say.

"Don't bother. By then I'll be too far gone."

"This isn't for you, it's for me."

"I'll bet." Bobbie laughs. "I know you, Graycat. You want to make up to the world for me."

"You're wrong. I used to want that, but now I want to do what pleases me."

"Perhaps." Bobbie lights a cigarette, lies back in the tall dark grass. "In therapy we're doing my sexual history. Did I ever tell you about the time I was raped?"

"No." I don't really want to be hearing this but what can I say, "Don't tell me"? There's something about the subject that makes me feel more than usually nervous, as if I'm in some way connected to Bobbie's story.

"I was fifteen and it was that guy Mack I used to go out with. I never liked him but I thought if I went out with somebody I could show the world that I was normal. Mack was a math genius and was legally blind. He wore these thick, Coke-bottle glasses. Anyhow, we'd been downtown to see a play—*Rhinoceros*, I think it was—and we had this flask we shared during the performance. Mack kept putting his hand in my lap and I left it there because I thought that was what girls were supposed to do."

"Right."

"Then we went back to Mack's house and he said there was something in the garage he wanted to show me. It never occurred to me he was going to rape me; maybe it hadn't occurred to *him* until we were inside the garage with the oily rag smell and his broken childhood bicycles and his father's old *National Geographics*, and somehow he got me down on this smelly mattress, pinned me with his arms, and pulled my underpants down with his teeth, and the whole time I was in such disbelief, I wanted to laugh, I even think I *did* laugh, the whole thing was so preposterous. He was much stronger than he looked, the wiry type."

"God, Bobbie. You never told me."

"There I was, being raped, and there was nothing I could do about it, except scream maybe, but that seemed so inadequate. The whole time it was happening I was thinking, How peculiar. I just stared at the chinks in the garage ceiling until I disappeared through one of them and went floating free, in the sky. It was like being anesthetized."

I stare at the grass, uncomfortable with Bobbie's confession. Is it because I identify so closely with Bobbie that I feel her experiences myself? In my head I can hear a familiar distant noise, a resonance, like a neighbor's buzz saw on a humid day, droning in and out of consciousness.

"Sorry," Bobbie says. "I didn't mean to ruin the tone of the day."

"You didn't," I say.

"Just like when you go to paint a canvas and the beautiful idea you started with unaccountably turns ugly," Bobbie says.

"I wouldn't know. I never paint."

"Jesus," Bobbie says, the tears coming in her eyes, "I can't even have one good afternoon."

"It's okay," I tell her.

She looks at me. "No, it isn't. What happened to both of us isn't okay. And I don't just mean my rape and Max's abandonment of us. I mean *everything*. The whole way we had to split ourselves and take sides to survive. The way I became wild and you grew more and more quiet. That's not normal, Gray."

"I often hated you for stealing all the attention. It was easier to hate you than to hate Max and Mudie for creating the situation in the first place," I say. "You see, both of us wanted the same thing, for them to be *parents*."

"Seems easy enough," Bobbie says.

two

hristmas is cold, especially for New Orleans. Nathan and I go for a drive together; the streets are filled with children on new bikes or roller skates. The sky is heavy, almost as if it might snow.

Nathan joins us for dinner. Being Jewish, his family doesn't celebrate the holiday; I'm glad to have him with me. I realize since my night with George things have been strained between us, but I hope Nathan will be forgiving.

After dinner Bobbie corners us in the kitchen.

"I'm having a party tonight around ten. Hope you and Nathan can come."

"Where? Here?" I ask.

"No, at the Royal Orleans. Theater people mostly."

"Bobbie, how can you afford the Royal Orleans Hotel?" I ask.

Bobbie smiles. "Never send to know," she says.

"But Bobbie—"

She blows me a kiss. "Don't worry about it, Gray. Just be there. And try to wear something imaginative."

"Do I have anything imaginative?"

"Raid Mudie's closet. Come on, Gray, when are you going to start having fun?"

"Okay," I say, "we'll be there. Around ten?"

"Suite fourteen-oh-six," Bobbie says.

"I don't believe this. The Royal Orleans."

Bobbie pinches my arm. "Don't tell Max," she says.

Nathan and I arrive at the Royal Orleans around ten. It is Christmas night; Max and Mudie are at home sleeping. I told them we were going to a school Christmas party, which is Nathan's alibi too. He is wearing his father's tuxedo; it is more than a size too big for him and the pants slither a little around his ankles. I am wearing an old Christian Dior dress of Mudie's, white silk with black trim. The doorman at the Royal Orleans gives us a supercilious sneer, which makes us giggle. Perhaps he thinks we don't belong here in our parents' party clothes, looking young and decadent.

"I'm not sure I want to go through with this," I mutter. "I have a bad feeling about it."

"Then we'll go home."

"No." I grab Nathan's arm. "We're here, we might as well go in for a minute."

"There's no law that says you *have* to," Nathan says. "But personally, I'm curious."

"It's more than curiosity," I say. "Something compels me."

We knock on the door of Bobbie's suite; a man dressed like a mime, in black leotard and tights and whiteface, bows and gestures for us to enter. We go in, and there are about forty or fifty people inside; everybody is in costume, but I recognize a few people I know. There's a bar in one of the rooms; I spot the waiter from the Boston

Club Max usually hires for his own parties. I hope he doesn't recognize me. The waiter gives me a glass of champagne, Nathan a glass of scotch.

"Where's Bobbie?" Nathan asks.

"I don't know. I'm not sure I'd recognize her if I saw her."

In the other room the pianist begins playing Cole Porter songs. The suite itself reminds me of one of those sugar Easter eggs, decorated in lilac and white and shades of green. "The Mardi Gras Suite," a man whispers, going by. He is dressed in silk and reminds me of the White Rabbit in *Alice in Wonderland* who was always late and in a hurry. When Bobbie and I were children Max used to read the story to us, and I would cling to him and cry because it was scary. I feel the same way about this party; nothing is right about any of these people.

We drink our drinks and stand nervously at the edge of things. Then Bobbie comes in; she looks just like Judy Garland in *The Wizard of Oz*, she's even wearing ruby slippers and those thin white socks Judy Garland wore in the movie. "It's uncanny," Nathan whispers to me. "She's a chameleon."

"Hey Graycat, Graycat, how's it going, where y'at?" Bobbie kisses me and squeezes my arm. "Glad you could make it, Nate."

Nathan nods.

I stand there staring at my sister; I can't think of anything to say. A man dressed half in white, half in black, with the two halves of his face made up to look sad on one side and happy on the other, comes up to us. Then I recognize the coppery hair underneath the powder: Bobbie's theater friend, Quentin.

Bobbie introduces us. "Quentin came as manic-depression."

Quentin bows. "Lovely party, Bobbie. Is there any more champagne?"

"There's loads"—Bobbie looks in the direction of the bar—"I ordered about a dozen cases."

"It was generous of you to share your inheritance," Quentin says to Bobbie.

"What inheritance?" I ask.

Bobbie gives me a warning look, then smiles at Quentin. "We had this marvelous great-uncle Stanton, who was a famous thoracic surgeon. You may have heard of him. He left an estate of thirty million dollars."

"To Tulane Medical School," I say.

"Uncle Stanton was really brilliant," Bobbie goes on. "His career was ruined when it got out that he'd let a patient die on the operating table deliberately, just to show his students what could happen if they messed up. Nobody knows if the story was true or not. I think it probably was."

Quentin looks confused, then excuses himself. I'm starting not to like the feeling of this party, of how Bobbie's acting.

"Bobbie, Uncle Stanton didn't leave us any money," I remind her.

Bobbie smiles. "Surprise. I wasn't going to tell you. Max specifically asked me not to mention it, seeing as Stanton only left money to me. Some kind of firstborn hang-up. It's nothing to get jealous about, Gray. Only a few thousand. Stanton had this crazy idea that I would give in and go to medical school. So he threw me a bone, to induce me to develop an interest in the sciences."

I have a strong feeling that Bobbie's making this up; if Uncle Stanton had left her any money she would probably have spent it before now.

"Christ, Gray, it's not that big a deal. Don't get so bent out of shape."

"Nobody in this goddamn family cares about me," I say.

Bobbie smiles craftily. "Join the club."

But she's wrong there. In a sense, everybody cares about Bobbie, because her actions and the desires behind them are so dramatic and visible. Bobbie craves love and attention and approval; she goes after them by testing us. While I hide away quietly digging a hole for myself, a space, maybe even a way out of the labyrinth.

Bobbie senses my anger and excuses herself. Maybe I got too close to something real, or maybe she just can't stand being reminded of the truth of our situation. I see her in the next room, talking to the piano player. Where has she found these people, how did she dream up this party? She's nineteen years old; this is a nineteen-year-old's idea of suave.

"That Quentin guy's a lunatic," Nathan says.

"Bobbie worships him."

"He's sure egging her on. I heard him on the phone to the caterers bawling them out about the caviar."

"What caviar?"

Nathan points; a bellhop is wheeling in a cart decorated with theater memorabilia, in the center of which is an enormous mound of caviar on ice.

Nathan says, "Those are very expensive fish eggs."

"You don't suppose what Bobbie said is true, about Uncle Stanton leaving her the money?" I say.

"What do you think?"

"I don't know. Probably not. But how is she paying for all this?" I look around. "The Mardi Gras Suite, the music, champagne, the caterers, caviar. Do you have any idea how much all of this cost?"

"At least six thousand dollars," Nathan says. "The same as a year at Harvard. Do you suppose this is Bobbie's way of getting back at Max?"

"Or at me."

I'm in the middle of this, wondering how to get out. It makes me feel like Alice in Wonderland; is there always a mixture of cleverness, cruelty, and pathos in any attempt to manipulate reality? Also, I realize I've been given a glimpse of a whole underworld that I knew existed but that I have tried to deny because Bobbie claimed it for herself first. More than she claims the Maubry family, or Harmony Street. For all those years of being sisters and growing up together, I now seem to hardly know her. The Bobbie I remember is only a small lost fragment.

I go in search of Bobbie. In the bedroom the bed is piled high with winter clothing; two people are having sex on top of all the hats and coats. They gaze blankly up at me as I go by into the bathroom. There Bobbie is sitting on the tiled floor, rolling a joint. "Graycat," she says, "I thought you were eternally pissed."

"Actually I'm confused."

Bobbie lights the joint, draws in the first smoke. "What is the source of your confusion, O brainy one?"

"This"—I gesture outward, in the direction of the party—"what does it mean?"

"Oh, we're going to have the Spanish Inquisition," Bobbie says. "Have a seat."

I sit down on the floor next to her and accept the joint. Outside, the party mood has intensified; the pianist is playing old Fred Astaire songs.

"The thing is," Bobbie says, "we fucked up so royally. All of us. Max, Mudie, me. The only one who hasn't is you."

"That's questionable," I say.

"We had it so sweet and we fucked up so royally I doubt it can ever be put right." Bobbie inhales and hands me back the joint. "All I can think to do is fuck up some more and some more until I can't fuck it up any worse. Do the maximum thing."

"The maximum thing."

"We had it sweet, though," Bobbie says, sounding rhapsodic.

I'm pretty stoned now, just at the point where anything serious might seem funny and anything funny, serious.

"Goddamn Max."

"What do you mean?" Bobbie says.

In a low voice I sing the opening lines of "You Made Me Love You."

Midway through, Bobbie joins in, so we sing the last two lines together. We start to laugh and then my mood switches abruptly and I start to cry.

"Graycat," Bobbie says, putting her arm around me, "this won't do. 'Cheerfulness in the face of dolor,' remember."

"Jesus Christ."

"Come." Bobbie jumps to her feet. She looks pretty ridiculous as Dorothy, but in a strange way the incongruity fits. "I've got a great idea," she says, "but I've got to talk to Quentin. He'll know how to pull it off."

In the main room someone has emptied a thousand pills into a crystal bowl. Fruit salad, it's called. The idea is to take a handful at random, swallow them down, and see what happens to you. I feel like taking two handfuls and washing them down with champagne, but I know it's too reckless. It might be dramatic enough to wake Max and Mudie up, but would it be worth it?

Nathan asks me to dance. "I noticed you eyeing the fruit salad," he says. "That's a good way to get brain damage."

"I didn't take any."

"Would swallowing a bunch of pills do *anybody* any good?" Nathan asks.

"I wouldn't mind jumping out of myself and being somebody else for a while."

"The only way to do that is gradually," Nathan says.

"Are you saying the project is a failure?"

"No, only a beginning."

While we dance Nathan kisses my neck. He knows I find this irresistible; together we go into the bedroom. This time it's two women making out on top of the coats. We withdraw into the hallway. "Lesbians and thespians," Nathan says. "I wonder if Bobbie knows any boring people."

"We're boring."

"Garden-variety humans," Nathan says, "I'm a string bean and you're—"

"—an artichoke, remember."

"Is your heart hidden behind thistles?" Nathan asks, kissing me.

"Definitely."

"And then there's the proper way to eat one, according to Max," Nathan says. He nibbles my ear.

Nathan's referring to the way Max likes to serve artichokes to guests he doesn't know very well. He claims the way people eat an artichoke is a key to character, to style. Some approach it cautiously, tipping the thing over with a knife. Others sit and watch us eating, to find out how we do it. There are people who approach artichokes analytically and others who simply try to feel their way. I wonder if Max has ever had that much curiosity about my character. Probably not; he probably thinks he has me all figured out.

The champagne is beginning to take effect. I seem to be growing smaller in relation to the room, as if the hotel suite were some elaborate decorated doll house. I'm starting to notice the details on the furniture, on people's costumes, the brass finials on the bed, the shape of the porcelain basin, the twisted silver knob of the ice bucket, Quentin's green false eyelashes.

In the living room Quentin is moving furniture around. He clears a big space in the middle of the rose-patterned carpet and then, from a huge red-and-white-striped bag, he produces a blow-up swimming pool.

"Interesting," Nathan says.

People take turns blowing up the pool; because of the cigarettes I've smoked I'm not very much help. It's a huge red pool with four rings and takes about fifteen minutes to blow up completely. Quentin sets the pool down in the middle of the living room and Bobbie produces a length of clear tubing and runs it into the bathroom and attaches it to the bath faucet. There's a knock on the door; a florist delivers a box of fresh gardenias. "To float in the swimming pool," Bobbie says. "I may not think of everything, but I think of *nearly* everything."

She goes into the bedroom and calls the front desk. "We're going to need more champagne," she says. There's a pause in the conversation and then she says, over-politely, "You may call whomever you please to get authorization but send the champagne. My guests are thirsty." She hangs up and looks at me.

"How are you pulling this off?" I ask.

Bobbie smiles. "You didn't buy the inheritance bit, did you?"

"No."

"God, I can smell those gardenias in here. They're a hothouse variety Quentin told me about."

"Who is paying for all this, Bobbie?"

"Max." Bobbie smiles. "Don't look so amazed. I was certain you knew. He extracts various favors from us and we in turn extract favors from him. You have no idea how ridiculously easy it was for me to arrange all this. 'Just charge it to Mr. Henry Maxwell Maubry,' I told them. 'I'm his daughter. He said for me to make any arrangements I liked.' That's the value of coming from a fine old New Orleans family."

"Jesus, Bobbie."

"No long faces. I think the swimming pool is about filled up. I'm going for a swim."

Bobbie begins to take off her clothes. She goes into the living room in her slip and in front of everybody starts to take it off. Several people are already naked, sitting among the gardenias in the pool. Bobbie looks at me, and some old, long-buried knowledge comes to the surface, just briefly. I start to take off my clothes too, even though Nathan's looking at me as if I've lost my mind. I don't care. I take off Mudie's old Dior gown and the slip and the garter belt and stockings and the pearl necklace and black patent-leather pumps. I take off my bra and the combs in my hair. Bobbie and I are just standing there like two little girls in our underpants, with no place to turn.

Then Quentin pushes Bobbie into the pool and I climb in after her, still in my underpants. . . . He made us love him in ways that were too powerful and charming for children, in ways that enslaved. The kernel of truth that lay revealed between us begins to sink and drift slowly out of my mind. The party gets louder and more raucous; complaints are made and ignored. The bowl of fruit salad diminishes as the night wears on. I know Nathan is watching out for me but I feel totally gone, lost to myself. I'm swimming naked in the pool without any shame. Eventually Nathan sees me shivering and brings me an oversized bath sheet. "I think you need to get out and put your clothes on," he says. "It's time to go home."

"What time is it?"

"Two-thirty."

I have no sense of time having passed, only of a blur of colors, of costumes and naked flesh and eyes and chunks of conversation. I let Nathan help me up and wrap me in the sheet. He leads me into the bathroom and sits me down and dries my hair off a little. "Where am I?" I ask.

"At the Royal Orleans Hotel. I'm going to take you home now."

"Max is going to kill me."

"I doubt it. He's probably asleep."

In the meantime Bobbie has ordered more food and liquor. The management is growing nervous; this time they tell Bobbie they will have to call Max for his approval. "Call Max and I'm dead meat," Bobbie says. She's wearing a dressing gown of Quentin's and has her hair wrapped in a turban. People are starting to straggle off.

"Okay, they've called Max and woken him up from his innocent slumber," Bobbie says. She goes over to the bowl of fruit salad and starts chugging handfuls of pills. "Next stop, the afterlife," she says, "Valium, Mellaril, Stelazine."

"Bobbie, stop."

"Percodan, Elavil, Nardil."

She's swallowing handfuls of pills so fast I can't stop her. It reminds me of when we were children and she would eat all of her candy and then mine too; no amount of prying at her fingers could make her turn it loose. Different-colored pills fall on the floor, and Bobbie's gulping down pills and sips of gin.

"I think I'd best be going," Quentin says.

I look at him, and see something malign in his coloring now that his makeup is removed: copper hair, copper eyes, copper-toned skin. It's as if there were only one material left to make him from, and that one not particularly fine. I feel like socking him.

"Rats are leaving the ship," Nathan says. He hands me my clothes; in all the confusion I've forgotten to put them on. Then the manager of the hotel knocks and comes in without waiting to be admitted. He takes one look at the scene—empty glasses, pills, gardenias floating in the swimming pool, broken furniture—and picks up the phone. "I want the police," he says.

"Forget the police. Call an ambulance," I say.

"An ambulance?"

"I think my sister's taken an overdose."

"You rich kids," the man says wearily.

"Never mind," I say, "I'll call. She's my sister."

The ambulance arrives first, then Max. As usual, he's impeccably dressed; I find myself wondering about the time it took him to shower, shave, and put on his white linen suit. Then it occurs to me: Maybe it's all he has, this image of himself as unblemished, a person who can do no wrong.

Max rides with Bobbie in the ambulance to Charity Hospital, and Nathan drives me home. The streets feel even emptier than usual this time of morning, and Nathan easily makes all the green lights. We're halfway home when Nathan lights each of us a cigarette and hands one to me. On Carondolet Street Nathan stops the engine.

"I had a wonderful time," he says.

"Nathan."

"That was some party. Typical New Orleans excess."

"Talk about Krewe of Dementia Praecox."

"I still don't think Bobbie is crazy, just flamboyant." He starts the car again and we sit feeling the engine idle, ourselves helpless and idle.

"I hope she's going to make it. Maybe I didn't try hard enough to stop her. All those pills. There was something alluring. This might sound funny but often when Bobbie does outrageous things it feels like she's doing them for me as well."

"A kind of dramatic language," Nathan says. "Bobbie acts out what you feel."

"Sometimes, yes. Sometimes, even before I know what I'm feeling. Earlier today I knew there was something peculiar about her. . . . She gave off that aura . . . like she'd left herself behind and gone on ahead, into another place."

"I feel like a skin has just been peeled off my brain. Am I wrong, or was that the weirdest party you've ever been to?" Nathan says.

"It was scary but it was kind of wonderful. Not your typical New Orleans fête."

"Your father didn't look too pleased," Nathan says.

"On Christmas morning he looked so jubilant having Bobbie home with us. He thought she was doing so much better."

Back on Harmony Street I don't want Nathan to go home but there is no real reason to keep him awake; it's past four now. I kiss him good-bye. My head jangles, thinking about Bobbie's party. If I hadn't drunk so much champagne I might know what to make of this. There's a curious connection between Bobbie's party and many other areas of our life: cleverness in execution; artistry; charm; secrecy; the attempt at deceit; misplaced romanticism; silliness; folly. Oh, the folly.

Mudie stands in the hallway, in moonlight.

"It's not your fault, Gray."

As soon as she says this, it *feels* like my fault; I am flooded with a sense of wrongdoing, of complicity, of shame. I know that Bobbie planned and orchestrated the party herself, that I had nothing to do with it. Yet there I was, drinking it all in, guzzling champagne, hoping *something* would happen to change the balance in our family. I'm as desperate in my way as Bobbie is.

Mudie offers me a cigarette and lights one for herself. She looks funny smoking, like a child trying to act grown-up. She is wearing a pair of Max's pajamas. We sit on the steps in the moonlight, smoking and talking. "When the manager of the Royal Orleans Hotel called us I knew it was about Bobbie. The situation was so surreal. You wake up at two in the morning because the phone is ringing, and when you answer it some man is asking you if your daughter has permission to charge more champagne. I just sat there on the edge of the bed wondering what it meant. Of course Max sprang into action and drove down there, as if the faster he went the more damage he could undo."

"That's Max."

"I had such a peculiar feeling yesterday, when Bobbie was here for Christmas dinner. It seemed to me that her behavior was all an act she put on, that she wasn't as happy as she seemed . . . those expensive presents. . . . There was something essentially false about her," Mudie says.

"A powerful odor of mendacity."

Mudie looks at me. "Yes, that was it."

The phone rings, with even worse news. Max is calling from the emergency room of Charity Hospital; they had to pump Bobbie's stomach but she is still unconscious. There's no way to assess if there's any permanent brain damage.

"Oh, God," Mudie says, "I should have known all along that Bobbie wasn't getting better, that she was getting *worse.* All fall I've had this premonition something like this would happen. But you just don't want to believe in anything this awful. Not again. I thought lightning wasn't supposed to strike twice in the same place."

"It doesn't," I say.

Mudie looks at me. I want to tell her everything I know, about Bobbie's and my lives and the pain she and Max inflict even as they are being charming. I want to tell her that I don't think Bobbie is sick, but Mudie depends so much upon this view of things to safeguard her own reality that I can't.

"Oh shit," Mudie says. "I wanted it all to be so perfect. Not perfect in some narrow nit-picking sense but beautiful, whole, alive. I wanted us to have such a good life."

Mudie and I cry in each other's arms. She's crying for her lost dream, for the daughter she doesn't recognize, the husband she changed the course of her life for, and most of all, for Bobbie's suffering, for Bobbie. I'm crying because I'm afraid Bobbie's going to die and I'm going to be part of the reason.

Around six in the morning Max calls back. "She's going to be okay," he says. "I don't know about the rest of us, but Bobbie's going to be okay."

I stay a few extra days in New Orleans; Nathan returns to Cambridge. He meets my plane, the red-eye, which arrives at two A.M. I wasn't expecting him; we drive back to school through soft, thickly falling snow. Nathan has a thermos of coffee and a joint for us to share. We end up parked in the farthest campus parking lot, our car completely blanketed with snow, making love to one another.

We miss our morning classes. Nathan lights a fire in the tiny fireplace in my room and we sit around inventing excuses to give our professors. "My mother died." "I got my hand caught in a meat slicer." "I'm having a panic attack." "*Playboy* canceled my contract to appear as Miss December." "I'm having sophomore slump, but then I always was precocious."

We laze around and smoke cigarettes and send out for coffee and buttered rolls. There's a delicatessen practically across the street from our dorm that's owned and run by a German family; they all speak with heavy German accents. Nathan calls it the Nazi Deli and swears the people who work there are all ex-Nazis. It doesn't keep us from buying their coffee and buttered rolls every morning.

We skip a few days' classes and then Nathan begins to wear his worried look. I've had a phone call from my Greek-tragedy professor, Dr. Atkin, wondering if I'm all right. "No, I'm fine," I tell him. "I was down in New Orleans and got a bad case of stomach flu."

"More like a bad case of bacchanal, I'd guess. Well, happy to hear you're on the mend. You understand the assignment for next week."

"What assignment?"

"Start reading Sophocles' *Antigone*. We're going to produce the play in Greek this spring."

I hang up, grab Nathan's arm. "Nathan, Professor Atkin wants us to read *Antigone*. Talk about nothing being accidental."

Nathan grunts and turns the page of his paper.

"I don't like it. I feel the strange circularity of things," I say.

"Too late to drop the course now," Nathan says, ever practical.

January begins, and I find myself reading *Antigone*. It makes me think a lot about Bobbie, what it would actually be like to be her. It's odd, but I find it harder to hide my own thoughts and feelings behind Bobbie's than I used to. I can still understand her, but now my own character takes precedence. I have the feeling Bobbie and I won't ever be as close as on our last visit together. And that for many years we'll be like planets orbiting out of proximity, on long elliptical journeys.

three

econd semester something happens to me. It begins gradually, so
I barely notice any change in myself. I'm signed up for five courses,
none of them really difficult, and I'm looking forward to watching
spring arrive in Cambridge. About six weeks into the term I start
having trouble getting out of bed in the morning.

"Come on, Oblomov," Nathan teases, "you can't just lie there and
be a symbol of the inner malaise of all the people."

"Nathan, I'm tired."

"Maybe you've got sleeping sickness. Be careful you don't go into
a permanent trance."

"I'm not kidding."

"Try harder," Nathan advises. "Get up, take a shower, go to class.
Shine your shoes."

"Fuck you."

Several mornings in a row I follow Nathan's advice, although I feel such lethargy and lack of energy I can barely get through a class. By the end of the week I get up, shower, get halfway to class, then turn around and go back to bed. Nathan starts bringing me food from the cafeteria, and he keeps me well supplied with coffee and rolls from the Nazi Deli.

One thing that drives me crazy is watching other students through my bedroom window, walking to class, going about their lives. I can't stand it. It's like being paralyzed from the neck down while everyone else is dancing.

Nathan is perplexed. "Your first semester was fairly typical," he says, "not exemplary but typical. You seemed to be enjoying yourself, more or less. I don't have anything to do with it, do I?"

"Don't be ridiculous."

"There's always the college psychiatrist."

"I'd rather buy some leeches. I think you can still get them through the Caswell-Massey catalogue, so Max tells me."

"Are you homesick?"

"God, no."

It's hard to describe. What's wrong with me is more like being lost. I feel estranged from my self, apart, separated, alienated, yet I have a distinct memory of my old self, like an amputee who has feelings in a phantom limb.

I finally drag myself to see the college psychiatrist. Remarkably, he is called Dr. Head, and he has a great smooth cranium to match his name. He prescribes me some pills but otherwise doesn't seem too interested in my case. I hear he does better with hysterics.

"Let's see those pills," Nathan says when I get back to the room. I hand him the bottle. "Thorazine?"

"Dr. Head says it will bring me into better contact with reality."

Nathan opens the pill bottle and goes into the bathroom and

flushes them down the toilet. "Some people don't know reality from fat meat."

"He said what I was going through was a kind of hallucination."

"Wouldn't it be pretty to think so?" Nathan says. "That you could fix what was wrong simply by taking a drug. I don't exactly know what the problem is, Gray, but those things will only take you further away from the solution."

I climb in bed, pull the covers up to my chin. "Would you mind pulling the shade down?"

"I won't do it," Nathan says.

"For Christ's sake. It's not like I'm shooting up heroin. All I want is sleep."

"It might as well be heroin," Nathan says.

In the following weeks Nathan takes over my treatment. He sets the alarm for seven every morning and drags me into the shower with him. He washes my hair, makes sure I put some makeup on and clean clothes. Half the time he's doing this I'm a zombie; the other half I'm crying. It feels excruciating, like being a Chinese woman having her feet unbound for the first time.

Nathan has a copy of my schedule. He walks me to each of my classes, even if it makes him late for his. He gets my assignments and tries to make me do the required reading. I can barely read, something I used to love. Gradually, with Nathan's help, my concentration returns. It's not as good as it once was, but it's an improvement. Every time I try to get back in bed or cut a class, Nathan reminds me, "Look, you only had a C average at midterms. You can't afford to miss that lab."

"But rat psych, Nathan. It's so boring."

"Most boring of all is doing nothing. I can't let that happen to you. What if you flunk out of here?"

"I might as well. I was never meant to be here."

"Make it yours," Nathan says, "you can take any experience and make it yours. Not to mention that I'd be lonesome without you."

"Lonesome. What a genteel, Southern word."

"Your lab's in fifteen minutes. Do you have last week's report ready?"

And so it goes. Nathan's relentless in his efforts to get me back to being a normal, functioning person. I let him help since it seems to make him happy but underneath I know that whatever sadness he is chasing away will probably return. People don't just stop getting out of bed for no reason.

As finals approach, we closet ourselves in our room and study. We make an occasional foray to the library, but there are too many other students there; it makes me nervous. I spread out my old faded lavender quilt from my bedroom at home on the floor of my closet and transform it into a study carrel. With a gooseneck lamp, my books and file cards, and a thermos of coffee, I can stay in there for however long it takes to review a unit's worth of material. Nathan lies nearby, flopped on his bed, his sneakered feet crossed on top of a stack of books. Every so often he looks up at me over his round tortoiseshell glasses and gives me a smile.

The night before exams begin I take a shower with lavender soap and climb into bed beside Nathan, my hair still wet. I'm surprised when he doesn't respond to being kissed.

"We can't have sex right before an exam," he says, "it spills the vital juices."

"Maybe yours, but not mine."

"A certain amount of tension is necessary to good performance."

"Nathan, I don't believe you."

"You don't have to." Nathan kisses me chastely on the cheek and rolls on his side to sleep.

By the time final grades come we are back in New Orleans, working for another of Nathan's hopeless political candidates. He rides by one day on his bicycle to see how I did. Three A's and two B's: I show him the card.

"Not bad."

"For someone who was about to flunk out. Thanks, Nathan."

"Somebody has to look out for you. Besides that lunatic shrink, Dr. Head."

"He meant well."

"About as well as a cottonmouth," Nathan says. "It worries me sometimes when I think about the profession we're going to be joining. The vast, shimmering field of mental health."

"It's kind of frightening."

"Only if you're a quack."

"What if you're a duck?—Someone who's still floating," I explain.

"I thought you *wanted* to be a psychiatrist," Nathan says.

"I want not to have to think about anything for the whole summer," I say.

"Okay," Nathan agrees.

It turns out to be impossible, not thinking. There are so many hours of mindless work—envelope-stuffing and telephone calls— that by the time we get off, my mind is full. My previous semester at Harvard haunts me; I want to understand why I became so depressed when I should have been elated to be there. Was I punishing myself? I don't think so; long ago I had gotten over feeling guilty about taking Bobbie's place, and it wasn't likely these feelings would return. No, my depression must have had more to do with me.

Maybe it happened because I wasn't doing anything differently; I'd left Bobbie's shadow only to find myself in some shadow of my own making. Look at the things I'd done: become Anna's friend, spent money wildly, slept with George . . . but I hadn't formed an opinion of anything. Here, I'd had all these expectations about Harvard, but Harvard hadn't done anything for me. It was there, like any other piece of the world, and once again I was retreating. I needed to decide things, not just experience them. I needed to mold experience with some response of my own.

The next morning on the way to work I told Nathan I didn't want to work in politics anymore. He looked stunned.

"But why not?"

"It bores me. If I have to stuff one more envelope, I'll scream."

"The end result is what counts," Nathan says.

"I know, but I just can't stand it. In fact, you can let me out here."

"Here?" Nathan says, looking around at the residential streets.

"I can walk home. It's not that far. I just had this revelation that I spend all my time pleasing other people, even you. I can't do this anymore."

"Okay, Gray," Nathan says. "Take it easy."

He lets me out, blinking in the sunshine. What I'm doing is so simple I have trouble believing how powerful it is. I have no idea how I'm going to spend today, or the rest of the summer, and that feels intoxicating.

four

've been back in Cambridge a week when Max calls to say that Bobbie left home in the middle of the night. She wrote a note that said she was severing all formal ties with her family.

"I'm sorry, Max," I say.

We hang on the line, but I don't have very much to say. Once, I would have offered to come home and help them find Bobbie, but I can't do that now. I care about Bobbie, but not to the extent that I'm willing to give up my education for her. She's probably just in some French Quarter apartment with some friends.

A week goes by, and no news of Bobbie. Nathan shows up in my doorway. I haven't seen him since New Orleans; he's been secretive, deliberate in his efforts to show me he can live either way, with or without me. "So," he says, "any news from home?"

"Not much. Bobbie's still missing."

Nathan sinks down on the bed beside me, into the jumble of notes, ashtrays, yesterday's paper, a creased edition of Dante. He opens to the first page and reads aloud, " 'In the middle of the journey of our life I found myself in a dark wood where the straight way was lost.' "

"Not now, please."

Nathan sighs, closes the book. "Can't escape, can you?"

"I wasn't trying to."

"No?" Nathan lifts eyebrows at what appears to be my life here: clothes he hates, books he hasn't read, friends he thinks are fatuous. Anna is in her bedroom, typing. She's just washed her hair and has it turbaned in a towel. "What's she writing now," he asks, "her autobiography?"

"You're so intolerant. Sometimes I get the feeling that whatever I do, it's wrong in your eyes. You're a little like Max, Nathan, do you know that? There's no pleasing you."

"I *was* pleased," Nathan says simply.

We look at each other. Friends since childhood, lovers, classmates at the same college, now we can barely have a conversation without arguing. How did it happen, I wonder. It used to be simple, being with Nathan. How do the simple things always slip from my grasp?

"I'll call you," Nathan says, and turns to go. It is clear his presence in my room is only another upsetting factor, although not so long ago I would have been happy to have him in my room with its mint-green walls and the ivy creeping through the leaded-glass windows.

"I'm sorry. Jesus, I'm sorry. I have to think. Please call," I say.

"I said I would."

"Okay then."

"Okay."

Nathan closes the door. Anna's typewriter stops clacking and she emerges, dressed in her funny-looking blue denim skirt and a black scoop-neck blouse. Her perfume arrives before she does. Then she leaves, and I am alone with the odd hour between the end of Anna's Russian class and her analyst's appointment. Anna has been in analysis for five years and has explained to me that you don't have to be crazy to need an analyst. Only rich, Nathan says. I wish Anna would stay here to keep me company. I'm chagrined about Nathan; already he seems hardened and set against me. And then there's the business about Bobbie missing. Anna would know what to say; even her exaggerated sympathy might be easier to take than Nathan's quiet empathy.

An hour later I dial Max's number. He answers the phone himself.

"There *is* something I want to tell you. Bobbie told me over the phone a month or so ago that she was considering going off her medication. She said it was turning her into a zombie. She felt slowed down."

"She needs to be slowed down," Max says.

"I tried to talk her out of it, but you know Bobbie. She said the medication was worse than the original disease. Told me about all kinds of side effects. I looked up the drugs in the *PDR* and she's right, there are hideous side effects. Shuffling when you walk. Slurping your tongue. Dry mouth. Amnesia."

Max says, "Gray, listen. Your mother and I have no wish to embroil you in Bobbie's difficulties. You can't do anything about her. Besides, I want you to concentrate on your work. College only comes once in a person's life and I want you to enjoy it."

"Thanks, Max."

"But if you hear from Bobbie, would you—"

"—let you and Mudie know. Sure, Max."

"Thank you."

In the morning I hear a discreet knock on my door. Anna is out—doubtless she didn't return from last night's medieval-wine tasting—and her unmade bed is heaped with bright-colored stockings and impressive-looking books, research materials for a paper she is writing on Freud and Poe.

"Come in."

Nathan again, this time dressed in his old wrinkled khakis from St. Rita's; at Harvard these clothes have a distinguished air.

"Any news?"

"No. But I have a strange feeling Bobbie might be here in Cambridge."

"May I sit down?"

Nathan sits on the end of my bed; his manner is almost chaste. He has a brown paper bag which he unrolls at the top, withdrawing, without spilling, two large coffees with milk. "Don't get any ideas about my being a sop," he says, "I just know you can't think straight without your coffee."

"You make me feel terrible."

"Not intentionally."

"No, I realize that. Here I've been so nasty to you and you come bringing café au lait."

"Native grace," Nathan says.

"You deserve better than me anyway."

"I was happy."

I let his words drop, light as a scattering of pins. I know I have hurt Nathan's feelings and he should not even be speaking to me, except that whatever bound us together in the first place must be stronger than I thought. And Nathan has always had a way of doing things that would make other people seem weak, things that done by Nathan seem exactly right. I wish I hadn't hurt him; it would make life so much easier.

We drink our coffee in an awkward silence and then I watch Nathan shred both our foam cups into tiny pieces. It must be a sort of release for him. "What are you going to do now?" Nathan asks.

"I don't know. Here I come all the way to Cambridge to escape my family, to get away from Bobbie and my duty to Max, and what happens?"

"I knew something would," Nathan says with a shrug. "It's just like life."

"You make things seem so inevitable. I thought you didn't believe in predestination."

"I don't," Nathan says. "Just in the tendency of things to happen in a certain way."

"Such as——?"

"What makes you think Bobbie is here?" Nathan asks.

"I have a kind of radar for Bobbie. It's hard to explain. I just get these vibrations. Little disturbances in the surface of my day."

"Not real scientific," Nathan says.

"Then little concrete things. Like pictures and books missing from my room. If I go out and forget to lock it, I have the feeling someone's been in here, going through my personal stuff. Two long-distance phone calls on the bill we can't account for. One to New York, the other to Tulsa, Oklahoma. *Tulsa, Oklahoma?* My shearling coat Max bought me is missing. Not that I would wear a dead sheep."

"Only a black sheep would wear a dead sheep."

"It's not funny, Nathan. This is starting to make me crazy. When I showed up for dinner last night they looked on the chart and said I'd already eaten."

"Those kitchen guys are morons," Nathan says.

"You don't believe me."

"I think you're mildly hysterical."

"Just wait. I bet you anything Bobbie surfaces."

Nathan shrugs. His point made, he stands up to go. I notice he is fully two inches taller than the previous year; his old St. Rita's trousers are too short.

"Your pants are too short," I say.

Nathan grins. "I was certain you would notice."

When he is gone I lie on my bed and stare at the dented plaster on the wall. Anna made the dent when she threw her Russian dictionary at the wall during a quarrel with her latest lover. I'm lying on the bed and staring at the dent and I can't help thinking that if I break up with Nathan I will lose my image of my own future. The image included graduate school with Nathan somewhere on the East

Coast, and later, marriage. I can see the children we would have together, children with straight hair the color of coffee and round, serious faces.

The first definite sign I have that Bobbie is in Cambridge comes from the bank. Near the end of November, when no leaves are left on the trees, I overdraw my banking account. I call up the bank to complain; there should be at least two hundred dollars there, I tell them. Politely, they ask me to look over my old bank statement. I fish the envelopes out of the bottom of my desk drawer and sort through; there, on the fifteenth of November, is a check for fifty dollars I didn't write. I recognize Bobbie's handwriting, though.

I call Nathan. "Bobbie's definitely here," I say. "She forged a couple of checks. What I want to know is, how does she get into my room?"

"Anna lets her in?"

"Possibly."

"Or she might have gotten a key," Nathan says. "She's very resourceful."

"Bobbie is just the kind of person Anna would be impressed by."

Around dinnertime Anna comes in. Her eyes are bright with the excitement that comes from some new shred of evidence about herself; as usual after her "analytical hour," she seems energized. In an hour's time she will have calmed down a bit and will be lecturing some undergraduate boy on the mysteries of life at Mink House, her childhood mansion.

"What's the matter?" Anna asks when she sees me.

"It's my sister, Bobbie. Remember I told you she disappeared again? Well, she's turned up. This time, in Cambridge. I can't seem to shake her."

"Bobbie?" Anna says vaguely. "The crazy one?" As usual, she treats everybody else's life like an insignificant blot on her own.

"I know she's here because she forged some of my checks. She used to do it to my father all the time. You haven't let anybody into the room lately, have you?"

Anna thinks. "Only the fire inspector."

"Man or woman?"

Anna's brown eyes widen with alarm. She lets out a shriek almost of amusement. "Don't tell me that was your sister! She had on this funny uniform like all the janitors wear, only it had some badges pinned to the pocket. Her hair was up under her hat. She claimed she was searching for illegal hot plates. Had this little clipboard and everything. Now I think about it, her voice sounded like yours. Yours is huskier, hers clearer."

"And someone turned a copy of my psych paper in to my professor early. I never turn anything in *early*. When I went in to give him the original, he got this startled look and said he thought I'd already handed mine in," I say.

Anna starts to laugh. She has this loud silly laugh that under better circumstances I find refreshing, but that now seems irritating. I realize it is pointless to try to explain to Anna how uneasy I feel with Bobbie lurking around Cambridge, nibbling at my life here. Anna is mostly interested in the drama of things, rather than how they feel to the person having the experience.

"What made her come *here*?" Anna asks.

"She's trying to take her life back. She has this idea I stole it from her."

"I'm sorry, Gray."

"For what?"

"For letting her in. I wasn't thinking."

"It's okay."

Let off the hook, Anna goes about showering; from the bathroom she shouts to me parts of what her psychiatrist said to her that day. "There's a lost genius trapped inside my body," Anna says. "Who knows, maybe I'll make films."

I don't listen very well to the unfolding drama of Anna's past. I'm angry and upset about Bobbie. We'd been writing and calling each other occasionally; Bobbie never mentioned that she might come to Cambridge. Then again, it was probably a move she never planned, just one of those impulsive actions that turn out later to have emotional significance.

I skip dinner. Hungry, I prowl the campus looking for signs of Bobbie, but now that I'm looking, there aren't any. Maybe I've been imagining Bobbie's presence; maybe someone else has been stealing my checks and forging them. Maybe someone stole the sheepskin coat. But who? Anna? She doesn't need any more things. Anna oozes money. The more I think about it, the more I am reminded of things Bobbie used to do when we were children and Hannah used to say my sister had the devil in her. Hannah used to say that there would come a time when she was dead and buried and I would have to protect myself from Bobbie. That time is here, even though Hannah's not dead, only old and sick and back in New Orleans, unable to help me. I'm nineteen years old, going on twenty. Bobbie's twenty-two.

It's kind of strange that I would need protection from somebody as fragile and unprotected as Bobbie, but there it is. Nathan says the fragile people break last, the others break trying to save them. In a way, he's right. But it doesn't do any good on a chilly New England night thinking in generalities. I want to find Bobbie. I want to find her and make her leave Cambridge so I can get on with my own life.

Bobbie has been going to classes; I know because my Shakespeare professor, Dr. Thoms, looked confused when I came for my conference and said he was sure he'd already spoken to Gray Maubry.

"Must be somebody else," I said.

"She was quite distinctive. Talked about Sophocles' Antigone as if she were in that character's skin. The idea of living death. Drew parallels to *Romeo and Juliet*, I recall. A singular girl, no doubt about it. But you say you're Gray Maubry? I wonder who that extraordinary girl was."

My sister, Antigone. I walk through the Cambridge rain wondering if I will ever be free of her, as Ismene did not escape alive, either. Bobbie haunts me. Every time I pass an empty classroom or go by a restaurant, I expect to see her face, perfectly pale and small, through the window.

Nathan meets me for coffee. The coffee shop is crowded with students, some arguing fiercely, others reading; beside them, Nathan looks serene. "What's up?" he asks.

"Bobbie's here, all right. Going to my classes, even. My Shakespeare lecturer said she'd been to see him. This is getting really creepy, Nathan. It's like she's trying to be me. When we were little I was always trying to be her. She got all the praise and attention. Now it's like she's trying to be me."

"What are you going to do?"

"What can I do?"

"You have a variety of options. It depends upon what you want to happen."

"What would you do?"

"I'd wait for her to seek me out, and then I'd persuade her to leave."

"My persuasive powers aren't as good as yours are."

"She's probably just jealous," Nathan says.

"I think it's more complicated than that. This whole thing has an aura . . . it *means* something. Bobbie's trying to tell me something, to work something out."

"The main thing Bobbie has to work out," Nathan says, "is that she isn't crazy. She's a distraction from the inadequacies of your father and mother."

We talk like this some more and then Nathan asks me what I'm taking this year. Shakespeare, and beginning ancient Greek, advanced biology and . . . "No psychology?" Nathan asks. "I thought you wanted to be a psychiatrist."

"I don't anymore. I don't know what I want." With only one cigarette left, we share it. I feel glum. Even worse than my betrayal of him with Anna's brother, this small betrayal seems mean, my not telling him of a change of heart. I know things like that matter to Nathan.

He withdraws now behind a patch of smoke. When he speaks at all, it's to say "I didn't realize you'd changed so much."

I don't answer. Presently Nathan gets up and leaves the coffee shop. I wasn't conscious of any radical change, but somehow by slipping one way or another, I've changed.

Now I want to run after Nathan the way French people do in charming black-and-white movies, run up behind him and throw my arms around him and say, if not "I love you" then something close, and keep the life I used to have preserved, as if on film. But of course, I don't. I sit where I am and brood about Bobbie.

Dr. Thoms calls me into his office. He paces nervously, a rabbity man dressed in a beautiful gray suit. The gossip about him is that he married a ballerina from the New York City Ballet and after the ceremony found out she had a hundred and fifty thousand dollars or more in debts. Which makes us both susceptible to the weaknesses of others, I suppose.

"Your work on *Troilus and Cressida* was absolutely magnificent," he says.

"Dr. Thoms, I keep telling you, it's not my work."

"Why are you so anxious to disclaim it?"

"Remember the extraordinary girl? *She* wrote the paper."

"There is no extraordinary girl. I haven't seen her since that first time. I must have had an hallucination."

"The girl was Bobbie, my sister."

Dr. Thoms smiles sadly and hands me my paper. Bobbie's paper. With an A+ on it. Since Bobbie arrived in Cambridge I've been doing great academically. Which isn't surprising.

. . .

Nathan stops by to report two sightings of Bobbie. The first was in town, in a bookshop. The second was at night, in a restaurant. Bobbie was wearing a tablecloth draped and pinned like a sari. She was with a Pakistani student famous for one-night stands. He never ate meat but he routinely slept with female undergraduates who wanted to lose their virginity. Which wasn't the case with Bobbie.

It is almost Christmas vacation when I actually see Bobbie. Here all this time I was looking for a flamboyant Bobbie instead of a subdued one. She is working in a health-food restaurant off campus; she looks like the young Russian comrade in *Dr. Zhivago*, whose small youthful face glowed under a babushka.

I spot her through the greasy window. Do I go in and sit down at one of the tables? Or keep walking? I end up going in. Bobbie comes over to take my order.

"I'll have the falafel," I say.

"Took you long enough to find me," Bobbie says.

"I'm a slow learner."

Bobbie shoots me a look that means *Later,* and goes off to place my order in the kitchen. She comes back with an iced tea I didn't order and a pack of Lucky Strikes. She sits down opposite me, tamping a cigarette on the linoleum counter with nervous agitation. "Will the real Gray Maubry please stand up," she says.

"What are you doing in Cambridge?" I ask.

"Don't you know? I thought you Harvard types knew everything."

"Why do you hate me?"

"I don't hate you. You're my sweet sister Gray."

"Look, Max and Mudie are worried about you. You might have told them where you were going."

Bobbie makes a gesture with her cigarette that signals agitation. "Before you go laying it on heavy, let me explain. I'll pay back the money from those kited checks."

"It's not the money. Jesus, you know that."

Bobbie composes herself. As always, she is theatrical whenever she wants to express things she feels strongly about; the combination sometimes leads me to think she is being false.

"Max is trying to turn me into his ideal daughter by making me take those drugs. He thinks when I'm on the drugs I don't do bizarre things and that means they make me well. It's easier on *him,* you see."

"I suppose you think that's all he cares about, himself? You don't think he wants you to be well from unselfish motives?"

"There is no such thing," Bobbie says.

"Maybe not. But I think it's cynical of you to suggest that Max wants you to take the drugs only to make his own life more peaceful. He's not like that. He's a lot more high-minded, for one thing."

"Yeah." Bobbie exhales smoke. "He's so high-minded that he sent me away to boarding school so I wouldn't tell Mudie about his affair with Kendra Hamilton. He thought I knew too much."

"He thought you were too smart for Rita's."

"You're such an innocent. Max wanted to shut me up."

"I don't believe it."

"Believe whatever you want. But it was part of the picture, let me tell you. Maybe he thought I'd go tell Mudie and then he'd lose his family, me, everything. You see, Max is always going on about how truth and beauty are the only things that count. He's willing to sacrifice his own image of himself but not other people's image of him. Charming Max, and damn it, he *is* charming. I don't suppose I'll ever love any man more, even if Electra did it first. Love is love, whatever kind it is, unfortunately."

"Still, Bobbie," I say, "you can't stay here."

"No?" Bobbie looks crestfallen, a child again. "Please don't make me go back to Max and Mudie. You don't understand. Those drugs they put me on are like having my mind wrapped in mummy rags. There's this dead, stiff feel to everything. So what if it makes me appear well? If feeling that way is being well, they can have it."

"Bobbie, look. You know I won't tell Max and Mudie you're here.

I couldn't. But you have to promise to make some kind of contact by Christmas."

"Big of you," Bobbie says.

"Personally, I'd rather you went home and cleared this up now. You can't run from Max and Mudie forever. They're your own parents."

"Some parents," Bobbie says. "The deadly duo. Have you ever seen two more narcissistic, self-concerned people than they are? What are they most involved with? Their own needs, that's what. And most of all, deadliest of all, is their need for me to be crazy and for you, Gray, to take care of everyone else. It takes their minds off the reality they've helped create. *They* are the ones with an altered sense of reality, not me."

I'm crying now, of course; it's as if all the sorrow I ever felt for Bobbie had been put aside and saved up for this moment. I can't believe the feeling could still be so fresh, so deep. Her point made, Bobbie sits quietly watching me cry. I suppose she's already felt the same grief I feel; only now it's changed because I know the grief is for myself as well as for Bobbie.

We leave the restaurant together. Bobbie tells me she's been living with a graduate student—"platonically," she claims, but I wonder. There's something too desperate, too urchinlike about Bobbie for this arrangement to be entirely innocent. Before we leave the restaurant, Bobbie goes into the bathroom and changes clothes; when she emerges, she looks like an entirely different person. Her hair is cut short like a boy's and she's wearing a white linen jacket—it makes her look like an Italian waiter—paisley pants, and a pair of handmade leather shoes, men's shoes, that are an exact copy of a pair Max had made for himself at Peal's in London. Sometimes I think Bobbie doesn't want to be the *daughter* Max wants, she wants to be a small replica of Max. I don't say anything, but I notice, of course.

five

"When I was at Bennington," Mudie says, "we had an unusually cold winter one year and between classes I used to hole up in my room reading—*Artists on Art*, Clive Bell, anything about art I could lay my hands on—and afterwards I'd work in the studio until the last light was gone from the sky. Weekends, I'd go in to New York. . . . I lived for that world, it felt like I didn't even need to eat. Then . . ."

"What happened?" I ask.

"The college closed down because of fuel costs. Sent all the students home to do work projects until spring. I found myself working with autistic children. It was very hard for me, I didn't have the qualities you need for that kind of therapy. I was afraid a lot. Then one day at one of the sessions, we were doing fingerpainting, or trying to, and one little boy who had never spoken, never even made eye contact with me in the past, crept over while nobody was looking and sat on my lap and just held me. I was completely undone. After that I went back to Bennington but it wasn't the same again. The world was different, not at all the intellectual sandbox I'd imagined."

I sit thinking while Mudie works. Sometimes she is so remote I can hardly believe she is part of this family, and then she says something to show me I am wrong; she is the heart of the family. When I think about the failures she has had to live with—in her marriage, her work, Bobbie's treatment—it makes me sad. But then there is Mudie, not feeling sorry for herself at all but sitting at her window, cool, rapt, fierce, as if she hasn't known a failure in her life. It makes me think I have given up on things in my own self I ought to look at longer.

I take the car and drive out to see Hannah, who is still living in her house on North Johnson Street. The neighborhood has gone down; Hannah's house is the only one on the block with shutters and a fresh coat of paint. She's retired now and spends most of her time doing church work.

I go up on the porch and tap the dusty screen. "Come on in," Hannah says. She grins when she sees me.

"Child, look. I never thought I'd see the day," she says, "you a college girl now."

"How's James?"

"The same. How's your daddy?"

"Mad at Bobbie."

"He's going to give hisself a conniption, the way he runs on. I tole him and tole him, ain't nothing he can do about Bobbie. Ask me. I raised her from a baby. Anything Bobbie get in her mind to do, it's done. No sense wasting time arguing."

We mix ourselves lemonade and go out on the porch. It's a warm winter day in December, the kind we sometimes have in New Orleans.

"How's that boy you used to run with?" Hannah asks.

"Nathan? I don't see him much."

"He married yet?"

"People in college don't get married."

Hannah ignores this remark. "I'd sure like to live to see your wedding day."

"I'm not ready to get married, Hannah."

"Who is? I was fourteen myself."

"I broke up with Nathan," I say.

"*Broke up?* You are swimming the wrong way in the stream, Gray. Marry him."

"He didn't ask me."

"Girl, you *are* blind."

"It's more complicated than that. My life's more complicated," I say.

"If you're talking about Mr. Max and your mother, I don't want to hear any more," Hannah says. "I know better than anyone what babies they are. Wanting all the attention, the love, for themselves. And the only thing I could do about it was stand by *you*. And Bobbie."

"I know that, Hannah," I say.

"You do?"

"Yes."

"What else do you know, Gray?"

"Probably the only way for someone like me to flourish is to stay with Nathan and let him love me. Stop driving him away. I don't know if I can help it, though," I say.

"Well, you said it," Hannah says. "It came from your mouth, not mine."

With Bobbie back on Harmony Street, the mood isn't much better. Max is locked in the library, listening to Brahms; in the room directly above him Bobbie radiates good humor. She offers me a joint, which I accept to be social. "Can you keep a secret?" she says.

"I've spent my life keeping secrets."

Bobbie smiles. "I've met somebody. His name is Franklin and he's a migrant farmworker in Arkansas. I met him at this coffee shop the other night. He's really an actor."

"God, Bobbie. Another theater type."

"You can make a lot of money picking apples in Arkansas," Bobbie says.

"I'll bet."

"Enough in one season to live on for a year. The rest of the time you're free to do whatever you want."

"Like?"

"Your empathy is killing, Gray. Like *whatever*. Write, design sets, get away from this dump."

"When are you leaving?"

"Soon, but don't tell Max. I want to take him by surprise."

"Who is this Franklin person?" Max asks over drinks. Lately he and Mudie seem to drink more than usual, and drinking has become more important than eating. Max is never without his pale amber scotch.

"Bobbie met him the other night at a coffeehouse," I say.

"What does Franklin do for a living?" Max asks.

"He picks apples."

"Apples?" Max raises his eyebrows.

"He's a migrant farmworker in season. Otherwise I guess he's an actor."

Mudie smiles approval at this. She pours herself another drink and samples it speculatively. "I thought I might go out today," she says. Nobody comments, although these days it is rare for Mudie to go out at all. How did it happen that Mudie got more and more afraid to go out, how did such a bold and delicate person become as stationary as one of her own sculptures? I think she's afraid of the family unraveling altogether; she thinks if she stays in, this can't happen.

Max says, "I suppose it's inevitable."

"What, darling?" Mudie asks.

"Bobbie leaving us. I mean, boarding school was one thing, and St. Vincent's is so close by. This departure seems more permanent. I can feel it in my bones the way another man might feel his rheumatism. I only wish she had finished school."

"Oh, Max, that's unrealistic," Mudie says.

"And Franklin? Franklin is realistic?" Max replies.

Even without a fight Max knows he is a beaten man, and Bobbie will fly into whatever wind finds her loose. For the moment it's Franklin and his artists' colony in Eureka Springs. Eureka, I found it. The only problem is that Bobbie hasn't managed to find an art that she stays interested in long enough to perfect her talent. Unless it's living by her wits; she certainly does that.

"Were you thinking of going out to lunch?" Max asks Mudie, his voice dreamy.

"Oh, I don't know if I can," Mudie says. "Where would we go?"

"How about Manale's?"

"The two of us?"

"The two of us," Max says.

"I'll try."

At Nathan's the electricity is off. Someone forgot to pay the bill for three months running; this kind of thing happens pretty frequently, so Nathan remains calm. "You two lovebirds forget about us and go on out to dinner," Darwin says.

"I thought we had a bottle of wine someplace," Nathan's mother says. She looks at me with wry humor, as if she understood the difficulty of our condition. We love each other, but certain character traits keep getting in the way.

"There's a dollar-and-forty-nine-cent special at Poco's," Nathan says. He looks as of he would like to crawl sideways out of his body. But then, he's always restless around his parents. Nathan looks at me. "How about it, Gray?"

"Poco's?"

"My treat," Nathan says.

Poco's is a Mexican joint a little way out of the Quarter. Nathan drives judiciously; the two of us share a joint. One way of really enjoying the food at Poco's is to arrive stoned. I feel a little self-conscious being with Nathan, but not too much. It's almost as if we need to feel unsettled with each other to feel connected. Maybe I've treated him too lightly, treated the idea of the two of us too lightly. Maybe that was why I needed to break up with him, so our relationship wouldn't be like an old married couple's before we had even begun.

After dinner we go to a movie in the French Quarter. Later, we walk down the street to the Morning Call for some coffee and beignets. The coffee shop is lined with mirrors, which makes our conversation seem more intense, yet ethereal.

"So," Nathan says, "what did you think of the movie?"

"Poignant," I say.

Nathan gives me a rueful smile. "Definitely poignant. And did you enjoy being with me? Did you enjoy dinner and the movie? Are you relishing this conversation?"

"Nathan, what are you doing?"

"Showing you what a mistake you made to break up with me," Nathan says.

"All I did was say I felt smothered and I wished you didn't have exclusive rights to me," I say.

"I forgave you," Nathan says. "You slept with a little twerp like George Mink, and I forgave you. Now, you're bludgeoning me because I want to be with you."

"All I want is some space," I say.

"You have powdered sugar on your upper lip." Nathan leans over and kisses me, wiping off the mustache. I have to admit, I like the kiss.

"Gray, look. You want space, right? Let me tell you what space is. Space is wino hippies who steal your poetry books and try to sleep with you. Space is football players worming their way into your affections and getting too rough with you after they've had a few beers. Space is starved graduate students, architecture majors with brilliant plans . . . all of these people are going to want you. You think you want space but I think you want the *idea* of space."

"Nathan, that's enough. I told you I was flexible about this. We can still see each other. I think it's good. I've spent my whole life in these intense, exclusive relationships. Max and Mudie's daughter, Bobbie's sister, her other half. Well, that's not enough."

"You're going to regret this," Nathan says.

"I don't think so."

"We disagree, then."

Back home, I go to bed early. Bobbie stays up late talking to Max and Mudie in the library. Interwoven with sleep come snatches of their conversation; fragments of anger fly like busted glass. I roll over and try to dream. I remember that when I was a girl and had nightmares I would wake myself up and try to think happy thoughts. I get so engrossed trying to remember what these happy thoughts were, I forget about Max and Bobbie's argument.

In the morning the house is quiet. I am the only one in the white kitchen; I grind coffee for Mudie's and my morning cup and carry them up to her on a tray. I knock on the studio door; "Come in," Mudie says. She is dressed in a pink bathrobe, the cuffs of which are streaked with clay. "Gray," she says, "I was just thinking how good coffee would taste."

She tells me the news: Bobbie's gone. Last night Bobbie and Max began to fight, and afterward, when it was over, Bobbie said she was leaving for good.

"What did they fight about?"

"Bobbie's life. Max is convinced if she doesn't resume treatment she'll get sick again. Bobbie's convinced Max is only trying to get her to take the medication for his own sake, so she won't go around doing bizarre things. She says it hampers her creativity. Max says she only wants to spite him. That kind of thing."

Of course, Bobbie leaves before I do. She wouldn't wait to say good-bye, or make less than a dramatic departure. This makes me feel deflated, like an empty sack. "Don't worry," Mudie tells me. "It will all work out."

"Yes, but the question is, which way?"

Max stands in the doorway. He has the light, haggard look of an overtired child; his robe and pajamas look freshly ironed, as if he hasn't slept. "Bobbie's gone," he says quietly, "anybody want breakfast?"

We brew a fresh pot of coffee; Max makes waffles that rival those at the Allgood, they are so light and buttery; Mudie even manages not to scorch the bacon. Sunlight falls in slabs through the long windows; we eat in the kitchen so as to be near that light as long as possible. When breakfast is over, Max sees me looking at him. "What happened?" I ask.

"Your sister and I had an argument last night. I guess it got pretty emotional, as these things go. I threw in her face everything she had ever done and she threw in mine everything I'd ever done, which made us even. Almost. She's had a shorter life but I've had more opportunity to do the wrong thing. Then about six-thirty this morning Franklin drove up in a Ford Falcon with no taillights. I imagine Bobbie had called him to come rescue her; when he said he was leaving for Arkansas right away, she looked startled, but she got in the car."

"What did you do then?" I ask.

"I let her go."

"You shouldn't have."

"She's twenty-two. It was time to let her go."

"Some people you never let go," I say.

"I guess we'll find out," Max says.

I can't believe it, Max taking this position. Here all our lives he's been keen to protect Bobbie; now he just lets her go. This doesn't fit in with the rest of Max's character, which is complicated, to say the least. He looks almost pleased with himself in his seersucker robe and white pajamas with the piping on them, and I am touched by what

I can only say is his angelic innocence. Max, a man of forty-nine, innocent? There isn't any other word for it; in some part of his heart he believes Bobbie is like some wild bird you cannot keep, only let her fly and she will find her life. And here all this time he was pretending to hold her.

Max drives me to the airport. We say good-bye outside the terminal; Max has an appointment at noon with a client about a new building. Already hope is rising in him like sap; he's trying to forget that Bobbie's gone, that I'm going, and that perhaps Mudie, even in hiding, was here all along. In our place is a series of plans, elevations, notations on solar heating, elegant fenestration. He has this much to save him.

Nathan is waiting for me on the plane. He gives me a shy nod as if to say his presence isn't entirely an accident, but he's keeping his distance. I slide in next to him; my Greek grammar bangs him on the shin. "Sorry."

"Already?"

"I had a terrible morning."

"Nothing the rain-washed streets of Cambridge can't fix," Nathan says. He doesn't even wait for takeoff; he unscrews his pocket flask and offers me a sip of gin.

"Are you going to tell me about it?" Nathan asks after our second drink.

"I don't know. There isn't much to tell, really."

"That's what Homer said when he sat down to write the *Iliad*."

"So he just started by telling what the trouble was."

"And before long, he was listing ships, and who had done what to whom," Nathan says.

"And that remarkable scene when Andromache tells how she's lost so many people to war, that only her husband is left and how he has to be father and mother, sister and brother to her."

"Well?"

"It's like that with Bobbie. She's lost so much to this family, I can see why she counts on me for so much. I can't just be myself, you see. I have to be father and mother, and sister. I even have to be Bobbie."

"Not if you don't want to."

We fall quiet. Outside our tiny aircraft window the gray runway speeds past, gives way to air, a tangle of light towers, rooftops, eventually whole houses and backyards with swimming pools in them, until finally we are looking at blue sky.

"You know, Nathan, there is no such thing as compensating for someone else," I say. "Not really."

"It's taken you this long to discover that?" Nathan says.

"I'm a late bloomer," I say.

six

n late January Max calls me. "I have a special favor to ask you, Gray. I hope you'll say yes."

"What favor, Max?"

"I've decided to make this my last year to ride the Carnival floats. I'm getting too old; let the younger men do it. All that excess and drunkenness, it's really too much for me. But I'd especially like you to see me ride in Comus one last time."

"I'd like to Max, but I have final exams."

"Oh, well, of course it isn't possible." His voice trails off and becomes dreamy, making me feel irrelevant.

"No way, Max. That Carnival stuff has bad associations for me. . . ."

Carnival. I think of when we were young and used to watch Max ride in three parades: Proteus, Momus, Comus. Those names suggest to me change, mockery, and sensual mirth; I can remember standing in wonder at the transformations people underwent to participate. They must have, like Max, felt some particular urgency I didn't understand.

In New Orleans Carnival week begins. It is unseasonably cold; the police are on strike, the hotels full. Mudie sends me clippings from the newspaper that amuse her; in the margins of the photographs are little amusing notes, like "This year's queen of Iris had her jaw wired shut in an attempt to change the krewe's image" and "Remember Bobbie's Krewe of Dementia Praecox at St. Vincent's?" I wad the envelopes up and stow them in my desk drawer; amid the seriousness of Harvard, New Orleans at Carnival time seems lurid and frivolous.

Carnival night Max plans to ride in the Comus parade. Comus, god of mirth, sits waiting in his den among the papier-mâché deities of Carnival. This year's theme is Gods and Heroes of the Empyrean. Max calls me on the phone the night before the parade; he sounds wistful.

"Sure you don't want to catch an early-morning flight?"

"Sorry, Max. I can't. Here I've spent all this time learning ancient Greek, I don't want to blow it now."

"Why did you spend all that time?" Max wants to know. "Were you unhappy with the present? Was it to make us feel inferior?"

I can tell Max has been drinking so I try not to prolong the conversation. But it irks me that both Max and Nathan have made the same suggestion about my life now, even though Nathan's was the more sober explanation. I'm learning ancient languages because there was something about my life that was intolerable to me. In truth, I learned Greek because I felt lost. And now I still feel lost, except when I'm translating Greek. It requires complete absorption.

Tuesday night in New Orleans, the parade edges its way down Claiborne Avenue, flambeaux burning crazily in the freezing air. I am in the library translating Homer. Somehow, between the squiggly lines of text, I see a miniature of the night parade: Max waving, a flare of satin costumes, fire on the February darkness. I have to concentrate to dispel the sensation. When I finish working for the night, I go back to my room. Anna is waiting for me.

"You better call home," she says. She looks serious.

"Why?"

"Just call."

Mudie answers, gives me the news. Max has fallen from the float he was riding and hit his head on the curb. His skull is fractured in three places; he was taken to Touro Infirmary still in his Hermes costume, unconscious. The doctors won't know how extensive the damage is until later. If the brain begins to swell, Mudie says, who knows what will happen? She is only home to pack a suitcase, Bobbie is waiting downstairs to take her back to the hospital.

"*Bobbie* is?"

"Yes, isn't it odd. At the last moment she decided to come home for Carnival," Mudie says. "Naturally she wasn't expecting Max to hurt himself."

The next day I fly home. I take a cab from the airport to Harmony Street, where Hannah is waiting for me; she makes me eat lunch before going to the hospital. To please her, I hide a half sandwich under my chair cushion and pour a cup of tea into Max's prize ficus.

Bobbie and Mudie are at the hospital; they meet me in the coffee shop before taking me to see Max. The whole time, I'm thinking, At least he is still alive, but when I see him, dressed in white pajamas, his head swathed in bandages, I don't feel optimistic. "Is he awake?" I ask Mudie. She shakes her head.

We wait. The pressure inside Max's skull is mounting, the neuro-surgeon says; he may have to operate to relieve it, but he is doubtful he can prevent brain damage altogether. Mudie listens to him, small and dutiful as an obedient child. Do anything, we say.

We wait. Bobbie and I have a cigarette alone in the hall outside Max's room. Bobbie says:

"I must be clairvoyant, Gray. When you mentioned about Max asking you to come home for Mardi Gras, I remembered thinking,

What the hell, these apples aren't going anywhere. I thought of the times he came for me, if you know what I mean. My botched suicides. So I flew home, but when I got here Max and I had this terrific fight, Sunday I think it was, and I went away furious with him. I disappeared into the Quarter—I still have old school friends there, you know—and Thursday night I watched the parade from my friend Toby Debo's balcony. I had no idea what had happened earlier. Then later, around two or three in the morning, I bumped into Toby again, we were both drunk, and he said, 'Bobbie, you better go home.' 'I can't go home,' I said. 'There's been an accident,' he said. 'Go home.' So I went. Hannah was waiting up for me, stiff as a cigar-store Indian in the front hall. She knew I'd come eventually. By then, of course, Max was here. Apparently he had a few and lost his balance on the float. He was supposed to be wearing a safety tether but I guess he forgot."

For two days Max is unconscious. Around midnight, the neurosurgeon comes in, still wearing his evening clothes, and drills four holes in Max's skull, then goes home to wait for results. In the morning, Max wakes up.

I am the last one allowed in to see him; we have been told his condition is still critical and have only been allowed three minutes apiece. When I go in, Max is in a kind of traction, bent at a twenty-degree angle to the bed. He looks pale and rosy; his eyes are unnaturally bright.

"Gray," he says, "glad you could take a few days off from college to see your old man."

"I'm sorry I didn't come earlier, Max. It seemed like the right thing to do."

"Funny, you always did the right thing and Bobbie did the wrong thing."

"And you always seemed to love Bobbie more."

Max closes his eyes, then opens them, with some effort. "Love," he says, "what a mismanaged state of affairs.

"Tell me, what have you been studying? The thing I miss most about my youth is learning things."

"I'm taking Greek."

"I'd forgotten. Say something to me in Greek."

"Oh, Max I don't think so."

"Come on. Anything. I just want to hear you say something in Greek. After all, there was a time I didn't think you'd make it to Harvard."

"Okay. *'Ta agatha kai ta kala diokosein.'* "

"What's it mean?"

" 'We pursue the good and beautiful.' "

Max smiles, closes his eyes. He lies very still, not even a flutter of eyelash, and then the nurse cranes her neck around the door, signaling me it's time to leave. Max's left eye flies open. "Plato," he says.

"Bye, Max, I'll see you later."

"Second daughter," he says, "second only in birth order."

"I'm Gray, remember."

"Gray. I remember we named you after the color of your eyes."

In the coffee shop Mudie is crying. "We have to be strong," she says, although I can tell she doesn't think very much of this wisdom herself; anyway, Mudie's particular frailties have always been a kind of strength, so why should she be different now?

"What'd he say?" Bobbie asks.

"He wanted me to say something in Greek."

"And?"

"So I did. It seemed to make him happy. It seemed to be what he wanted."

"I'm sure deep down, a person knows," Mudie says.

"What will make him happy? I didn't get that feeling," I say. "I got the feeling Max was still trying things out."

Bobbie smiles at this piece of honesty. The old rivalry between us shows like Hannah's gold tooth; the old misunderstanding flourishes. It makes both of us feel better. Mudie's just the opposite; Mudie would rather believe in harmony at a time like this and then have it crumble away later like a casting of lost wax. We all have our own ways.

"It's funny," Bobbie says, "Max seemed to think I was me at different ages. He remembered when I was four I wanted a spider you plugged in that spun its own web. He remembered the white-and-gray dresses we wore and the leather baby shoes. He kept having these crazy memories, completely lucid but crazy. I guess we all get a turn."

I am tempted to cry, but I see Mudie first. She has her fists balled up and is crying like a small child. Bobbie lights her a cigarette, and Mudie even looks like a naughty six-year-old smoking it; the gesture raises all our spirits.

In the downstairs lobby Bobbie gives me some money. I've flown in from Cambridge without any; as usual, Bobbie has these mysterious rolls of bills.

"He's going to die," I say.

"No."

That night Mudie and I go home to sleep; Bobbie waits at the hospital, in the hall outside Max's room. It is around midnight when we open the front door; the moon shining through the glass atrium casts long flickering shadows—first Mudie's, then mine—on Max's hardwood floor. "Plato wrote that we are all living inside a cave and that what we see and take for real are only shadows like these, but because we can never see the source of the light throwing the shadows, we don't know that they are only shadows, and not real." I hear myself giving Mudie this explanation, watch how she nods and watches the shadows herself.

"You know," she says, "the other morning before your father left, I got out of the shower and came into the bedroom naked, and he looked at me as if I were a fresh sight or as if he'd just seen something in me he'd never seen before, some loveliness I guess, and he didn't even have to say anything. I knew immediately." She smiles. "I suppose that's what marriage is. Shedding old layers."

Max is in the hospital three days; Mudie, Bobbie, and I take turns waiting in the corridor outside his room. At rare intervals one of us is allowed in to see him, but after my first conversation with him he doesn't say much. He lies banked in pillows, head swathed in white bandages, while the doctors monitor the pressure inside his skull. On the third day there is a crisis. Max develops a high fever and begins to vomit. He begins to speak in long wandering sentences about events and people that are entirely strange to us. The nurses don't want to let us in to see him, but Bobbie and I insist; Mudie is at home taking a bath.

We go in, and there is Max, looking the same as he has the past three days except there is something diminished about him, something that reminds me of an empty shirtsleeve. "My girls," he says fondly when we are close enough to be recognized; one of his eyes is covered by the bandages.

"We're here, Max," Bobbie says.

Max draws a relieved breath. "I was just going over the plans for the new shopping center with Virginia here . . ."

"Who's Virginia?" Bobbie whispers.

"I don't know."

". . . and I think it's going to be unlike any shopping development in the country."

"Yes, Max," Bobbie says.

Max goes on: "There is some trouble I'm having at the moment, a minor thing really, something I'm sure can be corrected later on. Something's leaking. It must be the damn—" Here he breaks off and looks in bewilderment around the room. "Where am I?" he demands.

"At Touro Infirmary, Max," Bobbie says. "You fell off a float, remember."

"No," Max says, "it's just this damn—"

Now we are converged on by a flurry of interns and nurses; one taking Max's pulse, another listening to his heartbeat, a third watching the monitors hooked up with electrodes to his temples. "I'm afraid we're going to have to ask you to leave the room," one of the interns says.

"Is he dying?" Bobbie asks.

"He could be."

"We're staying," Bobbie says.

"I'm afraid you're making things very difficult," the intern says.

"Good," Bobbie says.

We let them work around us. Max drifts back into sleep, the crisis passes, and soon Mudie returns from home with a fresh change of clothes. The minute she sees Max, she knows.

"When did this happen?" she asks.

"Just now," Bobbie says. "He was talking about some shopping center he was designing, and then he said something was leaking."

"They tried to get us to leave," I explained.

"Nobody's leaving," Mudie says.

We spend the night in the hospital. Around dawn, I am sleeping hunched in a chair in the hall when I see Mudie come out of Max's room. "He's gone," she says. "He had a very restless night and then about ten minutes ago he opened his eyes, and then he closed them again."

Bobbie and I are just sitting there in the hallway, which has begun to bustle with early-morning efficiency; Mudie just sinks down next to us on the floor like a child waiting for the camp bus, and around us flows a steady stream of nurses and residents, some going off duty, others coming on. Through the far windows slatted with venetian blinds, we can see the rosy sky turn a definite blue. Eventually Mudie says, "Where is everybody?" and the resident magically appears and reads Max's vital signs and pronounces him dead. I don't want to look at him but I do anyway in case later on I don't believe it happened, and then somebody covers him with a sheet. Mudie goes to sign forms; Bobbie and I sit in the coffee shop and read the *Times-Picayune* until Mudie returns. Then there's nothing left to do but drive home.

Hannah is waiting in the kitchen. Nobody had to tell her to polish the silver and make a huge urn of coffee; she's done that already, and laid out fresh clothes for me and Bobbie. Mudie goes in the library and starts making calls; I hear her voice, low and definite, through the library door. I stop in on my way upstairs to bathe. "Can I do anything?" I ask. Mudie shakes her head no. Then she says, "Does anybody know what Max's last words were?"

"I think Bobbie was the last one he spoke to."

Bobbie comes in and sits down. "Try to think," Mudie says, "what Max's last words were."

Bobbie thinks a minute. "He said, 'It's just this damn—' and then he broke off. I guess he couldn't think of the words."

" 'It's just this damn—?' " Mudie repeats.

"That's right," Bobbie says. "Those were his exact words."

Mudie sits thinking. She traces a few ivy leaves on the phone pad, doodling as if she has all the time in the world, and then a slow smile comes over her face. " 'It's just this damn—' " she says with amusement. "How like Max."

It only takes Mudie a few phone calls, and then by that mysterious process of gossip and telepathy in New Orleans, everybody seems to know the news. Flowers begin arriving, the phone rings, Max's picture gets printed on the front page of the afternoon *States Item* under the heading

PROMINENT ARCHITECT DIES
FALL PROVES FATAL

The house is thick with relatives—weird uncles and peculiar cousins I have never seen before or haven't seen since I was a child; they must be part of what Aunt Byrd called the vast ruinous empire of idiots and savants. Idiots mostly. Sunlight and relatives come pouring in the front door, where Hannah stands taking coats, directing casseroles and flowers to the kitchen. In the library a fire is burning; Bobbie and I lock the door to have a moment's privacy. Bobbie spots a box of chocolates on Max's desk.

"So," she says, "he wasn't too mad at me after all."

"Who, Max?"

"After we had that tremendous fight I sent him that box of chocolates, part joke, part peace offering." Bobbie opens the box and shows me that two chocolates are missing. "See, if he had been really mad at me, he wouldn't have eaten any."

"Funny, Max dying from a fall in a Carnival parade. In a way it seems so abrupt."

"You know," Bobbie says, "his death was entirely appropriate. He died from his love of old customs and gaieties."

"Stupid, his not wearing his safety vest."

"Exactly."

"You know, I always thought he would die young."

"I never thought he could die," Bobbie says.

"Gods and Heroes of the Empyrean," I say. "A fitting theme for the parade."

"I wonder what Max would have to say about a man who falls from a Carnival float and breaks his skull in three places," Bobbie says.

"So heroic. Have you ever noticed what ridiculous deaths heroes die? They never just have a heart attack or anything," I say.

"He was just pursuing the good and beautiful."

"By the way, the funeral parlor called. They want somebody to come pick out a casket."

"We'll both go," Bobbie says. "I can't imagine Mudie doing it, can you?"

"No."

Bobbie puts the lid back on the box of chocolates and gives a desultory poke at the fire. I think we both have the feeling that there is more to say than the things either one of us can think of, but our brains fail us. Bobbie traces Max's well-worn path on the rug, a perfect oval smoothed by years of worry. "The house that Max built," she says.

At the funeral parlor we are given cups of coffee in good English china cups and shown a variety of coffins. This embarrasses both of us; we have no idea which one to choose. We are only vaguely guided by the principle that Max wouldn't want anything tacky, but when it comes to coffins, who can tell? After about the fifteenth one, Bobbie starts poking me in the ribs, and I start feeling uncontrollable waves of laughter rise, like unbidden nausea. There is even one coffin, lead-gray and seamless-looking, that we're told is strong enough to survive a nuclear holocaust. This is the end. Bobbie drags me and the funeral-parlor director back into another room and points to a plain oak coffin. She doesn't say anything. The funeral director nods and makes a notation on his pad. Then Bobbie says, "Let's get out of here. Fast."

We drive down to the foot of Canal Street and sit watching the ferry negotiate the hard current of the river. The boat must make a wide arc upstream before gently eddying down to clank on target with the pier on the other bank. A cool rain comes up, so we leave; we stop for coffee at the Morning Call and then Bobbie says, "I guess we better go back. God, those people give me the creeps. All those aunts and uncles Max hated when he was alive, pawing over him like this."

"It's death. It makes people act funny."

Back on Harmony Street, the daytime visitors have been replaced by a fresh crop. Mudie is upstairs lying down, so there is a note of suppressed hilarity in the conversations, which I think Max would like. One of my first cousins, a boy I knew as Garner, now twenty-four, tall and loping as a Modigliani, corners me in the dining room near a *daube glacé*. "Gray," he says, more passionately than I like to hear, "you were always such a lovely girl. A shame we're cousins."

"Not really."

He doesn't take the hint. He is wearing a bow tie, in imitation of Max I suppose, and I can smell scotch on his breath. He leans over close to my ear,

"The heart is unexplored territory," he says.

"Not mine."

Bobbie smirks at me from behind a vase of heather. "That your sister Bobbie?" Garner asks.

"Yes."

"I thought she was a schizophrenic."

The word hurts, especially today. "Wasn't she in Mandeville or some place like that?" he says.

"There's no place *like* that," I say. "She was in Mandeville."

"Let's hope it doesn't run in families," Garner says.

I look right at him. "It does. And now, if you'll excuse me."

"Catch you later," Garner says.

"Not if I can help it."

I go and lock myself in an upstairs bathroom, sink down into the tub with all my clothes on, and cry. I've been in there about twenty-five minutes when Bobbie knocks on the door and says, "You all right? Not drowned, are you?"

I open the door. Bobbie has a plate of watercress sandwiches and a bottle of champagne. From the pocket of Mudie's silk dress (borrowed for the occasion) she produces a sturdy joint. We lock the door and sit in the bathtub and smoke the joint and drink the champagne and eat the sandwiches. It helps, a little.

"People are such jerks," I say eventually.

"That Garner Maubry. You know, he was practically trying to seduce me," Bobbie says. "He probably thinks former mental patients are easy prey."

"Just part of the vast ruinous empire."

"Guess what his line was? He came up to me and whispered in my ear, 'The heart is unexplored territory.'"

"Used the same line on me. What does he think he is, the D. H. Lawrence of the Delta?"

Bobbie giggles. Here in the white bathroom with the last of the poor sunshine and our unaccustomed good clothes and the last of Max's champagne and Max's fading presence and our two selves relieved for the first time since birth of the burden of pleasing Max, we feel curiously bereft and light. It is not sadness that overtakes us, nor yet loss, it is more like a subtle alteration in the earth's gravity that finally allows us to rise in unison from the enormous white bathtub and walk together down the back stairs to join the other guests.

Part 5

one

After Max dies Mudie moves to New York, becomes as skittery and shy as a spider. From her loft apartment she looks out at the night sky, against which the great web of a city stands illumined. "I'm finally here," she says, telephoning me in Cambridge. "It's possible I may be twenty-five years too late. Maybe not."

The house on Harmony Street is sold, Max and Mudie's artwork carefully crated and stored, Max's old Mercedes traded in. Mudie moved to New York with the idea of picking up her sculpting career where she left off, nearly twenty-five years earlier, when she met Max and moved back to New Orleans. She doesn't go out much; she spends two hours a week on the phone long-distance to Dr. Haven, her psychiatrist.

For some people as anxious as Mudie, New York would be a

nightmare; Mudie comes to find the narrow eyelets of light comforting, and the way people live tunneled in, streaming back and forth from work at regular intervals, suits her fine. Her loft faces north, with plenty of natural light.

I am in my last year at Harvard. It seems pointless with Max gone to be doing this, more pointless to quit, so I stay in Cambridge and work on my thesis. Bobbie is back in Eureka Springs, not picking apples anymore but running a shop that boasts 101 varieties of pasta.

After Max died my biggest fear was what his death would do to Bobbie, but Bobbie has not taken it the way I thought; she lives carefully, as if aware that at any moment her life could derail. It gives her a sense of purpose that I lack, a sense that Mudie finds in her work; of the three of us, Mudie seems the best. She *knows* she's lost without Max, and gives herself up to her new bewildering situation. She doesn't pretend to be whole; she lets herself be shattered like a carelessly fired piece of pottery.

One Friday she calls, asks me to come to New York for the weekend. I'm glad to get out of Cambridge, away from my notecards and my sense of having nothing important in my life. Nathan Kentor I rarely see anymore. He has girlfriends; he waves to me from across the Quadrangle. Occasionally he stops to talk, but not often. Sometimes I think I see in his sideways glance a twist of longing or at least curiosity, but I can't bring myself to act on it.

When Nathan told me he was ending our relationship, first he mocked the word "relationship," then he told me, somewhat gently, that he couldn't commit himself to someone he couldn't trust. I guess he meant the whole haphazard way I was living. "It was your idea in the first place," I told him, "wasn't it? 'Extend the borders of your personality'?"

Nathan smiled his rueful smile and kissed me. I could tell he wanted to sleep with me once more but the puritan splinter in his nature stopped him. Instead he shredded a cigarette butt. "I know I should be laid-back about this whole thing, like a Californian."

"Why can't you be?"

"I could try. But one day Southern pigheadedness would surface and I'd throw it in your face. I'm sorry, Gray."

On Friday night Mudie and I are sitting in her loft, which like most lofts has a big exposed-brick wall; the other walls are painted cerise, the floors white. Mudie sits wrapped in one of Max's old Brooks Brothers sweaters, charcoal gray with a hole in the elbow. She's wearing a denim skirt and black stockings; her hair, lustrous and unkempt as usual, has begun to sparkle with threads of white. She sits hunched in an armchair, drinking coffee.

"I signed up for a class today," she says casually, "a bronze class with a woman whose work I really admire."

"Mudie, that's tremendous."

"I don't know about tremendous, but it's a start. I'm a little uncertain about taking the bus, but I'll manage somehow. You know, some days I practically forget I'm agoraphobic."

"Max would be proud."

"*I'm proud*," Mudie says.

I know what she means. Here, all this time we were so concerned about pleasing Max, we sometimes lost ourselves. I'm one example. Since I gave up the idea of becoming a doctor I can't think what else to do. Sometimes, remembering Bobbie's private intensity, I write in my journal, but even writing seems an activity borrowed from Bobbie, something I will never do as well as she can.

"You know," Mudie says, as if she can tell what I'm thinking, "I like the things you write."

"Bobbie's a much better writer."

"I don't think so."

"No?"

"She was precocious when you girls were younger, yes. But your things are truer."

"I wrote a story once that got published in the St. Rita's paper," I say. "It was about the time Bobbie deliberately let my kite loose in the sky. I guess I thought if I wrote about it, I'd learn something I didn't know before. It's like dumping out the contents of an old drawer and sifting through the pieces."

"What did you learn?" Mudie asks.

"That it was okay to be angry at Bobbie. That she wasn't such a goddess. That my own perceptions were as valid as hers."

"I wish you'd write more," Mudie says.

"Max asked me not to. When my story came out in the paper he called me into the library and said I shouldn't write about Bobbie because I might say things that would hurt her. There didn't seem to be anything else to write about, so I stopped."

Mudie smiles. "There was one thing I never understood about your father until recently. He had this tremendous vulnerability, which he covered up. He tried to escape his own rigid expectations by foisting them off on other people; that way, he was left a measure of freedom. Here I was married to him for years and never grasped that simple thing about him."

"All that stuff about Bobbie, how she had to be a genius and go to some Ivy League school?"

"Fear, mostly," Mudie says. "When he realized that something was different about Bobbie, that she wasn't going to fit the mold, he got scared. He made impossible standards for her, not that she isn't gifted enough to fulfill them, but she can't because she isn't made that way emotionally. Max didn't see it."

"You mean, part of the reason he didn't have those same expectations for me was because he wasn't afraid for me?"

"Partly," Mudie says.

I sit thinking, realize that the reason Max didn't want me writing about Bobbie was that it hurt *him* to read what I wrote; most of all it bothered him that Bobbie wasn't the perfect child he'd envisioned. So many of his actions went to protect himself, not her, and maybe that's what protection is for parents. Someday, Hannah used to say, there will come a time when I'm dead and gone, and who will learn to look after you if you don't learn to yourself? Hannah knew about protection, more than Max did. Max was always living in buildings that, however beautiful, leaked when it rained. Maybe it was the desire for protection that led Max to become an architect in the first place; for what is a building, if not protection?

I go back to Cambridge missing Max less. Here I thought I'd devote my entire senior year to grieving for him; surprisingly, I find days on which I manage not to think about him. I have this one image that haunts me like a memory, only it isn't a memory since I wasn't there.

First, flambeaux carriers pad down St. Charles Avenue with their lolling aggressive gait, dripping flames so close to the Carnival floats it seems as if they catch on fire, only it isn't fire, it's the sparkle and gaiety of the floats themselves, a pocket of fire on a dark Thursday night. Max's float rounds the bend to make the journey up the opposite side of the street, and I follow it, yelling after the float, "Throw me something! Throw me something, mister!" only Max doesn't hear.

The crowd is roaring with that mixture of anger and satisfaction unique to Carnival parades, and just when I'm about to give up trying to catch Max's attention, he sees me, reaches into his satin bag of throws and flings a handful of glass beads high into the air, hitting me. Only somehow, at the height of his arc, he loses his balance and stumbles forward so that the favor he's throwing isn't a tangle of glass beads or a gold doubloon or even a child's fake rubber dagger, but himself, falling through the faces and hands and smiles and looks of amazement, and all the while he falls he wears a smile of perfect happiness, as if he knows he will never reach the ground.

He does, of course, and the rest is my memory of what really happened after I flew home to see Max. The events of those days are interleaved with my last year in Cambridge, illuminating or darkening the day according to no particular pattern. Grief isn't all unhappiness; I have days of unexplained bliss.

. . .

In early May Mudie calls me from New York. Bobbie has disappeared again; she wants to know whether I have heard from her recently and whether there was a postmark or anything that might tell us where she is.

"I'm not so much worried about her," Mudie says, "but I just don't like the feeling of not knowing where she is."

"Have we ever known?"

"Probably not. Frankly, I feel guilty toward Max's memory for letting her disappearance go this long. All her friends in Eureka Springs say they have no idea. 'You know Bobbie,' they told me. I don't know whether I do or not."

"Don't worry, she'll surface," I say.

My last term at Cambridge I spend writing my thesis and speculating about Bobbie. Maybe she's holed up in Europe somewhere, taking acting classes from a mysterious, talented director—his name was Ravenel—she once told me about. Maybe she has a car dealership. She could have done something like go to law school, or shave all her hair off and join some strange Eastern religion. I remember once she had her hair dyed blue, cerulean blue, to protest Max's desire for her conformity. That was in the days when he wanted us to conform; sometimes it was hard to tell *what* he wanted. But as usual, what Max wanted mattered to us both.

I go for walks by the Charles River and watch the crew team rowing; from a distance they look like ungainly spiders skating the dark water. There is something in these days that feels like fate; I have the sensation of beginning to separate from my life like a paper backing soaked in water. The layers separate and rise. Mudie calls again a few weeks later and says that she still hasn't found Bobbie and it's occurred to her we may never find Bobbie. "This may be her way to choose freedom," she says. "If she's not around people who know what her problem is, then the problem doesn't exist."

"Maybe we're the problem," I say.

"How could that be?" Mudie asks.

"Think about it."

Max isn't around to organize a search for her this time, and for some reason Mudie doesn't want to. Maybe she's in the process of separating, like me, only she has so many layers it's like stripping the wallpaper from an old house: You stand in pain and amazement at the evidence from the past.

One thing that happened after Max's funeral I think about a lot. It's a piece of information; I carry it around with me like a talisman, rubbing it for luck. The day of Max's funeral we walked back to the house from the church; guests had begun to arrive, and the house had a startled ungainly quality, as if it weren't used to the loss yet. Darwin Kentor rang the doorbell and I answered it. "Darwin," I said. He stood there in his tan raincoat, looking like a crane, and then folded his arms around me and said, "You know, Gray, you always were your father's favorite."

"Me?"

"I'll bet you didn't know that."

"No. I always thought Bobbie was."

Darwin chuckled, pleased at himself for having come to the funeral of his best friend bearing a gift; he touched my cheek and said, "No need to tell Bobbie."

"I won't."

I looked around for Darwin later on; I wanted to ask him more about what Max had confided to him about me, but he had gone. I wanted to throw my head back and laugh, the way you do at rain when it has already soaked through your clothes, because that was the way I felt about Max's love for me. He was a man of such secrets, of carefully prepared subterfuges and passions, a man whose actions couldn't be read as an index to his feelings. I thought, just briefly, of all I'd ever done to try to please him, to try to take Bobbie's place in his affections so that he wouldn't feel the loss of her as keenly, and what had I done? I'd robbed him of a second daughter. I'd robbed myself too, except that the life I'd stolen still seemed much better than the one I'd left behind, only loosely fitting and inconvenient, like having to be good, like taking certain vows and receiving, in return, a modest grace.

One afternoon, late in March, a letter comes from Bobbie. She is living in Tulsa, Oklahoma, learning to be a neon-sign artist. "I moved to Tulsa when Franklin ran over my dog named Blue and wiped out my bank account. I'm sharing an apartment with an Irish woman my age whose hair turned permanently white when she was nineteen. Her name's Chelsea. I hope you are finishing up at Harvard in fine style and will soon come visit me. On second thought, don't visit me. I'm afraid you'll find my circumstances both humble and bizarre. Love, Bobbie."

I call Mudie immediately. "Bobbie's in Tulsa, Oklahoma."

"In where?"

"Tulsa."

"I thought that was in the middle of the desert."

"Maybe it is."

Then we don't hear anything for a while. In June Max's lawyer calls me to get Bobbie's correct address. Five business days later a check arrives for sixty-four thousand dollars: my inheritance from Max. The phone rings.

"How can they do this?" Bobbie says.

"Do what?"

"Cut Max down to a piece of paper?"

"They can't."

"I guess not." Bobbie's end goes quiet. "The sixty-four-thousand-dollar question. How long will a man lie in the earth ere he rot?"

"It's been over a year since he died," I say.

"I wonder where Max is now. Looking down on us and thinking what a screwup I am." The rapid switch in tone is typical of Bobbie; I can't think of anything to say.

"What are you going to do with yours?" Bobbie asks.

"I don't know yet. Remember I once wanted to go to medical school? I don't have the heart for it, or anything."

"I'm buying a nightclub," Bobbie says, "I'm calling it Baby Green's Last Evening in Paris."

"Max would love it."

"No," Bobbie says, "Max wouldn't. Max wouldn't love it at all. He wanted me to be perfect, see, and now he's not here to badger me about it. I survived *him*."

We hang up and Mudie calls, worried that Bobbie is going to waste her inheritance on something frivolous. "I think she's buying a business," I reassure her, only partly lying.

"Yes, but you know Bobbie," Mudie says.

"Mudie, it's Bobbie's money. If she wants to lose it, let her."

"I guess so."

Graduation day in Cambridge it's ninety-four degrees. Mudie takes the train from New York to watch me receive my diploma; actually, there are too many students for each of us to be named personally, so I stand with the rest of my class while the sun beats down on us. Our names are printed in the program. The day has an aura of sadness, of festivity, like the puberty rites I read about in one of my anthropology classes. Across the trampled courtyard I see Nathan with his parents. He waves to me sheepishly, gesturing with his wrinkled copy of the program, congratulations, regret.

"Do you want to go talk to him?" Mudie asks.

"No."

Afterward we go to the president's reception. Mudie is wearing a blue-and-white silk dress and a straw hat. She looks like one of the students. I feel as if I'm Mudie's age. "I wish Max were here to see you," Mudie says.

"Me too. Max and Bobbie."

"I think it would be hard for her," Mudie says.

"You know, this whole thing was Bobbie's idea," I say.

"What, Harvard?"

"When Bobbie was hospitalized she told me I had to take her place, go on and do what Max wanted for her."

"I can't believe that," Mudie says, looking bewildered. The possibility that things didn't just happen to people, that people made plans and followed them, was always foreign to her.

"I wanted Max to love me, you see," I explain.

"He did."

"It's such a waste, his not being here to see me graduate."

"Nothing you do is ever a waste," Mudie says. She smiles and shakes the president's hand, and then we turn away toward a large cut-glass bowl of punch. "Only it sometimes takes years before we recognize the value of what we've done," Mudie adds.

We spend the night in Boston, at the Ritz. Mudie feels comfortable here. We stay in and order room service and watch television and talk about my future. I can't help thinking about Bobbie, and about how she stayed in this hotel when she was in Boston for psychiatric tests. How different our two lives are. I'm sure she doesn't wonder about me; she probably assumes I have everything worked out. I used to, but all that's changed. I don't have any plans now, only a way of seeing.

Mudie goes back to New York; I stay a few weeks in Boston. A few weeks become months; I can't seem to leave Cambridge. I get a job working in the university counsel's office; we mostly defend against claims by irate graduate students deprived of their doctorates. It's an easy job, with plenty of time off. My inheritance check from Max sits in my desk drawer, uncashed. Sixty-four thousand dollars. Sometimes I take it out and look at the number and wonder how it can seem so small, such scant compensation, for the man who left it to me.

Nathan goes on to graduate school at Johns Hopkins. He sends me postcards, to which I don't necessarily respond. For reasons I don't entirely understand, Nathan's ambitions are as strong as ever while mine seem to have evaporated. I spend a week at the end of August on Martha's Vineyard with Anna. She is going to study film at NYU; we build fires on the beach and watch the dry twigs twitch and burn far into the evening. Mornings, the fog is in; I walk around mute and damp, suffering the longings of every person who has ever grown up.

Fall in Cambridge is worse than expected; the infusion of new students reminds me that I don't belong here, that I am only borrowing time. With Max dead, Bobbie gone, and Nathan at Johns Hopkins, I can't seem to get a fix on things. I keep looking for a call from Bobbie—or, worse, a glimpse of Max on the street. I imagine that Max isn't dead, that he has only escaped his life and will show up eventually wearing that familiar suit the color of rice paper and his lavender bow tie: cheerfulness in the face of dolor.

One afternoon in November, I get the idea that what is wrong with my life has to do with Nathan Kentor. As soon as it strikes me, the idea that I am still in love with him seems fine. I get out a pen and write him a letter telling him that I was wrong, that I still love him, that it is scarlet and yellow in Cambridge, that I'm sorry for the nakedness of my letter. I mail the letter and sit on the edge of my bed. Ten days later, a letter comes back.

Baltimore
13 November

Dear Gray,

First of all let me say that I appreciated the openness of your letter. A letter like yours I'd certainly never write! It surprised me coming from you; you were always at least as reticent as I am, possibly more so.

To be honest, when I found out that you were still in love with me, I was not overjoyed; I didn't swirl a hat rack around the room in a series of mock dance steps as someone in my position would have done in the movies. I greeted your revelation with a mixture of sadness and happiness, the latter because the admission came at all, the former because it came too late.

To back up somewhat, you must know that after we drifted

apart in Cambridge, I was too stiff to come after you and say, "Hey, what is this?" Instead I tried to be philosophical. "These things happen," I thought, and figured in a few months, I'd rebound. After all, who can expect a love that began in childhood to survive into adulthood? So, I was modern. I got other girlfriends, I moved on.

And yet, the whole time there was this undercurrent of feeling reserved for you. I kept thinking I'd wake up from modern life and find you there. I was wrong. Then, when your father died, I had this inkling (forgive me) that there might be a chance. I wanted to come for the funeral, but common sense forbade me. After all, nobody wants to be a fool twice over. I bided my time but nothing came. I came to the conclusion that I was right, it really was the twentieth century.

Our graduation from Harvard was a freakish time for me. Here I was involved with a girl from Smith (her name's Vicky) and I was spending all this time with her, and she was in Cambridge a lot too. Well, when it came time for me to graduate, I'd been visiting Vicky at Smith and I got this manic urge to see you, so I hopped on my bicycle and rode all the way back to Cambridge. It was early morning when I got there, my parents were arriving shortly, I had a million things to do, but I sat in my empty room and dialed your number. There kept being no answer. I went outside and sat on the hood of a yellow Volkswagen and drank a carton of chocolate milk and watched the scene: jubilant students, workmen setting up a million folding chairs, Bach blaring from an open window, and then when a supercilious preppy sneered at me I thought, What the hell am I doing here waiting for Gray? I had things to do, people to say good-bye to, a girlfriend to make plans with, and here I was mooning after somebody who had forgotten I existed. Plus there was the anxiety that if I did find you, you might have changed. For all I knew you might have dyed your hair blond or have twisted sexual habits or be a member of the American Nazi Party or be into TM or chew tobacco. I took a deep breath. Then I slid off the hood of that Volkswagen and walked back to my room and called Vicky. She was wondering where I'd gone.

Did I tell you how I came to be involved with Vicky? Vicky I met halfway through college, maybe later, at some party. She had a good friend at Harvard who, as it happened, lived in my dorm.

I knew for a while she was interested in me, but I steered clear out of shyness; Vicky was sophisticated, had been around, lived on the East Side, wore contact lenses, dresses, and heels. Plus there was other-womanism; I knew she wouldn't want to see me as long as I was with somebody else, so I hung up my cleats with Joanna (your successor) and started sleeping with Vicky.

This year our affair blossomed. There was this jaded-seniors, end-of-college flavor to everything we did; we had lost our innocence and were scared about life. Vicky came every weekend. We had little to do, so we spent all day in bed. We sat up late and watched the May stars. We saw the sun rise and drove around the Boston suburbs taking in Little League games. I don't know what I thought, but somehow I imagined I'd have this last fling with Vicky conducted at breakneck speed and intensity and then it would be over. I guessed there'd be a note on the kitchen table some afternoon—"So long, it's been swell"—but I must have underestimated her. A week before graduation she declared herself In Love and asked me to marry her. Charmed by the reversal, I said yes. It was strange, but the moment I said it, I knew it wouldn't come true, the way certain spells in fairy tales make the opposite of the desired thing happen. I said yes, but I thought, What about Gray?

You probably have no idea what Vicky is like; perhaps you think she is just another Easterner with nervous habits; spoiled, with an overrefined sensibility and aspirations toward art. Her parents will (and do) do anything for her. She is the bright spot in an otherwise blighted marriage; next year she's going to France to study art restoration. And yet, neither is she the typical Jewish American Princess. Did you know that she makes great lemon chicken and hits a baseball farther than I can? She likes people to think she is frail, that she has delicate poise, and she has, but she has more. She is, additionally, the sort of person who remembers to say "neither/nor" on an answering machine and wraps her toenail clippings in a neat square of white gauze.

So where do we stand in all of this? Where do Nathan Kentor and Gray Maubry figure in the modern age? My conclusion is that you are mistaken: You don't really love me anymore, only the idea of me, and it is really nostalgia for your father that prompted you to write. I could be wrong but I don't think so.

It would have been a rare thing, marrying you. Our lives would have been one unbroken seam running back to childhood. I'm going to miss knowing everything about you, the narrative line your life will take; yet it strikes me that after all, mine is a journalist's regret, not a lover's.

As ever,

Nathan

two

The last day of November, Bobbie calls. She tells me she is back in Eureka Springs, in the hospital with a collapsed lung. She needs money. Her voice on the phone sounds offhand and faraway, a daydreaming child's. I tell her not to worry, I can send her some money, and then I think better of it and throw some clothes into the old Danish schoolboy's bag Mudie once gave her for Christmas. I get in the car and begin the drive to Eureka Springs, and the whole time I'm driving I have this tremendous sense of purpose, and there is nothing I wouldn't do for Bobbie.

The hills are still green this time of year, with piebald spots, and most of the leaves have fallen. When I get to Fayetteville, I ask where the hospital Bobbie mentioned is and drive there. The information desk tells me there is no patient registered by the name of Bobbie Maubry.

I go into town. There's a hotel called the New Orleans Hotel, and when I drive up in front, Bobbie's sitting on the front steps smoking a cigarette. She sees me and gives an embarrassed smile. "Graycat," she chides me, "I never thought you'd actually *come*."

"You said you were sick."

"I was. A mild exaggeration."

"A powerful odor of mendacity, if you ask me."

Bobbie smiles, throws an arm around me. I don't soften immediately. "I thought you were dying," I say.

"No more than usual," Bobbie says.

We both laugh, and then I know that it's happened. Bobbie and I are no longer fused. We're separate people. I can't point to the exact moment it happened. Maybe over time, as Bobbie pulled away, I got a chance to develop into Gray, something I'd been unable to do as a child.

Bobbie's even thinner than usual, and her hair is cut so short it stands out in little burrs; the sight of her, so vulnerable and so enduring, makes me think of a young saint. Bobbie dispels the idea immediately.

"Frankly, it'd have been a hell of a lot better if you'd just sent money," she says. "Not that I'm not thrilled to see you, Gray."

"Is Max's money all gone?" I ask.

"Mostly. I got involved with some people in Tulsa who were going to make me rich. Instead, they made me poor." Bobbie gives a slight laugh.

"I'm sorry," I say.

"I'm not. That money always gave me the creeps, as if Max was looking over my shoulder to see if I could handle it."

I take out my checkbook and write her a check for three hundred dollars and hand it over, to get this part of the afternoon over with right away. Bobbie takes the check. "Is it enough?" I ask.

"It's plenty. Thanks. I'll pay you back sometime. It's just this . . ."

"Just this damn," I say.

"Just this damn . . ." Bobbie looks away, up at the newly washed windows of the hotel, so clean they reflect the November sky back at us, and the fallen leaves, and the bright colors of our two down jackets, red and apple-green.

"I guess you want the truth," Bobbie says.

"Not necessarily."

"I was raped again. As if once wasn't enough. I borrowed money for an abortion. There's this old beauty parlor in town they turned into an abortion clinic."

"I'm sorry."

"The place still has hot pink walls and funky gold-drizzled tiles and mirrors everywhere."

"God."

"The guy who raped me. When he was done his friend started unzipping *his* pants. I just looked at him. 'If you had any idea what I've been though, you wouldn't do this,' I told him. And you know what? The guy looked miserably at the ground, sort of scuffed at the dirt with the toe of his boot, and zipped himself back up without touching me. So I guess there is mercy, of a limited sort."

"Jesus, Bobbie."

"Don't tell Mudie. I don't want her knowing."

"Why not?"

"I want to protect her from such ugliness."

"Okay."

"I'm going away for a while," Bobbie says.

"Any idea where?"

Bobbie thinks a minute, then smiles. I can tell she's thought of a place she wants to go, but doesn't like the idea of telling me; maybe she thinks as long as I know where she is, she won't be free.

"I'll send you a postcard when I get there," Bobbie says. "Wherever *it* is."

"Look, I understand."

Bobbie fixes me with her bright inquiring gaze. "I wonder if you really do."

"I try. I know I can't understand everything."

"Never mind," Bobbie says, waving, "you wouldn't want to."

We sit on the lawn and smoke. Now that I've been here and seen Bobbie and given her what money I have, there seems nothing else to do. Bobbie asks, "How's Mudie?"

"Doing better than I expected. I can't explain it, but since Max died she's come into her own. She has her first show next week."

"Is she going to be able to go to it?"

"I think so."

"Good. I always wondered if it had anything to do with me, her not being able to go places."

There are places I want to go, too, but I don't talk about them with Bobbie. It seems enough this afternoon for the two of us to sit on the lawn and feel the grass get cold, smoke cigarettes and exchange pieces of conversation that to anybody listening would be of no importance. Once, I tell Bobbie she shouldn't smoke so much, and she tells me I shouldn't be so critical, and then it gets too cold for both of us to stay out any longer, and Bobbie says, "Hey, I'll buy you dinner." The lights in the hotel have begun to come on, and from where we are sitting outside we can see through the long wavy windows the headwaiter polishing a spot on one of the glasses.

"Come on," Bobbie says, "I'm starving."

In New York Mudie sells her first sculpture. At the gallery opening she stands next to the owner, looking shy but radiant; she touches a wall with two fingers, as if for added support. The room is fairly full; she sells two more pieces, and there's interest in a fourth.

Afterward we make supper in her kitchen. It's midnight; Mudie draws the blinds on the muzzy all-night sky. "What do you hear from Bobbie?"

"I saw her three weeks ago."

Mudie cracks an egg. "How did you find her?"

"She called me. She needed some money."

"Already?"

I intend to lie but it's hard to lie to Mudie; she knows me too well. "Bobbie was raped and had to have an abortion. She'd borrowed some money—God knows what's happened to Max's money—and needed to pay the friend back."

"She told you she was raped."

"That's right."

"I'm sure in her mind she was," Mudie says.

"You mean, you don't believe her?"

"I don't know," Mudie says. "Bobbie sometimes invents things when they suit her needs."

"But this—?"

"I'm saying it's possible," Mudie says.

In bed that night I think it over. Bobbie's story, Mudie's refusal to believe the story, my trip to Eureka Springs to save Bobbie—which parts were true? At first it shocked me that Mudie seemed so callous about Bobbie, that her only response was to chop up more avocado for the salad and pour an extra glass of wine, but then what? Maybe Mudie is right and Bobbie has invented the story to satisfy something in her mind she needs. Maybe, too, Mudie is protecting herself from feeling for Bobbie; maybe in this new life she needs to spend all she has just on herself.

I meet Anna for lunch. She waves at me from a corner table; her current boyfriend, Raymond, is with her. Raymond is a piano student at Juilliard and looks shrunken next to Anna.

"Gray," Anna says, shoving a chair at me, "you won't believe the decision I've just made. I'm moving to Chicago."

"Chicago?"

"The Art Institute has a much better film program than the one here."

"But you like New York."

Anna makes a face and orders another glass of wine. "Make it a bottle," she tells the waiter, "we're celebrating."

Raymond looks at me. I shrug my shoulders; what did he expect of Anna? He must know how quickly she acts upon a whim. "My psychiatrist says it's an attempt to get away from my mother, but who cares?" Anna says. "I'm sick of being so analyzed all the time."

Raymond and I both laugh; nothing about Anna is predictable except her style of jumping from one enthusiasm to another.

"Why don't you come with me?" Anna asks me.

"To Chicago?"

"Why not?"

"What's in Chicago?"

"What's in Cambridge?"

"It's cold in Chicago," I remind her.

Anna blinks, impervious. "It's cold everyplace," she says. "The object is to find some point of warmth."

After lunch we say good-bye; I wish Raymond luck on his upcoming scholarship competition. He looks resigned to losing Anna; perhaps he's even relieved. Anna kisses me, gives me a sheet of paper with her Chicago address on it, and hails a cab. "You might find yourself calling me," she says.

"I might."

"There's Max's inheritance money. You can pretty much do what you want."

"I know."

"Saving that money won't bring Max back, Gray. He's gone."

"I know that, Anna."

"Just thought I'd remind you."

In Cambridge, students are clustered in tight knots, studying for exams. On my desk is a postcard from Bobbie. The front of the card is a photograph of a young woman about Bobbie's and my age boarding a bus in the middle of the desert. "Having a marvelous time," the card reads. "Wish you were here, or I were there. Or almost anything. Lv, etc, Bobbie."

I put the card in my desk drawer with Max's inheritance check. Sixty-four thousand dollars, a sum Max himself would have found amusing. Anna's right, though; keeping the check uncashed in my desk won't bring him back. Thinking about it, I'm amazed I let myself fall for that kind of thinking. There's no preserving any of us. People don't keep.

It's only four, still light out. I fold the check in half, deposit it in my purse, and walk three blocks to the corner bank.

Anna's apartment at Fifty-second and Dorchester in Hyde Park, Chicago, is in a smudged red-brick building with bars on all the windows. Like Anna, the place is oversized and overstated: enormous rooms painted turquoise, russet, nectarine; a lipstick-red bidet in one of the bathrooms; a collection of wild and impractical furniture. Amid all this, paradoxically, some beauty manages to survive. My room, rag-painted robin's-egg blue, faces east and collects silvery light in the morning and evening. I have a bed, an old bureau from the flea market on Maxwell Street, shelves full of books, botanical drawings framed on the walls.

The city itself is refreshing in its unfamiliarity. Nothing from home, or from New England, has prepared me for the shoreline of Chicago, the neat heft of skyscraper against sky, the broad strong streets. My first weeks there I spend learning the city; mornings I ride the Illinois Central north. I keep a map in my purse. The city is geographically easy, but a month passes before I decide I'm bored enough to need a job.

A professor at the University of Chicago hires me to illustrate a biology textbook. The work is tedious, engrossing, repetitive—"beneath you," as Anna says—but I like the quiet charm of it. When I talk to her long distance, Mudie suggests I take a class or two and I say it's a good idea, but I don't do anything about it.

"Or at least go to med school, if you like science so much," Anna suggests. Everybody thinks I should be doing more.

Then Nathan calls. "I wondered if you'd gotten my letter."

"I did. I just wasn't sure what to do next."

"I want to come to Chicago. Vicky threatened suicide if I saw you again but she's safely in Paris now and I think I can risk it."

"Nobody's forcing you."

"I'll check the bus schedules."

"You're sure you want to come?"

"Pretty sure."

"What about Vicky?"

"Emotional blackmail."

"Still, it might change things—"

"I know," Nathan says.

"—or might not."

"How's next week for you?"

"Next week's fine."

Nathan arrives with his knapsack full of papers, clothes, chewed pencil-ends, mismatched socks. Anna's gone for the weekend, up to Door County with her latest psychotherapist. The minute Nathan steps in the apartment I know it was a mistake for him to come here, but since he doesn't know it I have to let the next few days unfold. His hair is long; he's gained ten pounds and looks more substantial than he used to, but still. He kisses me. Under his hiking boots the waxed floorboards creak. He runs his index finger down my back. "I've missed you," he says. My clothes fall on the floor; he struggles out of his. Anna's bed is bigger than mine; we shove aside the clot of pillows and sheets and make love on the bare mattress. "Classical," Nathan says, finishing. He sleeps, face turned to the window, on one side.

When he wakes up, it's nearly dark. I'm at my desk near the window, using the last daylight to finish an illustration of the muscles of the hand. Propped on one elbow, Nathan watches me with his nearsighted gaze.

"When your father died, I wanted to come for the funeral but I didn't know if I'd be welcome. I even went out to the airport and bought a ticket, but at the last minute something stopped me."

"Your father came. I remember him standing in the doorway in his elegant old suit, and for a split second I thought it was you. He told me that I'd always been Max's favorite, not Bobbie. Can you believe that?"

"Yes."

"Then, when I wanted to talk to him some more about Max, he was gone."

"Just like Darwin," Nathan says. "The disappearing father. Oh, he makes himself obvious enough when he wants to lecture you or give you some piece of advice. He wrote me this long disapproving letter that pretty much said I would botch my life if I didn't marry you."

I lift the completed drawing up to the light. The pale, luminous outline of a hand shows through the translucent paper.

"Is it too late?" Nathan asks.

"I don't know if it's a question of time."

"Then what? We're not incompatible."

"No, we're not."

Sunday afternoon Nathan catches the bus back to school. We have a few minutes to spare in the terminal; we spend them reading and shredding the Sunday *New York Times*. Nathan's bus is number seventeen; the driver climbs in and flips the sign that says CLEVELAND to BALTIMORE. Nathan touches my shoulder, gives me his wry smile.

"Think about it," he says.

I look up, blind with a sort of confusion. I have the sense that the elements of my life are dissolving and becoming more solid at the same time; some invisible rearrangement of atoms is taking place. The light in the terminal is like the light at the end of a pier in early morning; kissing me, Nathan looms and then becomes invisible. The doors of the bus hiss shut. I stand and wave, but I can't see who I'm waving to, or tell exactly when to stop.

three

A letter from Bobbie.

"I got tired of living in the desert and have moved to San Francisco," she writes. "Enlarge the space of thy tent and all that. I'm for the moment living in a tiny garden apartment (read crypt) in the Castro and selling old clothes for a loving. Oops, meant 'living' but decided to leave the mistake. I live with my new pet, a gigantic scarlet macaw named Polly Ester, Ester for short. I hope this letter finds you thriving, or at least finds you. Love, B."

Winter in Chicago is glacial. In the early morning the nearly empty streets look white and wraithlike in the cold; waves slam against the shore of Lake Michigan and freeze in stiff peaks. Anna goes out and buys a fur coat that makes her look like an extra in *Dr. Zhivago*. She spends her days holed up in front of the fireplace, banging out scenes from her childhood on her red IBM typewriter. A package arrives for me from Mudie, something she found when going through the Harmony Street house, a twelve-foot-long woolen scarf that was a Christmas present from Max when I was twelve, knitted in a dozen muted colors. I hold the scarf to my nose; the wool has Max's smoky masculine smell.

Mudie telephones. "I had a letter from Bobbie."

"So did I."

"What did yours say?"

"That she's living in San Francisco. In a basement apartment with a parrot named Polly Ester."

"Mine was strange. Some sort of manifesto about her childhood, how Max and I didn't want her and locked her up in a mental hospital. How her diagnosis of schizophrenia was a fiction. Made up so Max and I could get rid of her."

"Maybe it felt that way."

"I always wondered, though, if Max was so keen to send Bobbie away to school for selfish reasons."

"Meaning . . . ?"

"Kendra Hamilton. I guess I didn't handle all that very well. If at all."

"Mudie, it's academic now."

"I suppose. But a sensitive person like Bobbie might have interpreted Max's actions the way she obviously has. She thinks we didn't want her."

"She thinks that now. Tomorrow she might think something else."

Mudie laughs agreement. The conversation runs on to other things: Mudie's work, the friend who was mugged in the subway, Anna's new screenplay. "It's called *Freud & Friends*," I explain to Mudie, "and it's about this overprivileged family living in New York and going to psychiatrists in a vain attempt to understand each other, and when the mother's analyst dies, she finds out her husband has all along been going to the same analyst. But now that the analyst is dead, some invisible barrier between them lifts. It's typical Anna," I say. "Nathan would hate it."

"Do you ever hear from Nathan?"

"Sometimes."

I don't tell her about the letters Nathan has written since his visit to Chicago; they sit unanswered in a basket on my drafting table. The first letter thanking me for the weekend, the second curious about why I haven't written, the third miffed, the fourth analytical ("Perhaps you should rethink your position"), the fifth accusatory ("The problem with you is that you lack a center, an essential core").

January brings twenty-eight days of below-zero weather; Anna takes to writing in bed under a huge purple down comforter. I ride the bus bundled in an old tweed overcoat of Mudie's. I'm too restless to stay indoors, too unhappy with my way of handling Nathan; maybe he's right, and I have some flaw in my character (inherited from Mudie?) that makes it impossible for me to come to terms with people who love me. I'm sitting intrigued by this possibility when the Clark Street bus lurches to a standstill with some sort of engine trouble and the driver makes all the passengers get off.

It's five degrees below zero. I'm standing at the corner of Clark and Webster streets on the city's north side when I remember reading about a bookstore fourteen blocks west that sounded promising, a place that sells poetry and small-press fiction. I start walking west in the cold wind, hunched and determined. The air is dry and razor sharp; my shinbones feel as if they might shatter. I've got Mudie's overcoat on and Max's scarf, and even though I know it's crazy to be walking all this way in the cold, something prods me. It's a good half-hour walk on icy sidewalks; my scarf gets moist with breath and freezes on my face. My fingers feel as if they've dropped off.

Then I see the sign TWO HANDS in a corner window. A bell above the door rings when I go inside; the soft aroma of coffee and books envelops me. Behind the desk a woman about my own age, in horn-rimmed glasses, looks up.

"You've come about the job."

"Is there one?"

"It's still open."

Deborah gives me coffee and an application form to fill out; I hold my hands against the radiator to warm them. The store is clean and well-lighted: one large room lined with books, two wicker chairs, a huge orange calico.

"She's called Catastrophe," Deborah says.

I smile, thinking of Bobbie's parrot. I don't tell Deborah that it's by complete accident I arrived here, that I had no intention of applying for a job, that I already *have* a job and an inconvenient apartment on the South Side, that my roommate, Anna, is such an egotist she drives out every thought I have of writing, that I lack a center, an essential core . . .

"When can you start?" Deborah says. She barely glances at my application.

"How about Monday?"

"We're closed Monday. Make it Tuesday. Only I have to come in to make sure the landlord doesn't turn the heat off. He did it once to save money and the whole place froze. All these beautiful books— hand-printed, some of them—and he turns off the heat. The books all swelled up and warped, just like people freezing." Almost as an afterthought Deborah says, "You'll hate the pay. It's only minimum wage."

"It's enough."

Bobbie calls from San Francisco to tell me the news. She's going to drama school. "I kept going around in this kind of eerie fog. Then I realized it was Max's old fear I was carrying around with me. He was afraid of the theater. Afraid of emotional exposure. I'm not. The only problem is, I don't have any money."

"What'll you do now? Ask Mudie?"

"I hate to, but what's the alternative."

"Me."

Bobbie draws an audible breath. "You know, Graycat, I was all set to ask you if you could float me a loan, but something invisible stopped me. You've done enough, I guess."

"Me? I haven't done anything."

"You've been *you*. Listen, don't worry about it. I'll get enough stashed away for a semester or two. The school has a loan program. I can make noodles, pick apples, do anything. It'll work out."

A few weeks later I have a letter from Bobbie. She sounds exuberant; classes are going well. Her teachers think a lot of her talent. "Out in California my past isn't such a handicap," she writes. "Nobody cares if you've been in a mental hospital, since probably most of the population has, at one time or another."

Spring comes, late even for Chicago. At the end of May Anna announces that she's moving back east; piles of her possessions start to accumulate in the apartment. Her departure doesn't surprise me, since I had a feeling that the Midwest was only another of Anna's experiments, and that when the novelty wore off she would get restless. Privately, I'm happy; the commute from the South Side was impractical. I scan the classifieds for an apartment near the bookstore. It doesn't occur to me to move back east with Anna, and since Max's death New Orleans seems to be closed, too characteristic of Max to ever belong to me.

I find a place near Two Hands, a small coach house in back of a three-flat, with bay windows and plenty of natural light. At the bookstore, Deborah asks me to be assistant manager; she wants to open another store in late summer. The three of us—Deborah, myself, and Paul, the bookkeeper—run the store, and at night Deborah and Paul lead writing workshops. "So," Paul asks me one Monday night when we're adding up the day's business, "when are you going to bring something to the workshop?"

"I don't have anything to bring. I've only written one story in my whole life and that was in high school."

"Bring it anyway," Paul says.

"I hate workshops."

"Maybe I can't even write anymore. Maybe I've forgotten how," I say.

"Maybe," Paul says in his quiet voice, "you've never learned."

May, June, July, my notebook begins to fill with pages. It is like the greening of dead lawns after winter; whole patches of memory that I thought were dead revive. With Anna gone, my inhibitions about writing lift; she always made it seem like a selfish activity, something done to win approval, capture love. "I don't know if this is any good," I say when I finally get up the nerve to show my story to Paul. "I can't seem to trust anything I've written recently. Feels like trampling on new grass."

"Gets easier, then tougher," Paul says. "Don't scare."

In late summer I stop hearing from Bobbie. At first I assume she's gone away on vacation, and then the phone calls start. From bill collectors mostly, from the bursar of the drama school. Bobbie dropped out owing five thousand dollars, do I know her whereabouts? Even if I did, I wouldn't tell them. I ignore their written pleas, the telephone threats. I don't tell Mudie anything; lately she's seemed so at ease in her new life I don't want to upset her equilibrium. I get a dunning phone call from Pacific Bell, wanting me to pay Bobbie's phone bill. "We have an outstanding balance here for a Miss Noblesse Oblige," the account manager says. "Are you a relative or something?"

Another of Bobbie's assumed names. These credit people have no sense of humor. "I'm her sister."

"And you mean to tell me you have no idea of her whereabouts?"

"That's correct."

The calls and letters worsen. Bobbie phones, sounds panicky. "I can't explain it all now," she says. "I've had to go under an assumed name."

"Don't worry, I won't give you away. Where are you, anyway?"

"Still in California," Bobbie says, "but just barely."

"Is there anything I can do?"

"Probably not," Bobbie says, her voice practically a whisper. "Just don't tell Mudie."

Mudie calls. We talk some about our work, compare the weather in New York to Chicago. Then Mudie says, "I have this funny feeling about Bobbie. You haven't heard from her?"

"Not lately. She's pretty busy."

"Don't laugh, but every morning I've been waking up with this anxiety. I know it's connected to Bobbie. She's in some kind of trouble. I know that in the past year or so I haven't seemed very connected to her or very concerned, but Gray, this sense is overpowering. I have to see her."

"What'll you do?"

"Go to San Francisco. Dr. Haven thinks I can manage it."

"Do you want me to come?"

"Not this time. But thanks."

More dunning letters, more phone calls in search of Bobbie. I try to reach her myself once or twice, but her phone's disconnected and she won't answer my letters. Mudie flies out to San Francisco, calls me from her hotel.

"It's very peculiar. I went to Bobbie's apartment and waited three hours. She knew I was coming because I wrote her. When I put my ear to the door I heard somebody talking in this dry cackling voice."

"Polly Ester."

"Bobbie's parrot? Oh, God, I'd forgotten. Well, at least I know I'm not crazy. But I'm worried, Gray. I know Bobbie's around, but for some reason she doesn't want to see me."

"Try again tomorrow," I tell her. "Get some sleep."

I don't hear any more and then a few days later Mudie calls and says she's coming through Chicago on her way back east.

"What about Bobbie?"

"I'll tell you when I get there."

Mudie arrives in time for a late supper. I almost don't recognize the person she's become, still shy but assured, buttoned into a black linen suit. She was always unkempt and trailing, Max's "ruined beauty." Now she looks like a person who has filled in her own outline with thoughtful, quiet strokes.

Mudie was in San Francisco five days. She camped out in front of Bobbie's apartment, left numerous notes, tried finding out who Bobbie's friends were. "It was obvious she'd gone into hiding, that she didn't want to see me. Do you have any idea why?"

"Maybe she wants us to leave her alone."

"The last day I was in San Francisco it rained. I didn't have an umbrella. I was waiting outside Bobbie's door getting drenched when I saw the caretaker come out of a basement door. I cornered him, said I was Bobbie's mother and worried about her, but he wouldn't unlock the door for me. Finally I told him Bobbie was a mental patient and if he didn't let me into her apartment to find her, if anything went wrong it would be on his conscience.

"He let me in, but Bobbie wasn't there. I went through everything, her clothes, books, records, diary . . . but there was only this great big parrot in a cage, shifting gloomily on her perch. The parrot did something I'll never forget—she laughed at me, in this tinny mechanical voice that I swear was an imitation of Bobbie's. I was completely spooked. Of course, the whole thing was wrong, my fault. I probably only made things worse."

"Bobbie's been in trouble. Financial mostly. I should have told you but I didn't want you to worry. You see, she'd been doing so well," I say.

"Don't," Mudie says. "I understand already. It's not up to you to keep us all safe."

I put coffee on the table, French roast with chicory in white porcelain mugs. Mudie stirs hers. "You see, the reason I went out there in the first place was that I felt I'd let Bobbie down somewhere along the way and I wanted to help. I was prepared for anything except what I found: She didn't want to see me. When it grew clear she was hiding out somewhere and knew I was trying to contact her, it made me frantic. I had to break in, had to *possess*, had to take hold of the daughter I'd lost."

"You haven't lost her. She's grown up."

"I lost her. Lost the chance to make her whole. Now she's out there drifting, and anything could happen to her."

"To any of us."

Mudie looks at me. "Do you think she'll hate me forever now?"

"She'll get over it. You know Bobbie. She'll go on to some other phase, dye her hair blue, and convince herself you did it out of altruism."

"Not Bobbie. She might dye her hair blue but she'll never give me an inch. You know what she said to me once? It was during some interminable session with Dr. Cavendish or Dr. Fergus, I forget which. She looked directly at me and said, 'I never knew a mother and daughter could be wrong for each other.' "

"Mudie, it's late."

"I know, and I have an early plane to catch. Sounds pretty surreal, coming from me, doesn't it?"

"It sounds good."

They arrive in the mail on the same day, identical letters from Bobbie. Postmarked San Francisco, that's how we know she's still living there, in one guise or another. "Dear Graycat, Dear Mudie. I want you to know that from now on I am no longer a member of this family. Please don't try to write or call or contact me in any way. Especially do not hire any guards, detectives, social workers, or police on my behalf. Consider me dead, as dead as poor Max in his ivy-covered grave. Only know that I will be well and flourishing, that despite all your efforts, I have escaped alive. Yours, Bobbie."

The next day a box arrives. It contains the wooden madonna Max found on a trip to Mexico and gave to Mudie. The arms are broken off, the madonna has no child to hold, no arms to hold one with.

Mudie gave the sculpture to Bobbie when the house was sold. I think she was trying to make amends. As far as Bobbie's concerned, nothing Mudie does can ever be right. "You made me wrong," Bobbie told Mudie, on more than one occasion. The time I heard her say it, I thought Bobbie was saying, "You *made* me wrong," as if Bobbie had been born perfect and Mudie had never been able to love her the way she was.

I unwrap the madonna and place it on my mantel. If anything, the sculpture is more lovely broken than whole. I dial Mudie in New York, and just when I think she isn't home, she answers. I tell her about Bobbie's latest gesture.

"I guess that's typical," she says. "We may hear from Bobbie one of these days, but don't hold your breath."

I put the phone back in its cradle and walk to the front of the room, stand near the window. It's that time of day when I can't be sure whether people are standing still or moving. Then the doorbell rings: Paul and Deborah, bringing me news from outside.

"Come to the reading."

"You don't get out enough," Deborah says. "It's not good for your writing."

"It's not good for you," Paul says. He gives me a chaste kiss on the back of my neck. Paul is six foot seven and has a dark beard. I think of him as Paul Bunyan from my childhood, a benign and happy giant.

"It's snowing," I point out.

"It's always snowing in Chicago," Deborah says. "There's a party afterward."

I go with them to the reading. The novelist is a young woman in her thirties. Her book is about Alaska. I am at the point in my discovery of writing where I can barely stand to read someone else's work; my own keeps breaking through. Also, I've begun to want more out of my writing than scattered memories. "Don't worry," Paul tells me. "If it's there, it will happen."

At the party afterward I meet a man named Robert, a lawyer. I don't know that many lawyers yet; most of my friends are still in school of one kind or another, or trying things out. No one is anything yet. Robert is tall like Paul, but with a slender frame. He seems completely trustworthy. He takes me to breakfast after the party; we sit in a greasy spoon on Clark Street talking about the things we like. Ancient Greek. I can't believe I've found someone else who studied ancient Greek. What funny things bond people together.

Robert brings me back to my apartment. It's very early in the morning. I practically run from the car. When I get inside I hide under the down comforter and try to sleep. The store opens at eleven and I'll be in no shape to do anything. I start to cry. I'm so certain that I'll never see Robert again, that he will never call me.

He waits three weeks, and then he calls me at the store. "I lost my nerve," he confesses. "Funny thing for a trial lawyer to lose."

The next weeks I see Robert nearly every day. He comes by the store and buys a book just to make me feel good, or else he takes me to dinner or the movies. We look funny together; Robert in his suit and me in a leather skirt and boots. We look as if we come from two different worlds that have only by accident managed to meet.

The following summer we drive through Canada together; standing on the boardwalk overlooking the St. Lawrence, Robert and I decide to get married. It takes about a year to accomplish this, with Mudie in New York; Bobbie appearing and disappearing, work, parents, friends. Bobbie can't seem to stay away. In the midst of this, Robert tries cases. I move in to his simple, uncluttered apartment with all my books.

He owns one towel. Robert is determined not to put emphasis on material things. He lets me have my writing instead of insisting that I get a job so we can live in a fancier apartment. He encourages me to keep writing even when I want to give up, go to some graduate school or other. "How about law school?" I say. "Child psychology? Culinary arts?"

"What about writing?" Robert always says.

Then I get a story published, my first. This comes long after I'd despaired of ever seeing it happen. In the same way we come to have Cal, our son, who is born after we are told we can't have children. We don't know what to make of this, how sometimes you can't have the things you want the most, and sometimes you get the things you want least: delays, uncertainty, unwanted complications. Robert holds Cal under the lights in the delivery room and admires his full head of black hair, his sturdiness. "I'll always do right by you," I whisper to my son at two in the morning when neither of us can sleep. Do I believe this? Is it a promise or a lullaby?

four

hen Cal was four months old, Bobbie came to visit me. I hadn't seen her since my wedding nearly five years earlier, when she and Mudie had quarreled again and Bobbie had stormed away, vowing never to speak to any of us. Now she wanted Mudie to lend her twenty thousand dollars, the down payment for a house. Bobbie had never had any sense of money; it drifted through her hands like stardust. Perhaps she never trusted the future to save for; to be thrifty meant planning for the next bad episode, and this she was incapable of doing. Mudie tried to persuade her to "get help"; Bobbie refused to admit she was a schizophrenic. "It was Max," she shouted at Mudie, "it was you. You two were my disease."

For several years there was no contact between Bobbie and Mudie. I was the go-between, but even my communication with Bobbie was scant; she seemed to go along for a while doing one thing, and then she would suddenly change course. Those were often the times we lost touch. Then one day I'd get a postcard or letter or a phone call, and there Bobbie would be, as if she had spoken to me only the day before.

Then Bobbie called and said she wanted to come visit; I was living in Chicago with Robert and Cal, trying to write during Cal's naptimes, more often than not falling exhausted on the bed in my room. I had mixed feelings about Bobbie coming; I wanted to see her, but I didn't want any trouble, any pain. I had the irrational fear that her presence would somehow make my own life dissolve, that however permanent and real anything of mine was, Bobbie could etch it away like acid; that's how powerful she was. Then I remembered some of the things Alan Cavendish used to tell me about wanting to lose my own self in the face of Bobbie's illness, how the impulse came from guilt. "You can't hide under a rock simply because your sister is flamboyant," he told me, "especially not if you're doing it for Bobbie's sake. Besides, something tells me you see right through to the core of things sometimes, so don't waste your gift."

Bobbie was still living in San Francisco; she flew in on a late-night flight, and by midnight was standing in my living room. She was smaller than I remembered, and had cut her blond hair short and spiky, which made her look both glamorous and vulnerable. She was wearing bright-green eyeglasses; her suitcases stood in the hallway, metallic gold photographer's cases plastered with stickers from countries around the world. I found myself wondering if she had really been to any of these places; knowing Bobbie, she probably had.

"Jesus, it's good to see you," she said.

"It's good to see you."

"I was a little *intimidated*," she admitted.

"So was I."

There was Cal, four months old, his small face puckered in an intense frown. Bobbie leaned over and tickled his fist. "Small babies make me nervous," she said. "There are so many things that can go wrong."

"They make me nervous too," I said. "At first I used to dwell on the possibility of disaster a lot. After Cal was born and had been pronounced perfect I was relieved, but it wasn't long before I found myself standing by his crib in the middle of the night. 'All right,' I'd say to God, 'so far, so good. I'll accept my share of evening colic. Just don't let anything worse happen.' "

Bobbie knew what I was afraid of, but neither one of us mentioned schizophrenia; it was as if even breathing the word might unleash the possibility. Both of us knew that Bobbie was born perfect too; it was only in her fourteenth year that signs of trouble began to show. Schizophrenia, or something else?

Unfortunately, Max and Mudie didn't know what Bobbie's behavior meant; it made Mudie draw into herself and Max begin to make plans to send Bobbie away to school. Perhaps underneath, they suspected something unmanageable. Perhaps they thought that if they changed Bobbie's life for her, she couldn't change theirs. What they didn't realize was that Bobbie was only reacting to their problems; they thought it was the other way around.

Bobbie stayed with us a week. At night when Cal was asleep in one room and Robert in another, she and I stayed up and talked. She told me something of her life in California. There were pieces missing from the narrative, odd conjunctions of events, and I realized with sadness that what I had hoped for had not happened: Bobbie had not changed. She was able, miraculously, to hold jobs and keep an apartment, but just when she'd been at a job long enough to accrue any benefits, she'd slide sideways into some kind of episode. She told me this was due to alcoholism; that was why she periodically went to live at a mission in the Bay Area, to dry out. When she told me this, I didn't know what to say. Her episodes corresponded in some way to what I used to think of as my black spells. She whirled around in a fit of activity; I sat looking out the window. Except that over time I had become more than an anxious depressive, more than the dark sister. I hoped Bobbie had found a way out of her trap, but I couldn't be sure.

In the daytime we went for walks. Bobbie pushed Cal around in his carriage. In Chicago, the light sometimes reminds me of the light in Paris; it has this flat silvery quality. Bobbie noticed it right away; we were in the backyard, and leaves were blowing into the open carriage. "Remember when we were little," I said, "Mudie used to stand at the window and look out at us playing in the yard, and there was always this absorbed expression on her face, as if she were seeing something that wasn't there. I used to try waving to her but she never seemed to see me."

"You know, Gray," Bobbie said, "when Max fell off that Carnival float and was taken to the hospital, do you remember what his last words were?"

" 'Just this damn—'?"

"Right before he died, when he leaned over and said, 'It's just this damn—' I think he was trying to deliver a message, something witty and elegant probably, but it had gotten lodged in some remote cavern of his brain and refused to come to light."

"Graycat," Bobbie says over breakfast, "You have no idea what it's like, being me."

"I have some idea."

"You have no idea what it feels like to have your whole family think you're crazy; it's like they're against you."

"I'm not."

"Max and Mudie were, from the start. Maybe I turned out to be more than either one of them could handle, and they just retreated, Max into his affair, Mudie into her studio—both of them into whatever private world suited at the time. I got sent to St. Vincent's, then Mandeville. I was too much for them. Believe me, I've thought about it all a lot. I'm not schizophrenic."

We left it at that. Maybe if Bobbie thought she was schizophrenic, it would paralyze her. She would have no way to live, no part of her life would be untouched by illness. Bobbie's periodic disappearances, her absences—what are they, compared to that more basic loss?

The thing that used to bother me most was that I could see Bobbie without any disease; I had a strong sense of what she could have done if she hadn't gotten sick. This phantom life of hers haunted me, and prevented Max and Mudie from accepting her as she was. Bobbie sensed this, I think; it set up a kind of reverberation between her and Max—and between her and Mudie—that prevented each one from ever seeing the other whole. They lived by myths.

Mudie tried to be more realistic, but over time developed such thick armor toward Bobbie that Bobbie could no longer feel her love. "All Mudie can see is what she's been told by psychiatrists," Bobbie told me one afternoon. We were in the kitchen making bread. "She's used the diagnosis of schizophrenia to keep me at arm's length. What if one day she found out she was wrong and I'm not schizophrenic? There would be no explanation for me."

I believed Bobbie; she had the ability all good actresses have, of making their audience want to believe their version of events. Besides, why would she want to deceive herself about something so central to her life? Several times after one of our talks I had the eerie feeling that what she was saying about her past superseded all other accounts, including my own. What was true about Bobbie? I found it harder and harder to know, and yet there was this whole vast history between us, events I thought were fixed, understood. The more she talked about not being sick, the more my memory of her behavior changed, so much so that by the time she was ready to return to San Francisco, I was beginning to see that Bobbie might be right. I was so used to accepting Max and Mudie's viewpoint that my new vision felt odd, startling. Like coming out of a movie in broad daylight, having forgotten in the darkness that it was light all along.

"Well Graycat," Bobbie said when she was getting ready to leave, "you done good. You made a good baby." She grabbed Cal's tiny fist and leaned over to whisper something in his ear. Cal smiled his first real smile.

"What did you say to him?" I asked.

"A secret," Bobbie said.

Right then I had a powerful sense of the complicity between us; Bobbie had somehow helped to make the good life I have and she didn't begrudge me it. All along, through all our upheavals, she was showing me that it was possible to occupy my own place on earth. I had stopped being her other half and had become myself.

The taxi pulled up in front of the house; we said good-bye, and Cal waved a frantic fist. I watched Bobbie cross the lawn littered with fallen leaves and get in the waiting car. Grinning, she rolled down the passenger window.

"You know," she said, "for so long I felt as if a magic circle had been drawn through our family and I was outside of that circle. I don't feel that way now."

"Neither do I."

When she was gone I wheeled Cal back into the kitchen for supper. I kept thinking about Bobbie and me while I peeled the carrots and chopped handfuls of parsley. And I thought about us all that night and into the next morning, without coming to the end of my thoughts.

About the Author

LEE WALMSLEY grew up in New Orleans, Louisiana, and was educated at Princeton University. Her poetry has appeared in *Antaeus,* and her short stories in *The North American Review. Light Sister, Dark Sister* is her first novel. She now lives north of Chicago with her husband and three children.